BLUE

SUE-ELLEN PASHLEY

For Mum and Dad,
For your belief, your support and your love.

CHAPTER 1

This is what I know about me for sure.

I am seventeen.

I am a twin.

And I am an invader of homes. A thief who takes people's things, including their peace of mind. It's not what I want to do. It's not who I want to be. But I don't have a choice.

I stare out the window of the car, head on my palm. I can feel the vibrations of the road through my elbow, resting on the door sill. Every bump nearly slams my head into the window, but I don't move. Maybe I can knock myself out. Then I won't have to think.

This town looks like every other one we've been to. House after house, all of them basically the same, everyone living their normal, ordinary lives. We've been to so many of these little nothing towns now, I'm starting to lose track. Just once, I'd like to go somewhere where things are different. Not just the town, but our lives too. A normal, ordinary life – that's what I want.

Not that there's any chance of that.

I glance over at Gep. He's concentrating so hard on the road it looks like he's trying to make it bend to his will. His dark hair is grey at the edges and the lines on his face look like they've well and truly settled in. Weathered, I think they call it. He's looked like this for as long as I can remember. I think it's because we've moved around so much that we're the only ones who realise he never seems to age…

I watch him, making sure I keep my face void of emotion, and try to work out when I actually started to hate him. Not just be scared of him but actually hate him. A hate that's a churning anger, deep in my gut, gnawing at me. Probably when I was fourteen. When he really started to take it out on Jimmy. When he showed how much of a sadistic bastard he is. Three years of burning rage with no way to get rid of it. Can't be good for my health.

He looks over at me, the lines in his forehead furrowing deeper.

'What the fuck's wrong with you?'

I look away, not stupid enough to answer, and stick my earphones in, letting the music wash over me, fill up my brain. My eyes shut out the bright, noon-day light. For a moment, I can pretend I'm somewhere else; pretend I'm some*one* else. The beat pounds in my ears, taking me away, drowning out my life.

The tap on my shoulder brings me back to reality. I pretend to ignore it, even though now it's all I can think about. When I feel the second tap, I know there's no point in continuing the sham. I reef an earphone out and twist in my seat. Jimmy's grinning at me, his green eyes bright, his blond hair all messed and sticking up like a frigging halo around his head. I can't help but grin back. He's the only one who can do that to me.

'What?'

'Do you think there'll be cute girls?'

The words slur out of his mouth and I can see he's trying hard not to let his left arm fly into Fox, sitting next to him. Not that he can help any of it. Brain damage from the car accident that killed our mum left him like this. That's what Gep's told me anyway.

God knows if it's true. Not that it matters. He's my brother. My twin. It's as simple as that.

'Yeah, and they'll all be flocking around, running their fingers through your hair, trying to do things for you, make things easier. Frigging underdog shit always works.'

He grins at me again and turns to Fox.

'Did you hear that?' he says. 'Penn reckons I'm going to outplay you again.'

Fox shakes his head, his red hair a fiery mess in the sun.

'You're a freak, man. God, makes me sick the way the girls want to talk to you all the time.'

'You're just jealous,' I say. 'He can't help it if he's got normal coloured hair and the girls can't work out if you're a guy or a monkey.'

'Fuck you,' he says, but there's no real feeling to it. He doesn't want to be here anymore than I do.

'It's a pointless conversation anyway.' Gep's voice is loud in the car, dominating the space around us. 'Jimmy's not going to school this time.'

My heart sinks, spiralling down like it's not controlled by my body anymore, making me nauseous. Not again. Not after last time.

'That's shit,' I say.

I know I should keep my mouth shut – in fact, every cell in my body is begging me to do just that – but my anger makes me stupid.

He looks over at me, eyes narrowed.

'What did you say?'

I take a deep breath. The other boys in the car – Jimmy, Fox and Kat – are silent. I can feel them watching me; feel their tension. And I know if I turned around to look at Jimmy, his eyes would be telling me to shut up. But I can't. The words spew out of my mouth like I'm a suicidal moron.

'I said that's shit. He should be able to go to school. I'll do what you want me to do. You don't have to worry about it, alright? I'll do it.'

'Damn right you'll do it. But after the little…rebellion you had last time, Jimmy's my insurance. So, you'd better be a good boy.'

He leans over to pat my cheek like I'm five years old. I try not to jerk away at his touch but it's hard. He smirks, like he knows. It's that smirk that does my head in. I whack his hand away with my forearm.

'Fucking psycho.'

It's muttered under my breath but I know he'll hear it. Even then, I'm not ready for what he does next. You'd think I would be. After living with him, day in and day out, for the last sixteen years, you'd think I'd be able to predict his actions.

But he moves so quickly, I don't react until his hand is on the bare skin of my arm. And I know what's going to happen, even if I don't know how he does it. I feel his energy burning into me, coursing through my body, like it's charring my veins, leaving only ash in its wake. It takes all of my strength to not scream out, even though it feels like my whole body is on fire, the heat engulfing me, burning every organ to a crisp, until I'm just a shell. But I keep it in, not giving him the satisfaction, like I've done so many times before. And, even more important than that, not letting Jimmy hear it – not putting him through that.

It seems to go on and on, until there's only the heat, the burn.

I hear Jimmy yell out and it's the last thing I hear before the blackness takes me.

CHAPTER 2

My mouth feels like a desert. I move my tongue against the fur on my teeth, trying to get some saliva happening before I even think about opening my eyes.

'About time you woke up,' a voice says. 'We had to do all the moving in and carry your sorry arse into the house as well.'

'Shut up, Kat.'

He ignores me, like always. It's a rare moment when he actually has nothing to say.

'God, Penn, why couldn't you have just shut the hell up? Gep was an arsehole all night.'

I open my eyes a crack, letting the light creep in for a second before I open them fully. The room we're in has no personality. Unless you can call the bright yellow walls personality rather than a gross lack of taste.

'Jesus,' I say, leaning up onto my elbow, 'what sun threw up in here?'

Kat grins.

'You should see Jimmy and Fox's room. It's purple. Like bright purple. We got off lightly.'

I flop back down on the bed again and shut my eyes with a groan. At least it's not a bad bed. The last one I had felt like it was a hundred years old, the springs almost sagging to the floor. How sad is it that I've never had my own bed? Only ever slept on somebody else's crappy furniture that comes with the rental houses Gep finds.

'Come on,' Kat says. 'We're supposed to leave for school in half an hour. Gep's already got the uniforms. Yours is on the desk.'

I open one eye to look at what he's wearing. Blue sports shirt with white stripes at the side and blue shorts. Better than last time. A brown and cream combo. Don't know what idiot thought that one up.

I sit up as he goes out and contemplate my options. Even though I know I'm kidding myself. There are no options. I need to get up, get dressed and go to school, mingling and finding out information, just like Gep wants me to. Just like he's forcing me to. Because he never does his own dirty work. Ever. Not when he can make us do it. All he's interested in is the power that comes with the things we steal.

I grab the pile of clothes off the desk and go look for the bathroom. Not that it's hard to find. It's a small house, even by our usual standards. I can hear everyone else out in the kitchen and shut the door, locking it before any of them can intrude. A few minutes of privacy is like gold around here.

Stripping off, I run the water, waiting forever for the hot to come in, and then step under, letting it wash over me, running in warm rivers down my head, my face. I shut my eyes, trying not to think about the fact that it's starting all over again. Another town, another fact finding mission and another robbery. I'm sick of it. Sick of our life. There has to be more than this. God, I don't even have any friends other than Kat, Fox and Jimmy. And they're family, so they don't count. How is it that I'm seventeen years old and have no one else in my life except them? It's crap.

I sigh and turn off the shower. Feeling sorry for myself isn't going to help. Suck it up, princess. Two minutes flat and I'm dried and dressed. I don't even bother looking in the mirror. What's the point? Even if I impress a girl, we never hang around long enough for anything to really develop.

The door sticks as I try to open it and I have to reef on it, little bits of paint flaking off the door jamb as I do. Piece of crap house. Everything in our life is shit. No, I'll rephrase that – our life is shit.

They're all still in the kitchen when I go out.

'Morning, pretty boy,' Fox says, stuffing a piece of toast into his mouth.

I ignore him and grab the other half of the toast on his plate.

'Hey!' he says, but what's he going to do? I'm taller and stronger – he's got no chance. He knows it too. He slumps back in his seat.

'Arsehole.'

I grin at him.

'And proud of it.'

Jimmy's sitting in his wheelchair at the end of the table, and I can see that either Fox or Gep have already helped him with breakfast. I wish we could share a room. I'd even put up with the purple to do that. But Gep's never allowed it. Not since we were little anyway. I think he's worried we'll make up a plan to escape or something. Yeah, like it'd be that easy. Identical guys, with one in a wheelchair – we wouldn't be noticed at all. Jimmy's not grinning this morning and I know he's bummed about not being able to go to school. I sneak a glance at Gep, who's busy making a coffee at the bench. It looks like he's ignoring us but I know better than that. He'll be listening to every word we say.

'I'll bring you some work home,' I say.

Jimmy gives me a half smile – something, at least – and I shake my head at him in mock disappointment. I can't understand why he enjoys school work but he does. He's the brain, I'm the brawn. He's the good one, I'm…not. That's how the egg split, I guess.

'Thanks.'

I know it's not enough. I know he wants to go to school and feel like a normal kid – well, as much as possible anyway – but there's nothing we can do. Not after yesterday. The burn still feels too real.

I stand, ready to make a getaway. Not quick enough though.

'Penn.'

Gep's voice stops me in my tracks and I turn to look at him, holding myself stiff, trying to keep the hatred from showing in my eyes.

'I'm sorry about yesterday,' he says. 'I went too far. I know that.'

I nod. I've heard too many apologies in the past to think that this one means anything.

'You need to do what I say, that's all. I feed you, dress you, look after you. We're family. We need to stick together.'

I don't even nod this time, just look at him.

He watches me for a few seconds, staring me down, before nodding like he thinks he's won. He stands straighter, looking at everyone else. Apology done obviously. He's in full leader mode now.

'Right, boys. We're looking for a book this time. Old; really old. Brown leather cover. It'll have a gold symbol on the front. No words. Just a symbol. And we've been led here so it's some-where in this town. That's all I know.'

'What's the symbol?' Kat asks.

'It's just a gold symbol.' Gep's mouth is tight. I want to tell Kat to shut up but I'm too late.

'Yeah but –'

Gep rounds on him, hands in fists, angry as all shit. First mood swing of the day and it's only eight o'clock. I've got a feeling it's a good day to be going to school. Which makes me feel even worse for Jimmy.

'It doesn't matter what it is! It's just a fucking gold symbol! Got it?'

Kat looks away, down at the table. He's never been brave when it comes to Gep. Or maybe he's the smart one. The one who can actually shut up when he knows he's crossed the line, even if that line is never in the same place. I start to walk away again while Gep's focus is on Kat.

'Penn.'

I don't stop this time. I just want to get out of here. But he catches me before I get to the door and holds it shut, his other hand on my upper arm. I refuse to look at him. Just stare straight ahead. And try really hard not to shake his hold off, even though I can feel his fingers bitting into my skin and my brain is trying to desperately retreat from memories of yesterday's burn.

'Don't forget,' he says, his voice low and deep, invading my ears like it's trying to get right into my head. 'You want to make sure Jimmy stays safe.'

I look at him now. I know my eyes are hard and he'll be able to see how I feel. But I don't care.

'He better be safe.'

He moves closer, taking my space, towering over me. Even though I'm six foot one, he's still taller than me. And powerful. It feels like that power's pushing into me, testing me. I struggle not to step back.

'Is that a threat?'

I try to hold eye contact but it's too hard. He wears me down like he's eroding my soul with each second his eyes are locked onto mine. I look at the floor, hating the fact he can do this to me.

'No,' I say. 'But I'll do what you want. There's no need to do anything to him.'

He nods.

'Just remember, we're family. We stick together. We don't let anyone in. We keep to ourselves and we keep our *business* to ourselves.'

'Fine.' I push past him now, desperate to get out to the fresh air, away from him. He lets me go.

Family. What a fucking joke!

I've only managed to go one block before Fox and Kat catch up. Part of me is glad for the company but the other part just wants to be alone. Alone with all the thoughts of what I'd like to do to Gep if I ever got the chance. Maybe it's better they're here.

I can see Kat looking at me out of the corner of my eye.

'What?' I say finally.

He shrugs, his face going red, like he's embarrassed about being caught out.

'Nothing. Just…do what he says, okay?'

'Sure.'

I don't realise how angry I sound until that word comes out of my mouth. And then I feel bad. It's not Kat's fault Gep's an arsehole. We all have to put up with him.

'Sure,' I say again and this time, it's better. Nicer.

'Sure,' Kat says in return and I can hear the relief in his voice. 'We'll find the book he wants and then we'll be out of here and everyone will be okay. And this might be the last thing we need to get. Maybe after this, we'll be able to…you know…live like normal kids, like he's always said.'

I can't stop the snort that shoots out of me, even though I feel like an arse for taking that dream away from him. He's only twelve, for Christ's sake. And I used to have dreams like that myself. Kat ignores it anyway.

'I wonder what the school will be like. I hope there's metal-work. I got to make a toolbox at the last one, remember. It was awesome, especially when –'

'Shut up, Kat,' Fox and I say in union and I grin at him. He grins back for a moment before the smile falls away.

'So, what'd you do last time? You know, the rebellion that Gep talked about in the car yesterday? And why's he so psycho about it? I mean, not sending Jimmy to school – holding him hostage. That's shit.'

My grin's replaced by a scowl. I don't answer. I'm not sure why. Maybe I don't want them to know what a loser I am.

'Come on, tell us,' Fox says. 'At least then, we'll know not to do it ourselves.'

I stare ahead, still not answering. Because they'd never do it anyway – never do something that'd bring Gep to the attention of anyone in authority. They get angry at him, sure, but they've been with him since birth basically. All I remember is Gep going away for a day or two and then coming home with a baby. Fox first and then Kat. Telling us they were our brothers, even though Jimmy and I aren't Gep's blood relatives. A fact which gives me a slight tremor of relief. I've wondered sometimes, where the hell Fox and Kat came from – did he steal them? Pay a surrogate to have them? But I decided a long time ago not to ask. It's safer. And he'd never tell me anyway. So he's the only parent they know. They'd never try to get him in trouble for what he forces us to do. Whereas I can still remember my mum. Sort of anyway. I remember her smell – vanilla and flowers – and the way she used to hold me…

Fox sighs.

'Whatever then. Just don't be an idiot this time.'

I try not to take offence at that. Mainly because he's right. There're times when I feel like the King of Idiots.

'We'll find the book and get out of here.'

I know that's what we need to do to make sure Gep doesn't get angry; to make sure Jimmy's safe. I know all of that. And yet… there must be some way we can stop this. Jesus. How does he manage to have this hold over us? How can he make me be someone I don't want to be? I shake my head again. Pathetic. It didn't work last time – it only made it worse. Just do what he wants and suck it up. Keep Jimmy safe. Protect him. That's all I have to think about.

The school grounds are teaming with kids. It looks like a typical school. A collection of single and double story buildings, a lame attempt at a garden, low chain mesh fence that fools no one. I sigh.

'Come on, may as well get this over and done with.'

Fox and Kat follow behind me, like I'm the unofficial leader. I wish they wouldn't. Because even though I call them my brothers, we truly aren't related. And I don't want to have to look after anyone else. It's hard enough keeping Jimmy safe. But they don't give me a choice and I don't say anything.

I pull open the door to the admin building, trying to ignore the stares as we walk in. There's something wrong about always being the new kids. Always being subjected to the whispers and looks – never really being part of the group.

The woman sitting at the desk looks up as we enter, her eyes flicking to each of us. She's not smiling but she's not scowling either, so that's a good start. Sometimes, they're scowling from the start, like we're polluting the school just by walking into the grounds.

'Can I help you boys?'

'Um, yeah, hi. We're new to town, just moved in yesterday, and we're here to register.'

She looks behind us and out the door, craning her neck, before looking back at me.

'Do you have a parent with you?'

'No. Our dad's sick and couldn't make it this morning. So, we thought, if we could take the paper work home for him to sign…'

I try my nicest smile, the one that says 'trust me, I'm a good kid'. She seems to fall for it. If only she knew…

'Well, it's a bit irregular…I guess it'd be okay if he comes in over the next couple of weeks.'

'Sure, he'll definitely try.' I sigh. 'He's got cancer though and he has his good days but, you know…'

I shrug like I'm being stoic and strong. Trying to ignore the sadistic pleasure I get in giving Gep cancer, even if it's only part of a story.

'Oh, you poor things. That's terrible.'

Fox and Kat nod, sad expressions on their faces. Actually, they look more like they're constipated. Bad actors, both of them. I clear my throat, trying to get her attention back on me.

'Yeah, it's hard, so if we could take the paperwork home for him, I can bring it back next week. And he'll come up as soon as he can.'

It's a lie. Gep never comes to the school. The fewer people who can identify him, the better. And usually, it doesn't take us long to get the information we need, make the steal and move on.

'Of course.' The admin lady's pulling the keyboard towards her. 'What grades are you boys in?'

We give her all the information. Our names, our grades, our last school, our subject selections. She's giving us a real smile by the end.

'Your father should be proud of you. There aren't too many kids who would turn up by themselves to the first day of school.'

I smile at her.

'We just try and make it easy for him.'

I feel like I want to chuck – I can't believe she's swallowing all this, but then, I've found most people want to believe the best, especially if you play the part well enough. And I've played the part for a long time now…

'Right,' she says, 'now we need to get someone to show you the way to your classes.'

'That's alright. I'm sure we'll find them.'

'Nonsense.' She stands up from behind her desk, smoothing her dress around her hips like she means business, and heading to the door at the back of the building. I look at Fox and Kat and roll my eyes. This is the worst bit. I hate being the new kid. Sucks the big one, especially when you have to do it over and over.

'Alex!' she calls out. 'Would you come here please?'

I wait until I see the kid that walks in before I know what sort of image to give off. We want to fit in as soon as possible – be the kid that everyone's okay with – that's the easiest way to get the information we need to find Gep's latest object.

And that keeps him happy.

Which keeps Jimmy safe.

It's like an endless cycle I'm never able to get off.

The kid who walks in looks to be about my age. And sporty – house captain or something. I almost turn around to high-five Kat when I notice the leader's badge on his chest. After doing this so many times, I can pick them. It's like my superpower.

He eyes us all up and I try my best to look non-threatening. It's hard when you're over six foot, so I slouch a little and give him a half grin. He nods at me but I can see he's still not warmed to me yet. At the last school, Fox reckoned all the girls were talking about me and wondering who I'd ask out. I'm pretty sure he exaggerated but I know I'm not bad looking. The blond hair and green eyes and the fact that I'm new blood seems to do something to the female student population, even if I can't figure out what it actually is – but it can also have a negative effect on the guys. Like they see me as a possible threat. It's shit. I don't have time for girls. Not if I want to keep

Jimmy safe. That'll have to wait until Jimmy and I can get out on our own.

'Alex,' the admin lady says again. 'This is Penn, who'll be in your year, and –'

'Fox,' Fox says quickly. He hates his first name. Can't say I blame him. Kat's is almost as bad. You'd have thought when Gep brought them home as babies, he'd at least have given them better names than the crap ones he did. Like some sort of compensation for having to live with him.

'Right…Fox,' the lady says, like she's worried about his sanity, 'and Katana.'

'Kat.' I say, because I know how much he hates it.

'So I need you to show them to their classes.' She hands him a piece of paper she's printed up. 'I think Penn has English with you next, is that right?'

Alex nods.

'Good, well, I'll leave you to it then.' She turns back to me. 'I'll have the documents for your father to sign ready for you this afternoon, so if you can come back in before you go home?'

I smile at her. 'Sure. Thanks.'

Alex is already waiting outside for us. I hitch my bag further up my shoulder as I fall into step beside him. Fox and Kat are walking behind us, like they're trying not to be noticed. Alex clears his throat.

'So, new kids, huh?'

I resist the temptation to roll my eyes.

'Yep. Moved in to town yesterday.'

'Oh, yeah. Where are you living?'

'Blue house. End of Tumbler Street, I think it is?'

'Yeah,' he says, 'I know where that is. Right on the edge of town.'

I nod. Time for a change of subject before he tries to get too much info on us. I need to be careful not to make it obvious though. Not like I'm avoiding questions.

'So, what are the teachers like here?'

'Not bad. Mr Mac, the one we've got for English, he's pretty good. Try and steer clear of Miss Styman though. She's a real bitch.'

'Had a few of them before,' I say. 'Noted. Thanks. What sports do you guys play?'

His face lights up like I've asked him to help me spend a million dollars.

'Our basketball team's really good – we just made it to the state finals. We go down there in four weeks' time. And football, of course.'

He says it like it's an afterthought. I'm guessing he's not a footy head, then.

'Any room on the basketball team or are you guys all pretty tight?'

He eyes me up and down.

'Yeah, you can come and train if you like.'

I nod, giving him a half 'gee-thanks-I'm-so-grateful' smile. Letting him think he's the alpha dog. We drop Fox and Kat off on the way to our classroom and he doesn't have much else to say as we go into ours. I like him just because he doesn't ask the usual twenty questions I have to work to avoid.

The classroom's half full when we go in there. Everyone turns and watches us walk in but again, I'm used to that. I give the self-depreciating smile again as find a seat at the side of the room and get my stuff out of my bag, letting it fall on the desk with a muted thump. Alex sits behind me.

'Practice is this afternoon at four if you're interested in coming,' he says and I nod my agreement.

The guy sitting next to him leans forward across the desk.

'Rory,' he says and I bump fists with him. Stupid ritual but if it makes him feel better… 'So, do you play basketball then?'

'Yeah.'

'What position?'

I shrug.

'I've played most of them. Depends on what the team needs.'

He nods, like he approves of my answer. I want to tell him I really don't care what he thinks but I've done this enough to know I need to shut the hell up. I don't know what's with me this morning…why I'm so shitty about having to do this…why I just want to tell them to all shove it when they actually haven't done anything. Usually it's almost like a sport. Suck them in, get them telling me exactly the information I need, trusting me, liking me.

But, at this moment, I don't want to be here. And I don't want to be doing this…pretending to be their friend so I can get what Gep wants. I'm sick of the game. I would like, for once in my life, to know what it actually feels like to just…feel something real.

I turn back around as the teacher enters the classroom. He looks pretty young and has one of those stupid earrings that makes the hole in his ear stretch right out. But I won't hold that against him. Not yet anyway.

He's about to start talking when the door opens again and a girl walks in. She mutters a quiet apology before sitting down at a desk at the front. Then he starts to talk. But I don't hear anything he says.

I'm too busy trying to work out why it feels like my whole world has tipped on its axis.

CHAPTER 4

I can't understand what's going on. What's happening to me?

My heart's banging so hard in my chest it feels like I'm going to have a heart attack. And I have to tell myself to breathe, suck in a lung full of air, let it back out, now do it again. I want to get up and go over to her. So badly the muscles in my legs are tight, like they're ready to stand up the instant my brain says it's okay. Which it's not!

But all I can think about is going over there and sitting next to her, hearing her talk, seeing what colour her eyes are, up close. When she bunches her freaky long, blue hair – who the hell has blue hair, for Christ sake! – in her hand and flicks it out, all I can imagine is letting it run through my fingers.

Fuck!

Something is seriously wrong with me!

I grip my pen, trying to concentrate really hard on not snapping it. I can see the veins in the back of my hand and try to focus on them instead, but my eyes keep flicking over to her, like they have a life of their freaking own.

For God's sake, get a grip!

She chews on the end of her pen, lost in thought, before she starts to write again, a small frown on her face as she concentrates. It snaps me back to the classroom. Crap, we're supposed to be doing something. I look around me...everyone's writing. I'm going to look like a moron. Jesus. I shut my eyes for a moment, picturing Jimmy, remembering the tears that slipped down his face even though he was trying to be tough, the agony on his face, the last time Gep did the burn on him because *I* stuffed up. That's what I need to focus on. Not some stupid, weird, blue-haired girl.

Find out where the book is, take it, give it to Gep and then, we can get out of here and Jimmy will be safe. It's not hard. Same pattern I've followed for most of my life. I clench my jaw, forcing myself not to look at her.

I look up at the teacher instead, and it only takes a few seconds before he notices. He smiles at me and walks over.

'I'm Mr MacCrombie. But you can call me Mr Mac. You must be Penn.'

I nod and glance down at my still blank page.

'I'm not sure...you know...what we're supposed to be doing.'

He raises his eyebrows, not in a bad way, just like he's listening, but I can feel the heat come to my face. I wonder how many other people are listening. Like an idiot, my eyes dart towards her again and she's looking. She's got brown eyes. Even from here, I can see that. I suck in another breath and force my eyes back to the teacher.

'What were you doing in your last class?' he asks.

'Book review,' I mumble. '*To Kill a Mockingbird.*'

He smiles.

'Then you're in luck. That's what we're in the middle of now. Do you have a copy of the book already or do you need a school copy?'

'No, I need a school copy.'

I want this conversation over and done with so everyone can stop looking at us. I stare at my page, focusing on the blue lines as he finds a copy. He puts it on the desk in front of me along with an assessment page.

'It's all pretty self-explanatory,' he says, 'but let me know if you need a hand.'

I nod, glancing up at him, and he smiles at me again before going back to his desk.

I pull the sheet over, attempting to make sense of the words written on it. But it's like my brain won't co-operate. Come on, it says, one look. Just one. Just to see if she's still looking over. I clench my teeth, refusing to give in.

It's not working though. My brain refuses to be distracted. And there's no point in staring at a page and reading the first sentence over and over. I huff and shut my eyes for a second and then look over at her. She's staring at me. I don't understand why the thought of her watching me has my stomach doing summersaults, rolling around like I'm going to be sick, but it does. When she sees my eyes on her, she looks away quickly, frowning at her page again, her face going red. She flicks her hand up to her hair, drawing it down over her shoulder so I can't see her face anymore.

Which is as frustrating as all hell.

I lean forward to see if I can see her better, when I hear a laugh behind me. I don't know if it's directed at me but I sit back so quickly, I almost rock the chair back over. I can feel my face get hot again.

Christ! Way to make a stupid impression.

Anger rears up and washes over me and I actually have to stop myself from screwing up the assessment sheet and stalking out. Years of practice of not showing how I feel – keeping everything in – is the only thing that saves me from making a total idiot of myself.

I press the palms of my hands against the top of the desk instead and take a deep breath. This girl is not important. She's nothing. Jimmy is the important one. And keeping him safe is important. I'm the only one he can rely on. I need to keep it together. I can't afford to get side tracked. I need to be focused. Stick to the plan. If I do it well, we could be out of here in a fortnight and then I'll never have to see her again. I try not to think about how my chest tightens at that thought.

Jimmy, I write in big letters at the top of my page.

I shift forward, putting my hand on my head and leaning into it, covering my eyes on her side to shield my view. Now I won't be able to look at her – even if I'm tempted.

I read the assessment page again. It only takes the first paragraph for me to realize that it's exactly the same as the one I did in my last school. I even finished the assignment for once in my life. Got a B for it too. Which is great, except it means I've got nothing to do for the whole lesson. Except think of her…

I drag the book over, opening to the first page, forcing myself to read each word. It's like torture. But I don't look at her. I manage that, at least.

The relief racing through me when the bell goes at the end of the lesson is not like anything I've ever felt before. Bigger even than when I was nearly caught nicking something for Gep and just managed to get away. I stuff my things in my bag, so keen to get out of the room – to escape – that I don't even look at what's going on around me. That's how I'm clueless about the fact that she's standing right by my desk until I look up. I stop breathing for a moment. Like literally, stop breathing. She's taken my breath away. I'm like a bad frigging romance novel, for Christ sake!

My hand tightens on my bag, the straps digging into my flesh. In a weird way, the pain is good. At least it's a distraction.

'Hi,' she says, sticking out her hand. She's tall, for a girl. It's not often that I don't need to really look down. 'I'm Selti.'

I want to take her hand so much it hurts. Physically. Deep down in my guts. I want the feel of her skin on mine. And then an image of Jimmy pops into my head. Strapped into his chair, his face pulled into the agony of a silent scream, Gep's hand on the side of his neck, Gep's eyes as he looks at me and tells me that it's all my fault. That if I just did what he expected me to do then he wouldn't have to hurt Jimmy.

So instead of taking her hand, I stare down at it until she drops hers.

'Nice hair,' I say and I can feel the sneer on my face, even though I don't want it there. 'What, did a smurf die on your head?'

I feel like an arsehole. Like the biggest arsehole on the face of the planet as I watch her face go through shock and then anger in the space of a few seconds. And I want to rewind the last minute. Redo it. Take her hand. Not disappoint her. But I can't do that to Jimmy either.

'Excuse me?' she says and I can hear the attitude clearly in her voice. It just makes me want to know her more.

'You heard me,' I say.

Everyone is leaving around us when she leans forward and jabs her finger into my chest. The contact delivers an electric shock to my heart.

'I don't know who the hell you think you are,' she says, 'but you need to stop being a dickhead and get over yourself.'

And then she spins on her heel and walks away from me. I stand there for a moment, watching her walk out the door. She doesn't even look back. Not that I would if I was her. But the fact that I did that to her makes my heart sore, like it's got a crack in it.

'Way to make a good first impression,' Alex laughs, clapping me on the shoulder as he walks past me. 'Come on, we've got PE together next.'

I guess he doesn't see me as a threat anymore then. Which is good.

So why do I feel so bad?

It's only when I walk past her desk, following Alex outside, that I notice a blue hair on the laminated top. Without even thinking, I scoop it up and hold it between my finger and thumb, feeling the shaft roll between the tips, before I wrap it around my fingers. I have a part of her. A part of Selti. And, for some reason, it makes me feel better.

CHAPTER 5

I truly don't know how I get through the rest of the day. I'm so distracted by the thought I might see her again, I'm pretty sure Alex and Rory, who seem happy to be my unofficial guides, think I am some sort of numb-nutted idiot.

But I don't see her.

Not once.

Even though I catch myself searching for a glimpse of blue hair so often it's embarrassing. It's like she's a ghost – only existing in some screwed up part of my imagination. And I don't know how to feel about that. It's like a wash of relief and a stab of disappointment all at the same time, making me feel schitzo. And I don't want to ask anyone about her either. Not after the way I'd spoken to her in class. Mainly because that'd require me to answer questions I didn't want to even think about, let alone talk about.

But somehow, and God knows how, I've managed to bluff Alex and Rory enough that they still want me to come to training. So I haven't totally stuffed it, which is something at least. Fox and Kat are waiting for me at the front of the school.

'How was your day?' I ask.

Fox shrugs.

'You know, another school…'

I nod. He doesn't need to finish the sentence for me to know what he's saying.

'I met this guy who's been telling me all about the bikes he has,' Kat says, practically bouncing out of his skin in excitement. 'He said I could come over and go for a ride on the weekend. Do you think Gep will let me?'

I don't want to tell him that he probably won't have a chance in hell because I don't want to crush the excitement out of him. Not when they don't get that much to be excited about. I don't want to be like Gep. And anyway, who knows, maybe it's only me Gep hates. Maybe he'll let Kat have a life…sort of…

And so I shrug.

'Don't know. Maybe. You should ask him. Tell him you think this guy might be a possibility for owning the book.'

Kat nods like he thinks it's a great idea.

'Listen,' I say, 'I'm going to go to the courts this arv for some basketball training. There are nine guys on the team apparently, so that should give me a good start for collecting some info. Can you guys let Gep know for me?'

Kat and Fox both nod and turn to walk down the path. But they only go four steps before Fox turns around again. I can see the worry on his face.

'Don't forget it's the second Friday,' he says. 'Gep will want you home by six so he can do the…' he looks around him, like he's checking that no one's close enough to hear. 'You know, the thing.'

I nod, trying to look nonchalant, even though it feels like my insides have turned to ice.

'Yeah, I know. Tell him I'll be there in time.'

He nods back and looks at me for a second, as if he's trying to work out if he should say something else, before they both turn again and start to walk. I can hear Kat talking about the motor-bikes already and grin to myself, feeling sorry for Fox.

I visit the office quickly to grab the paperwork I need for Gep before looping around the school and heading towards the basketball courts in the far corner, over to the side of the main oval. They've been pretty well maintained, so it's obvious that basketball is a big deal for this school. I can see some guys there already, hanging around, taking shots, talking. Never thinking they wouldn't be included. I feel apart from it already. Like an intruder. Ready to put on my mask and become someone who is never really me but gets the information Gep needs.

Alex throws the ball at me as I step onto the court and I catch it and lob it towards the hoop. It misses, but only just.

'Oww,' he says, 'not bad, considering how far back you are.'

I shrug and grin at him.

'I meant to do that, just so you didn't feel threatened with how good I really am.'

He grins back.

'Sure you did.'

He turns to the rest of the guys on the court.

'Hey, everyone, this is Penn. We thought we'd give him a chance on the team and see how he goes.'

There's a couple of 'heys' and half-hearted waves. It's what I'd expect.

'Mr Mac's our coach,' Alex says. 'He should be here soon.'

For the next five minutes, we take it in turns to shoot hoops. I don't do too bad – don't disgrace myself but don't stand out from the crowd either. Which is exactly what I'm trying for. The easy-going, non-threating kid you're happy to talk to and maybe make part of the team. When Mr Mac shows up, everyone stops and turns to look at him. He smiles at me.

'Penn. Good to see you. Alex told me you were interested in being part of the team. Have you been playing long?'

'Four or five years,' I say.

'Good. Well, let's see what you can do, then I'll know where we might be able to fit you in the team.'

He divides us up into two teams and for the next fifty minutes all I can think about is what I need to be doing on the court. I don't think about Jimmy. Or Gep. Or what's going to be happening tonight when I get home. For almost an hour, I don't have to think about any of it.

Alex wasn't overselling it when he said they were good. They are. One of the best teams I've played on. Almost makes me wish I could be part of it for longer than a couple of months. But my whole life is a jigsaw of unfulfilled wishes.

I'm sweating my guts out at the end of play, feeling it trickle down my back in miniature rivers, my shirt sticking to my back. These guys play hard. And I realise that for a whole fifty minutes, not only haven't I thought about my life, I also haven't thought about the girl with the blue hair. Wow, a whole fifty minutes. What a frigging feat!

I stand with my hands on my hips, breathing hard, trying not to show it. Alex grins at me. He looks just as stuffed so it doesn't make me feel too bad.

'Jesus,' I say. 'Was that a normal training session?'

He punches my arm and laughs like I'm making a joke.

'You did well,' Mr Mac says to me. 'I think we can find a place on the team for you.'

'Cool.'

'Training's Wednesday and Friday afternoons.'

'Great.'

And just like that, I'm part of the team. Shame it's not for real. A sham. Make believe. A con. Whatever...

'Do you want to come back to my place?' Alex says. 'My parents own the general store and me and a few of the guys usually go back after practice for a coke.'

I look at my watch. It's quarter past five already. Cutting it too fine to get back home by six. And it's not worth having Gep mad at Jimmy for my stuff ups.

'Nah, sorry, I better get home. You know…first day and every-thing. Maybe next time.'

'Yeah, okay.'

I wave to the other guys. Nearly all of them respond, which is a good sign, and then I'm walking away, back to the house.

Back to Gep.

CHAPTER 6

*E*very step I take on my way back to the house makes me feel heavier, like extra kilos are being added to my body…or maybe to my soul…weighing me down. I don't want to go back. If it wasn't for Jimmy, I wouldn't. Not even for Kat and Fox. Which means basically, that I'm a bastard. But they're not true family. Not like Jimmy. And they're still young. They'd be fine.

It feels like it's getting worse with each town we go to – harder to do what Gep wants me to do, harder not to tell him to get stuffed and just leave, harder to stay so at least Jimmy has a bed and food and the occasional therapy when Gep pays for it and doesn't have to put up with living on the streets. Which I could do but Jimmy couldn't. It wouldn't be fair. And separation from him is not an option. Ever. Which is obviously why Gep's keeping Jimmy with him…

Finally, the house is in front of me. Everything's quiet inside. I don't know if that's a good thing or not. But at least I'm not late. Even by walking as slow as I possibly can, I'm still a good twenty minutes early.

I stand there for a moment longer, taking in the sounds of the

30

insects around me, the low hum of a lawn mower a couple of streets over, the shadows on the grass. Wasting time. Screwing up courage. Sometimes they feel like the same thing. No use putting it off though.

I take the four steps up to the veranda, dragging my feet, and open the door. I can hear talking from the back. They must all be in the kitchen. I debate, for a second, whether to go into my room and pretend I'm not here. But I can't do that to Jimmy when he's been home with only Gep for company most of the day – and not when I know it'd piss Gep off. So I dump my bag and make my way out there.

Gep looks up as I come in. He's doing something on the bench. But it's Friday night, so I know it's not dinner.

'How did you go?' he asks, looking back to what he's doing.

I wait until I've grabbed some juice out the fridge, drinking out of the bottle, before answering him.

'Yeah, alright. I'm a part of the basketball team now so, you know…' I shrug.

It's what he expects us to do – integrate ourselves into the community pretty quickly – so telling him about the team will keep him off my back. But that's all he's getting. I'm not telling him about Selti and all the things I've felt since I saw her. It's none of his business and I want it to stay that way.

'I only want to be here a month or two,' he says. 'Three months at the most.'

Jesus, that long? This book must be really important. Usually he gives us a month. Two at the very tops. I try not to think about spending three months trying to get glimpses of Selti. Or even talking to her again. Like a normal conversation rather than insulting her. Seeing her smile. At me, maybe. I realise I'm still standing there with the juice and haven't answered him yet.

'Okay.'

I look at Jimmy.

'How was your day?'

'It was alright,' he says and his eyes flick to Gep. I know he was probably bored out of his brain but there's no point whinging. All that'll do is make Gep angry and it's better to be bored than in pain.

I sit on the chair next to Jimmy at the table.

'I brought some work home for you.' I keep my voice quiet, although Gep always seems to have a way of hearing things anyway. 'It's in my bag. I'll get it for you later.'

He smiles, the twisted one that means I'd do anything for him.

'Good to see that you've got the servant thing down pat.'

I smile back at him.

'You're a dick.'

'Yeah, and we're identical twins so what does that mean?'

Dinner is a 'get-your-own' affair like it is most nights, so I stick some flavoured pasta in a packet in the microwave for Jimmy and me and Fox and Kat get in line behind me. Gep's not eating anything, which is what happens more times than not. I've given up trying to understand why. Because really, I don't want to know. I divide the pasta into two bowls and plonk them down in front of me on the table, ignoring what Gep's doing on the bench – trying to ignore it, anyway – and focusing on Jimmy and helping him to eat dinner instead. It takes a while but I don't care.

'Penn,' Gep says, shooting my name out like bullet from a pistol. I look up at him, even though I don't want to. 'You'll be conduit tonight.'

Jimmy's face falls at Gep's words and I can feel my guts twisting, rolling, making me feel like I'm going to throw up. I don't answer him. Just stare at the top of the table and think about how much I hate him. He mustn't like the silence though.

'Do you have a problem with that?'

I know he's waiting for me to say yes; waiting to assert his dominance over me once again. I force the word out of my mouth.

'No.'

He smiles, like he knows he's won.

'Good.'

I help Jimmy with another mouthful, trying not to think about tonight. Trying not to think about the last time…

'You aren't eating much,' Jimmy says between forkfuls.

'Not really hungry.'

Which isn't a lie. Gep's demands have made my appetite flee like a little girl from the big, bad wolf and the smell of the pasta is suddenly sickening…cloying. If it wasn't for the fact that Jimmy needed to eat, I'd probably go to my room and wait for Gep to call me. But I don't tell Jimmy this. It's hard enough to get him to eat as it is. I clean the bowls in the sink when he's finished and sit back down, watching Fox and Kat flick their pasta at each other.

'Stop it.' It comes out as a growl and I feel bad for a split second, but I can't help it. My nerves have been tensioned to their absolute limit. Any minute now, they're going to snap and that'll be the end of me.

Jimmy kicks me under the table and because he can't control his movements so well, it's harder than he probably means. I'm about to lose it at him when I see his face. He looks scared. For me. This is the seventh fortnight in a row I've had to be the conduit and each time it gets harder and harder to get myself out of it.

'Don't worry. It'll be fine,' I say. But even *I* don't believe it.

'I'll be the conduit,' Jimmy says, twisting in his chair slightly and looking at Gep.

'No!' I couldn't stand it – watching Jimmy be taken in by Gep's power, watching him struggle to try and keep himself present. I figure it's sort of selfish, but I want to be the one to do it rather than have to be the one watching.

Gep looks at both of us, like he's weighing up his options. I hold my breath, waiting for him to answer.

'No,' he says finally. 'Penn's doing it.'

I want to punch the air in celebration, which is stupid. Really stupid. Being the conduit to any of Gep's connections is not fun. Not even close. In fact, totally the opposite. And yet every fortnight we do them – every fortnight he forces us. Usually me. Although he's been getting Fox to do them more often lately. Which I'm glad of, except I feel guilty about it too. Like it's my fault somehow. Not that Gep cares he's screwing us up more and more every time we do it. All he cares about is the power. How strong it makes him. When he'll get his next hit. Like a God damn junkie.

I wonder what he'll do when we all finally leave. He told me once, ages ago in a rare moment when he was actually more human than psycho, that sometimes he felt bad for getting us to do it. But the power hit was better when he had one of us do it rather than being the conduit himself. And that's why he'd wanted the stuff we'd stolen. Apparently they'd make him stronger – he'd be able to use them rather than having to make us conduits. And like a bunch of naïve idiots, we'd believed him. It hadn't stopped though, no matter how much we'd stolen. And the power was always more important than we were.

We sit in silence, waiting for him. Even Kat's quiet for once. Finally, Gep's finished and he goes over to the sink to wash his hands. I can feel my heart starting to pound. Don't do it, don't do it, don't do it – the words echo in my body in time with my heart beat. Except that's not an option. If it's not me, then it'll be Jimmy… That's what Gep will do to punish me.

He turns to look at me.

'Well,' he says. 'What are you waiting for? Come and get it.'

I stand up from the table, the chair raking its way across the lino like it's playing the death march. I can see what's in the dish from here and I don't want to go any closer. Not again – no, no, no. But I walk over to it anyway, making sure Gep doesn't see my reluctance – not wanting to give him that pleasure. And I try to focus on what I need to do rather than the deep silence that seems to be filling up the room.

It's as nasty as it always is. The entrails of the chicken Gep killed today are wrapped around its bones, and then topped with honey and butter and this weird salty, grainy mix. There's bile in the back of my throat and I swallow hard, refusing to give into it. I can feel Gep's eyes on me but I don't turn to look at him. Instead, I slide my hands underneath, feeling the honey and butter coating my fingers like it's trying to become a part of me. I can feel the power in it. The power Gep wants for himself, over and over, because it never seems to be enough. The power that keeps us tied to him.

The smell of the honey and raw chicken grabs at the back of my throat and I have the desperate urge to throw it on the ground, grind it into the lino with my feet so he can't use it. Can't make me be conduit. But it's just delaying the inevitable. I wrap my fingers tighter around it and turn to look at Gep.

'Are we going to do this or not?' I'm stupidly proud of the fact that there's no waver in my voice.

He grins at me, like we're partners in crime. My throat tightens, swells up like the tears want to in my eyes if I'd let them. Weak. I wait for him to say something but he leads us into the lounge room and I follow, just like that.

Weak.

I can hear the squeak of Jimmy's wheels as either Fox or Kat pushes him in. I don't look at him, not wanting to see in his face what'd be in mine if he was the one doing this instead. As long as he's safe, I can do it though. As long as he's safe…

Gep already has the fireplace going. It's one of those old black ones with the door at the front. The only requirement in any house we rent – no thought about our comfort – as long as it has a fireplace so he can get his power hit.

He bends down and opens the door to stoke the flames higher. I can feel the heat on my cheeks and struggle not to turn away. I watch as he stands back up and faces me, bringing his hands so they sit under mine, mushing the honey and fat that's dripping down onto the back of my hand. I can feel the power already – not painful – but there, waiting. My heart's thrashing in my chest like it's trying to pull me away from this spot, make me move, move, move. My feet stay stubbornly still though. I twist my lips, trying get rid of the sweat that's forming on top of them.

Gep smiles at me and his eyes are full of anticipation. He pushes my hands together even more, like he wants me to share his excitement. Like he thinks I already am.

'It's going to be a good one tonight. I can feel it. Can you? Can you feel the power, Penn?'

I shrug, not wanting to answer him. Not wanting him to see how shit scared I am, even after years of being forced to do this. Not wanting to show him just how much I want to run out into the fresh air and scrub the stickiness from my fingers and feel the cool air in my lungs, on my face, through my hair. Cleanse myself of the feel of Gep's power that's surrounding me like a beast stalking its prey.

My eyes flick to my right. I can see Jimmy out of the corner of my eye. His face is white, his eyes wide. Scared, that's how he looks. For me. I look away before I give into my own fear, waiting just below the surface, ready to claim me if I'd let it.

Gep lets go of my hands to pick up an old black pan, holding it in front of me. The edges are darker than the middle, where the multitude of fires it's been in have licked at the sides, the flames hungry to consume. He holds it by its two metal handles and shuts his eyes for a moment, his lips moving quickly to form the words I can only just hear. Not that any of them make sense. And not that I want to know what they mean anyway.

But I can feel it already. I can feel the power increasing, pushing on me from every side. I fight to keep my eyes open against it. And then he's holding the pan under my hands and I drop the tangled mess into it, hearing the wet, sucking sound as it settles into the pan. He turns and puts it in the fire and I'm left with dripping fingers, watching him.

Waiting. Waiting for something I don't want to happen.

The silence stretches on, punctuated only by the sound of the entrails cooking, until I'm almost ready to scream. How is it possible time seems to be moving so frigging slow and really fast at the same time? My stomach cramps at the thought of what's to come.

Gep gives me another smile before he turns and grabs the pan out of the fire. He doesn't have any protection on his hands but he's never had to. The heat doesn't burn him. He grips the handles like they're cool to touch and holds the pan in front of me again; the chicken cooked to almost a blackened crisp, the smell of the burnt honey sickly sweet in the air.

I shut my eyes against the sight of it, wishing myself away.

'Do it!' Gep's voice cuts through me, dragging my eyes open.

My hands are shaking as they move towards the pan. There's nothing I can do to keep them steady. No way to hide it. But Gep's too far gone to notice anyway. His eyes are wide; manic. Fucking psycho.

'Do it!' he says again.

And my hands are reaching towards the chicken, like I don't have any will of my own, grabbing a piece of the entrails from around the bone, feeling it squelch under my fingers, feeling the heat on my skin, and ripping it off from the rest. And then, my fingers are bringing it up to my mouth, closer and closer. I open my lips, my breath fast, panting, sucking in a lungful of the acrid smell as I do.

I don't want to do this!

Fuck!

I can't. Don't make me.

My fingers are shaking like they're having their own personal earthquake. And then Gep's hand is pushing in to mine, jamming the chicken between my teeth. I can taste the burnt honey on my tongue, feel the juices run down the back of my throat and struggle not to throw up, knowing he'll make me do it again, over and over until I actually swallow some. I force it down, not wanting it to be in my mouth for any longer than it needs to be. Just wanting it over and done with.

And then the power's not around me anymore. It's in me. Fighting to get out.

CHAPTER 7

I can feel the power pulsing in me, like it's trying to take over from my heart, trying to become the essence of who I am. It feels poisonous, filling me with a blackness that creeps over my body, and I want to reach in and rip it out before it can take any more of me.

'Tell me what I need to know,' Gep's saying.

I clamp my teeth shut, grinding them together, trying to keep it in, but it's no good. It's there. A part of me even though it's not. And then a voice is spewing out of my mouth. A voice that doesn't belong to me and that I can't control.

'The item you seek is here.'

Gep smiles.

'I know that. Is it the last thing we need?'

'Yes.'

I can see Gep's eyes shining as he takes in the power, pulling it to him. Psycho shining, like he's got no basis in reality and could easily pull out a knife and end it for all of us. And there'd be absolutely nothing I could do. I'm helpless, controlled by whatever's in me. Unable to look after myself let alone Jimmy. Shit. Shit!

My body isn't mine – it feels like my soul's been crammed

into the back of my skull and I'm just hanging in there. Watching what's going on without being able to control it. It's worse than last time. A lot worse. I push back against the power but it holds me down, pinning me.

And the voice speaks again.

'There is another power.'

This is a first. It's never spoken about anything like this before. Gep freezes, his eyes narrowing. He looks at all of us, like he expects us to jump up and do the burn on him. He stares in my direction the longest but I don't actually know if he's staring at me or the thing that's occupying me.

'What?'

'There is another power. Not yet developed. It is waiting for the blue to claim its hold. But it will be strong.'

Blue? The word shocks me, swamping me with images of Selti, chewing her pen, glaring at me, jabbing me with her finger...

And if I'm thinking about her, then she's open to the thing that's in me. They'll be able to see her, if they want. If they're paying attention.

I push against the power, harder than I ever have before. Aggressive. Forceful. Until, with a roar that's all me, I throw up on the living room floor, falling to my knees while I spew until there's nothing left. Even if all of this has nothing to do with her, I'm not willing to take the risk. I don't want any of her to belong to Gep – not even through second hand knowledge. I need to keep her safe, even if I don't really know why.

I wipe my mouth with the back of my hand, my breath still coming in gasps, and finally look up. Everyone is looking at me. But it's Gep I'm focused on. Call it a matter of survival. Because I don't know how he's going to react to this. Whether he'll see it as a betrayal – that not only have I taken away his power fix but also the possibility of answers – or whether he'll take it as something that's happened and move on.

He leans down to me, his face only inches from mine, his breath hot on my skin.

'You're weak,' he says. 'Pathetic. What a joke. Fucking weak. How could I ever think that you...'

But he doesn't finish the sentence. He pushes into me instead, knocking me fully to the ground. And then he's walking away. Looks like I've got off easy. For once.

'And clean up that fucking mess,' he yells back to me.

I sit back on my haunches and take a deep breath. Even if I do have to clean it up it was worth it. I don't know why I did it, but I do know it feels right to have protected Selti from Gep. Which doesn't make sense at all! Jesus! What's happened to me? One day! That's all it's been. One day – one stupid meeting where I made her hate me – and I'm thinking about how I need to protect her? It's nuts!

And the worse thing is, I don't even know if I had to. One stupid word for Christ's sake! A colour. It could mean anything!

'Are you okay?' The worry is clear on Jimmy's face and the emotion makes his words slur a bit more than normal – make it harder for him to keep control.

All I can do is nod. Anything else feels like too much energy. There's silence, hanging around us like a cloud, until Kat speaks.

'Did you hear what the spirit said, Penn? Did you hear it?'

I look at him. But all I think about is the blue reference, which shouldn't mean anything to him. He must see the blank look on my face.

'He said it was the last thing we need. The last thing! Do you think that'll mean we can stay here?'

My heart jumps at the thought. Could we stay here? Could I make friends finally? Actually play on the basketball team? But as I'm saying that in my head, all I'm picturing is Selti. And yet, I can't imagine not moving...can't imagine actually having a life. Not with Gep in the picture anyway. I'm saved from answering by Fox.

'Don't be stupid, Kat. We've got to steal the frigging book from here. Gep will want to leave as soon as we've got it.'

'Do you think the next place then?'

Jimmy's not even listening to them. He's looking at me instead.

'What happened?' he says.

'Nothing.' The word croaks out of my throat, still burning from the vomit. I feel bad keeping things from him but I don't want to tell him about Selti. Not in front of Fox and Kat anyway. And definitely not where Gep might over hear.

I know he doesn't believe me. I can see on his face that he knows there's something going on. Stupid twin thing. He always knows. I shrug.

'It was hard, that's all.'

That stops Kat and Fox's conversation. They're not the conduit as much as I am but they understand how shitty it is to be forced to do it. To feel like you don't own your body any more. To not be able to do anything until the spirit's sent away by Gep. This is the first time he hasn't had to finish it for us to be free again. The first time I've ever been able to force it out, even if I have no frigging idea how I did it.

As if he can read my thoughts, Fox sits on the seat in front of me.

'How did you do that? Force it out?'

I shrug. 'I seriously have no idea.'

I feel bad. It'd be good to be able to share what I did so maybe they could do it too. He squints at me, like he needs glasses or something.

'Do you feel different?' His voice has a spark of suspiciousness, like he thinks I'm lying to him.

'No. Just drop it, okay? I don't know what happened.'

He looks at me for a moment, mouth open like he's about to say something else, and then flops back in the seat. Disappointed.

But it's not my fault. I can't tell him what I don't know. He sighs and looks at Jimmy.

'Do you think we'll need to do it anymore?' He says it cautiously – on guard – like he has to stop himself from being too hopeful.

'Probably not. Not if what the…thing said is true. About it being the last object,' Jimmy says, but he's looking at me with doubt in his face and I know what he's thinking.

'Unless he wants to find out more about the other power,' I finish for him and he nods.

'Yeah, what was that all about?' Kat is screwing up his face like thinking is painful for him.

I stand up, not wanting to answer him.

'I'm getting a bucket.'

'Fox and Kat will get it,' Jimmy says.

They look at each other and grumble about it but do what he asks anyway. It's funny how we're all happy to do things for him. How everyone he meets tries to make him happy. It's because he's the good one…the nice one.

I go and sit on the chair next to Jimmy. He hands me the box of wipes that Gep buys just for this – how screwed up is that – and I try and get all the crap off my hands. I slump back and shut my eyes, even though I can see he wants to talk.

'What's going on?' Jimmy asks. I know he's trying to be quiet but tone control's never been one of his strengths.

'I don't know.'

'Bullshit.'

I open my eyes now and look at him.

'Nothing's going on, okay? Nothing I can't handle. We'll find the book and be out of here. And then we'll have a normal life, like Kat said.'

Jimmy snorts like he knows what a crock of shit that is.

'How did you do it? Get it out of you? Are you okay?'

I try a grin. It feels twisted but it's there.

'Well apart from bringing up my dinner, I'm good.' He doesn't smile back at me and I sigh. 'I don't know. That's the truth. I just...pushed it. Really hard.'

'You've never done that before though. What if it hurts you?'

I shrug. 'It didn't.'

'You've got to stay safe,' he says to me, his left hand spasming off the arm of his chair like it's backing him up.

I try another smile. It fits better on my face this time.

'Sure, bro. Safe is my middle name.'

He rolls his eyes but he's smiling now, and the pressure decreases from my chest. Maybe I can do this. Keep Jimmy safe and keep away from Selti so I can keep her safe too. Maybe.

CHAPTER 8

I jerk awake, the feeling of pain so intense I'm expecting Gep to be standing over me, hand on my skin. But I'm alone in the room, which means only one thing.

Jimmy!

I'm out of the bed so quickly it's like I'm running before my feet even hit the floor. Using the door frame as a swinging pole, I'm in the kitchen before I feel like I've had enough time to draw a real breath. Jimmy's at the table, panting, hair all sweaty, left arm so tight he can barely keep it down on his armrest – it's sticking out in front of him, locked at his elbow.

I look at Gep and he grins at me, like he's sharing a joke I haven't even begun to understand.

'Thought that'd get you out of bed.'

I want to hit him – launch myself across the table and take him down – pummel him until he begs for mercy and even then, I don't know if I'd stop.

But Jimmy needs me more. I sit beside him and start to massage his arm, trying to make the muscles loosen up to ease the pain.

'You know, most normal people just yell to wake someone up.'

I struggle to keep the anger out of my voice but I need to. Even though my head is so full of rage it feels like my brains are going to explode all over the kitchen table. One big, red hot mess.

'Yes, but this is much more effective. It's fun to see how fast you can get out here, especially when it's not even you I'm doing it to. That twin thing is amazing, don't you think? Imagine the research the scientists could do on you two.'

I don't answer. I just focus on Jimmy, looking into his eyes, which are still filled with pain. My fingers press into his skin, trying to make his muscles respond. It's like he's got walnuts under his skin. Press and slide, press and slide. That's all I need to focus on.

'I'm going out,' Gep says. 'I wanted you awake before I left.'

I still don't respond. I don't even want to know where he's going, except if he's disappearing for good. Getting the hell out of our lives. That'd be something I'd be happy to hear. Sitting across the table from us, Fox's eyes flick between me and Gep. He looks scared but then, who wouldn't be when the man who's supposed to be a father to you is nothing more than a fucking psychopath.

'You coming back?' he says.

'Not until later this afternoon. I expect you to have learned something about the whereabouts of the book by then.'

He moves over behind Jimmy and I tense, my own muscles as tight as my brother's, but he just ruffles his hair. Jimmy's eyes are wide, and I know he's waiting for the next burn. But Gep isn't looking at Jimmy. He's looking at me, waiting to see what I'll do. Testing me. Watching me as if he expects me to do something stupid. Except I don't know what I'm being tested on. I'm here, doing what he wants. So, I wait, fingers still for the moment. He smiles.

'Take good care of Jimmy while I'm gone,' he says. 'He seems to be a little tight.'

And then he's walking out the door and I have to actually think about relaxing my jaw before my teeth break under the pressure. When we hear the car start, it's like the stress, fear, anger; whatever it is – maybe a mixture of all of them – melts out of the room. Gep's gone and we're safe. For the moment, anyway.

'Hey,' Fox says, like it's the first time he's seen me this morning and nothing else has happened. 'You okay after last night?'

'Yeah, alright.' I don't want to tell him my brain feels like it's swollen to twice its normal size and it's pressing painfully against my skull. But Fox knows anyway. Probably because he's experienced it himself. He gets up and grabs the packet of painkillers from the cupboard above the fridge. I nod at him as he puts them in front of me.

'I'm guessing Kat's already gone.' I have vague memories of hearing him chattering to me when I was still half asleep. Something about going over to the friend's house with the bikes and how much he wants to be able to ride one. Even the fact that his audience was, for all intents and purposes, unconscious, didn't stop the flow of words.

'Yeah, he took off early. Probably the smart one.'

All I can do is nod in agreement.

'So, what are you up to today?' I say to Fox as I pop some pills from their packet. He shrugs.

'I think I'm a geek in this town,' he says but he doesn't look happy about it. 'There are some gamers in my grade. Into role playing and crap. They're the only ones I can think of that might have the book. They've invited me over today. I should go.'

'Man, that sucks,' I say.

We've only got access to one computer between us all and it's a pretty crap one, so none of us have ever really got into anything like that. Sometimes I forget that it's not just me who has to pretend to be a different person in every town we go to.

'Yeah. But whatever. If it keeps Gep happy…'

I nod. That's the premise we all work on, not that we're very successful at it. I look at Jimmy. He's started to relax a little now Gep's not here.

'Are you okay?'

He nods, and a grimace screws up his face. 'I told him he should let you sleep. Told him he was being stupid. Sorry.'

I grip the edge of the table, pressing down until the pads of my fingers hurt.

'You don't need to apologise. Jesus, he keeps you in here like a fucking prisoner and then hurts you. And it's all to get at me. He hates me and you're the one who suffers.'

Jimmy grins, like he's trying to be brave.

'Guess that means you owe me then.'

I can't help but smile back, even though I don't want to. I want to get us out of here. Safe. Protected. Away.

'Yeah. Guess I'll have to be your servant for life.'

'Good,' he says. 'Then I order you to take me outside. I'm sick of being in here. I want to get out in the sun and fresh air rather than being in this shit box house all the time.'

I hesitate, but just for a second. Stuff Gep. This is my brother and if he wants to go outside, he'll go outside.

So much for keeping Gep happy…

'Sure. It looks like there's a creek down the bottom of the yard. Do you want me to take you down there?'

He nods, a big one, which moves his upper body too.

'Make sure no one sees you,' Fox says. 'Gep will lose it if someone comes knocking and starts talking about wanting to help Jimmy or something, or asking about why he's not in school. Might be better to stay in here.'

'I fucking hate this,' Jimmy says and bangs his hand on the table, elbow stiff again. 'If I can't go to school, I want to go outside. I'm not a vampire, for Christ sake. And I'm not a bad person. I haven't done anything wrong!'

'We'll go outside,' I say. 'The back yard's private. And big. No one's going to see us. We can stay out there for as long as you want.'

He nods but I can tell he's not happy. My chest tightens in response. It's not right. He's not a frigging prisoner...well, he shouldn't be, even if Gep treats him like one. He deserves to go wherever he wants.

'Or we can go somewhere else. Yeah, let's do that. We'll go down to the café, get a coke, whatever.'

He sighs and shakes his head.

'No. Fox is right. Gep will flip. The back yard is good. I just want to get some fresh air.'

Part of me is relieved he says that. And then I feel like a real shit. Like I'm as bad as Gep, wanting to keep him hidden. But Gep will hurt him again if I do the wrong thing. And I don't think I could control my response next time, which probably won't lead to good things for any of us. Even when he's not here, he still seems to be able to control us.

'Well, I'm out of here,' Fox says. 'One of us better come back with something for Gep. Otherwise it won't be worth coming home.'

We watch him go out and I turn to Jimmy.

'So are we going to struggle with the chair or am I going to help you.'

'Stuff the chair. I feel like I haven't stood up in ages.'

I nod and push his chair to the back door, next to the fridge in the kitchen. It feels weird to just be the two of us. That hasn't happened for a long time and the squeak of the chair tyres on the floor only seems to bring home how quiet the house is.

I swing open the door and then turn, putting my arm under Jimmy's and pulling him up. He's unsteady, and for a second, I think we're going to go down. We both laugh as I catch us. It feels good. Normal. Well, normal for us anyway.

We start down the few stairs and it's pretty obvious that, from being in his chair so long, Jimmy's legs aren't going to do what they're supposed to. Maybe it's a twin thing, or maybe it's because he's my brother, but I know that each step he tries to take is full of frustration and pain. Pain he doesn't want to say anything about because that's the type of person he is – the kind who suck it up and try not to create any problems. Without warning, I grab him and put him over my shoulder in a fireman's lift.

'Jerk!' he says, struggling to get out of my hold but I just laugh. He's so light, it's not a problem to hold him.

'Stop flinging yourself around. I'm just taking you down the stairs.'

I put him down on the ground, my arm still around him to keep him stable.

'Arsehole! Don't do that again without telling me. I'm not some frigging damsel in distress!'

'Okay. Okay. Sorry.'

We walk over the dried-out grass and it crunches under our feet, pricking into our skin like it's trying to protect itself from invasion. Jimmy struggles with every step, although it's definitely easier for him on the flat than the stairs. Not that I care how long it takes. The hedges on either side of us are tall and no one can see. And the sun's warm on my skin.

Finally we make it down to the edge of the property where a creek winds its way through the rocks and grass that litter its bottom. I help Jimmy sit down, back leaning against a tree, and stick my feet in the water. It's cold and I can feel the goose pimples travel along my skin.

We sit there for a while in silence, enjoying being on our own together and listen to the crickets and birds starting to call again, fooled by our quietness.

Finally, he sighs.

'So what's the school like?'

I shrug.

'Same as any other school. You're not missing much.'

But we both know that's not true. Anything would be better than having to be stuck inside with Gep day in and day out.

'Any cute girls?'

'Some.' I try not to think of Selti, chewing on the end of her pen before I was an arsehole and said all the things to make her angry.

He knows me better than that though – just like I know him. He watches me, waiting for me to say something else. I try to stare him out but then I feel guilty. At least I'm allowed out to experience some sort of life – to get away from our psycho pseudo-parent. What sort of crappy brother would I be to keep it from him?

'There's this one girl in my English class. She's got blue hair...'

'Blue!' Jimmy laughs. 'God, you can pick them.'

'It's not like I really like her or anything. Just...you know... she's different. Not that it means anything anyway. As soon as Gep's got the book, we're out of here and it doesn't matter who's at school or how different they are.'

'Where do you think we'll go next?'

I snort.

'Christ, who knows. When has Gep ever told us what his plans are? I don't think he's going to start now. It'll only be till the end of the year for us anyway, then you and I are out of here. I'll get a job somewhere and we'll get a flat and you can get some proper treatment.'

He's quiet and I'm suddenly worried about what he's thinking. What if he doesn't want to leave? I can't go without him. He needs me to look after him.

'What?' I say. 'Don't you want to get out of here?'

He nods and then shrugs in a way that makes my chest feel like it's collapsing in on itself. Because it's always been about me and Jimmy, getting away. Having a life. But if he doesn't want to go...well, shit.

'Yeah. Of course. But what about Fox and Kat? Are we going to leave them?'

It's my turn to shrug now, but the guilt stabs into me like a samurai warrior with a finely honed sword. Jimmy's always been better than me. Always more concerned with everyone else. The one with a conscience that actually works. Maybe I should've been the one injured in the accident.

'They'll be okay,' I say. 'They have each other. It's not like we're going to leave only one of them. And if this book is the last thing Gep needs, then maybe they'll be better than okay. Maybe they'll have a chance at a normal life.'

'Do you think? What's he going to do with it all though? All the stuff you stole for him?' He struggles to get the words out, his tongue and mouth not wanting to co-operate the more he tries to rush the words. I wait for him to finish. 'What if he does more than just the rituals once he's got everything he needs? Worse stuff? What if he hurts them? Really hurts them? More than the burn?'

I squirm against the thought, taking my feet out of the water and sitting cross legged, ripping a leaf to pieces while I avoid answering him. I don't want to tell him I'd been thinking about that too. All these things Gep's had us steal over the years…they have to be for something, don't they? He said it's for his power – so we don't have to do the rituals – but what if it's not? He lies all the time – how do I know he isn't now? Or what if all this stuff makes him more powerful? Or more sadistic? How can we leave Fox and Kat to that? Which is why I don't want to think about it. I need to get Jimmy out…before he gets hurt even more. He's my priority. My real family. He's the only one I need to protect.

'They'll be fine,' I say but I can hear the doubt in my own voice, even if he can't. 'Gep actually likes them. Look how often it's me doing the ritual. It's hardly ever them.'

Except it has been Fox. More and more over the last year, Gep's been getting him to do it. And when that's happened, all

I've felt is relief. Every time Gep doesn't pick Jimmy or me, it's like a get out of jail free card. I am a sucky human being.

'They're our brothers,' he says, and I can hear the determination in his voice. He's not going to let it go.

My heart sinks to my stomach, cramping so much it feels like it's being eaten by the stomach acid.

'They're not though. Not really. And we can't take them. How am I going to make enough money to support them too?' But I feel like such an arsehole for even saying those words.

'Then we need to stay.'

'Fuck, Jimmy! Are you crazy? We need to get out!' I screw the rest of the leaf up in my fist and throw it away. 'How am I supposed to keep you safe when we're trapped here with Gep? I can't do it!'

'You don't need to keep me safe. I'm not a baby, Penn. I'm the older one, remember.'

Only by two freaking minutes. I flop back on the grass behind me and cover my eyes with my arm, blocking the sun flickering through the leaves overhead. Blocking out my world. It's not working. All I can think about is Jimmy's face this morning, when Gep did the burn on him. How can he protect himself against a psycho like Gep, especially when he can't move very fast? He needs me, even if he doesn't want to acknowledge it.

'Whatever.'

'No, not whatever. I get to make decisions too. And I'm not leaving without Fox and Kat. You can leave if you want.'

'I'm not going to frigging leave without you.' I'm guessing he knew this was what I'd say. Part of me hates him for knowing how to make me do what he wants.

'So what about this blue haired girl?' It's his peace offering. A change in subject, something to make me feel better.

'What about her?' I can hear the sulkiness in my voice and he laughs.

'Stop being such a frigging baby! Do you want to get with her or what?'

'No.'

'Bullshit. You should. You've never gone out with anyone.'

'Yeah, unlike you, the man-whore.'

He laughs again. It's something he's always been proud of. Doesn't matter which school we've gone to, he's always the first to get a girlfriend. I don't know what it is, but all the girls seem to love him.

'Are you going to ask her out?'

'Jesus, you don't let up, do you? No, I'm not going to ask her out. I need to get the book for Gep.'

'You can find the book and have a girlfriend.'

I don't want to even think about what he's said. Because if I allow myself even that little bit of hope that I could have both, I'm worried I'll get...distracted. And that I won't want to leave when Gep tells us it's time to go. Besides, even if Jimmy *was* right, there'd be no way she'd be interested now. Not after I was such a dick and said what I did.

'I'm going to concentrate on finding the book. It's the last thing Gep needs. Then, who knows?'

'Loser. Admit it. You're just afraid of girls.' He wriggles around and flops down beside me. 'What do you reckon all that stuff about the other power was about? Do you think we're going to have to be worried about someone else? Someone like Gep?'

'Who the hell knows? I'm sick of even thinking about it. I want our own life.'

But I know I'm not going to get it. Not yet anyway.

CHAPTER 9

Fox and Kat are in front of me, pushing each other as they walk to school, acting like idiots. It's sort of nice to see they're not stressed anymore. That the ritual's over for another fortnight...maybe forever, if what we hoped over the weekend comes true. I'm reluctant to be easy about it though. Like letting my guard down will give something else the opportunity to come up and slap me in the face – and usually that something else has to do with Gep.

My shoe drags across the gravel at the edge of the bitumen road. I wish Jimmy was here, sitting in his chair while I pushed him as fast as I could without tipping him out, both of us laughing at the thrill of it. Coming to school with us. Getting away from Gep...

He was quiet this morning. Quieter than normal. I think it's wearing him down – us going to school and leaving him there. I don't know what to do or say to make him feel better... Not that there's really anything, I guess. It's shit, and it's all Gep's fault. Another reason to hate him.

And yet, what's even shittier is the way my heart's beating out a frigging drum solo at the thought I might see Selti today. Total fucking, selfish loser – that's me. How can I even be a little bit excited about that when Jimmy's so screwed?

I just need to find the book and get the hell out of this town so I can get through the next seven months and turn eighteen and make a life for Jimmy and me…if I can convince him Fox and Kat will be okay. Then no one can come and give us shit about the type of care Jimmy needs and how we should stay with our father and want to put us in the 'system' to make sure they can keep tabs on us. That happened when we were thirteen and ran away. The punishment Gep dealt out for that little show of rebellion still makes me go cold. It was only because we moved so much that they lost track of us again.

No complications. No distractions. That's it. I've waited too long to get out of here to be side-tracked by some girl with funky hair. I square my shoulders, mind made up, and follow Kat and Fox through the front gates.

'See you this arv,' Kat calls out to me and I wave as I make my way towards the back of the school, where I sat with the guys for lunch on Friday.

Alex and Rory are both there, tossing grapes up into the air and trying to catch them in their mouths. They suck at it and so I grab one as I walk up to them, lobbing it up in the air and catching it between my teeth.

'Frigging show off,' Alex says but he's smiling and I smile back at him around the grape.

And it's time to get to work. Time to get the information I need – something I'm good at. I slouch on the bench next to him and start the process, pretending to be the person they want me to be even if they don't know it. To be one of them, even though I never feel like I am.

'So, what's the go with the other students here? Anyone interesting?'

'What? You mean, apart from stupid slags with blue hair? Man, that was such a slap down you gave Selti Friday!'

Rory has his hand up for a high five and I have to force myself to slap his hand rather than punch him. What the hell's wrong with me?

'Yeah, what's her story?' I'm trying to tell myself this is just about getting information. After all, I need to find out about everyone in this town – try and work out where the book might have the greatest possibility of being.

'Well, she's had the good sense to tell Rory to get lost twice,' Alex says with a laugh. That fact actually makes me feel better. Even though it shouldn't.

'Shut up.' Rory punches him in the arm.

'What's with the blue hair?'

Alex shrugs.

'Don't know. She started doing it at the end of last year. Just turned up at school one day with it like that.'

'Right. And what's she like? Smart? Stuck up?'

'Smart, I guess. She pretty much keeps to herself. Her and another girl, Emily – they're tight, but that's about it. She's always been a bit weird. Her dad's a uni lecturer and her mum's a hippie. Guess she probably can't help it.'

My antennae start whirring at this information. But I'm interested in this for the sake of the book – that's all. It's what I'd normally be interested in. It has nothing to do with her. Nothing at all.

'Oh yeah. What's he teach?'

Alex raised his eyebrows. 'Why the interest?'

It's my turn to shrug.

'No interest. Just…you know…curious about everyone here. Move into a new place – it's good to get a feel for it.'

'Yeah, well, ask Alex about *Sarah* then.' Rory's making gestures with his hands that aren't leaving a lot to the imagination.

'Stuff off.' Alex turns away from him and looks at me. 'It's a small town. Not much to learn really. Most of us have lived here all of our lives. That's why I can't wait to get away next year.'

'You're not going to follow in your parents' footsteps and manage the store?'

Alex laughs.

'Not a chance in hell. I'm going to uni to do sports physio.'

I nod. A man with a plan – you've got to respect that.

'Sweet. What about you, Rory?'

'I've already got an apprenticeship lined up for next year,' he says, puffing his chest out like he's the man.

'Yeah, with your dad in his electrical business,' Alex says.

'So? It's still an apprenticeship. I'll be earning money before you do.'

I have to stop myself from rolling my eyes. They're like a bickering old couple. Obviously, that's what it's like to actually have friends, but it's not getting me the information I need. I dig my hands into my pockets.

'So what then? Normal collection of nerds, footy heads, princesses and cultural freaks?'

'Yeah. Pretty much.' Rory points to a group of three guys sitting in a group at the edge of a building. They're huddled together, looking at something, before they all sit back and laugh. 'Role players,' he says. It doesn't sound like he thinks it's a good thing. 'You know, Dungeons and Dragons. Or some crap like that anyway.'

'Right.' I look at the three guys with more interest. Anyone into role playing might have an interest in an old book on all things mystic and spiritual…an old book like the one Gep wants. Well, I'm guessing that's what it's about anyway. All of the stuff we've stolen seems to be in that general category. Maybe I don't need to go anywhere near Selti after all. I can keep myself away from her and avoid all sorts of really dumb, pathetic decisions that'll probably impact on Jimmy. And I've been a part of this sort of group in another school. It was actually kind of interesting. Fun even.

'Are they the only ones in the school?'

'Another guy, Kenneth, is usually with them,' Alex says. 'But I think they're the only ones in year twelve. Don't know about the other grades … there probably are. Why, you interested in joining?'

He's grinning at me, like he's just waiting to call me out as a loser. I debate, just for a second, telling him I am and seeing what happens, but it's too soon yet to align myself with one group. And the popular kids usually have the most useful information to start with.

'Nah, I'm good.' I grin back at him. 'And is there someone who's a big deal around town?'

He laughs. 'Yeah, that'd be Henry Williams. He owns most of the stuff in town. You know, businesses and things. He owns the sawmill, so he thinks he's pretty shit hot. Personally, I think he's a bit of a wanker. His daughter's in year nine. She'll tell you how great they are.'

I nod, trying not to look too interested. A couple of people to start with then – rich or nerdy or hippie or book smart. Not a bad morning. That's when the bell goes.

'Come on,' Alex says, slapping me on the arm as he goes past. 'We've got maths.'

I follow him into the main part of the school, trying really hard not to look around me to see if I can catch a glimpse of blue hair. It's harder than I thought it'd be. And my stomach clenches in anticipation as I go into the classroom – I'm not sure if it's because I don't want to see her or if I do. But she's not there anyway. It only takes a quick scan to see that. I stuff the disappointment way down so that it's almost unrecognisable.

Find the book. It's a mantra I have to keep telling myself.

The class drags. Maths is definitely not my strong point and having a double lesson makes it that much crappier. What sort of sadistic idiot schedules a double maths first up Monday? I have to force myself to pay attention and my mind wanders more than I'd like it to. Wondering where Selti is, what class she's doing, if she enjoys it... I can't understand why my brain's devoting so much time to her! I've never been affected this much by a girl before. Ever. Even by the ones I thought were pretty hot at the other schools we've been too.

What is it about this girl that has me so preoccupied, for Christ's sake? A girl I've seen once! It's pathetic.

I'm so angry with myself I don't even wait for Alex when the class is over. I just slam my way out the door. And literally run into the very person I've been trying not to think about.

CHAPTER 10

The force of our bodies meeting knocks her to the ground and I hear the air leave her lungs in one sharp rush when she connects with the floor. For a few seconds, I stand there like an idiot – like my brain's misfired. That's what it feels like anyway. And then, without even thinking about it, I'm bending down to offer her a hand up. She looks at it and then looks back up at me, her eyebrows raised.

'Given up being a total jerk, have you?'

I don't know what to say. I should pull my hand away. I should. But somehow, I can't. And then, before I do anything, her fingers are wrapping around mine.

Her touch makes everything in my body clench and zing at the same time, like my body's freaked out by any connection with her but is revelling in it as well. Just as confused as my brain then.

And yet, in a weird way, it feels good too. Really good. Better, even, than being with Jimmy. But she's just a girl. And one I don't even know. What have I said – maybe ten words to her if I'm lucky?

Christ!

It has me wanting to run a million miles in the other direction and yet, I stay right where I am.

She's staring at me, mouth slightly open so I can just see the tips of her teeth. Probably because I'm still holding her hand. I drop it quickly. She rubs that palm with her other hand and my stomach cramps as I watch her, making me suck in a breath with the overwhelming need to hold her hand again. Her cheeks go red. I'm not sure why, can't even begin to understand, but I watch them anyway, like I've never seen anything so fascinating.

And then I realise I haven't spoken yet. Instead, I'm standing here like an idiot, looking at her.

'Sorry.' The word tumbles out of my mouth as if it wasn't meant to be in there in the first place. 'I, um, I didn't see you there.'

She gives me a half smile that quickly disappears. 'I was guessing that.'

She sounds breathless, like she's run a race. But then, I guess I did just knock the wind out of her. I don't know what else to say and sling my bag further up my back, trying to get my brain into gear. It's pretty obvious the cogs are stuck and might need some major maintenance work to get them going again.

'Well, see you 'round.'

But despite the words coming out of my mouth, my feet don't seem to be in connection with my brain. Or they're refusing to comply. Because I just keep standing there, looking at her. She's still standing there too. I don't know why she's not walking away. That's what I'd be doing if I was her.

'So, Penn, isn't it?'

I nod, stupidly thrilled she knows my name. Although, truly how hard could that be. One of three new kids in the school – it doesn't take Sherlock Holmes to figure out my name. She cocks her head at me, her blue hair falling across her forehead. My fingers itch to smooth it away from her eyes. It feels like my whole being, every cell in my body, is drawn to her. Like paper-clips to a magnet. Fuck!

'So are you always such a jerk when you meet people for the first time or was I just one of the lucky ones?'

I can feel my own cheeks getting hot.

'Sorry.'

Jeez, definitely wowing her with my wit. Way to go, idiot! I clear my throat and try again.

'I mean, I was having a bad day. You know. Sorry. I was a jerk.'

Slightly better but only just. She nods.

'Yeah, you were. But, whatever.'

Still, neither of us are moving. I don't know why she's not, but for me, I don't want it to end like this. Which is pathetic. I go to talk at the same time she does and we both stop and laugh. I try to ignore how good that feels.

'You go,' I say.

She takes a breath. 'Should we start again?'

It feels like she's offering me the world or something. I try and think of Jimmy and how much he needs me to stay focused, but it's hard to even picture his face at the moment. Besides, her mum and dad might be prime candidates for the book. I *have* to be nice to her. It shows how stupid I'm being that that makes sense in my head. I smile.

'That'd be great.'

She smiles back at me.

'Hi, I'm Selti.'

'Penn. Nice to meet you.'

She narrows her eyes at me, the smile still touching the corner of her lips.

'So, do you want to ask me why I've got blue hair?'

I shake my head. 'No. It's…good. Individual. It doesn't matter why.'

'Nice come back.'

I shrug and laugh.

'Sometimes, I do okay. When I'm not being a total arsehole.'

She laughs with me and my stomach falls away until it feels like I've got an empty hole there that can only be filled with the sound of her laugh. That's when I feel a hand land on my shoulder from behind. It's Alex, and he's looking at me with a cocky smile on his face.

'Wondered why you got out of there so quick,' he says. 'But I can see it was so you wouldn't miss our little artist. You should've said something. I could've introduced you properly.'

The sarcasm is hard to miss and I wonder how she'll take it. She puts her hand on her hips and looks at him in a way that makes me like her even more.

'Shove it, Alex.'

There's an awkward silence that I don't know how to fill. I want to tell him to shove it too, but I can't. Not yet. Until I find the book, I need to keep as many people onside as I can. So instead, I stand there, wishing he'd leave. I shrug his hand off my shoulder though.

Selti looks at me. I can't work out what the look means but it's gone pretty quickly anyway, replaced by a half smile.

'Well, I guess I'll see you around.'

'Yeah. Absolutely.'

She does her half smile again and walks off. I actually have to think about not watching her walk away. Alex comes around in front of me, a frown on his face. He looks confused. That makes two of us.

'Absolutely? What was that about? After that burn yesterday, I thought you weren't interested.'

I frown back at him.

'I'm not interested. But, you know, can't be an arsehole all the time.'

'Yeah, sure. If you want to go after the resident weird girl, that's up to you.' His voice makes it perfectly clear he thinks that'd be a bad idea.

I want to punch him. But I don't. Of course. Maintain the pretence. That's what my life is about. Nothing real; no sharing of feelings; no telling him what I really think – it's all about the front.

'Why's she weird? I mean, the hair, I'll give you that. But she seems pretty normal.'

He laughs.

'You know what? I'm not even going to tell you. I'm going to let you find out all on your own. It'll be more fun that way.'

I snort.

'Whatever.'

But I really want to know now. I want to know everything about her – what she does when she goes home in the afternoon, what sort of artist she is, what her favourite food is, what books she reads, why she decided to dye her hair blue…everything.

It's hard to focus on my next class. At this rate, the teachers are going to put me in the he's-stupid, don't-worry-about-putting-any-energy-into-him category. Which would be okay, except I'd like to be able to pass school. It'd make getting a job to support Jimmy and me easier.

When the break bell goes, I can hardly contain myself. All I can think is that I might get to see her, talk to her, hear her laugh.

I stop in at the toilets on the way to the communal area where everyone hangs out. Checking first that there's no one in here with me, I lean forward over the sinks, closer to the rust flecked mirror, and stare at myself. I look the same. There's absolutely no physical evidence I've changed in any way. And yet I feel different. So different I hardly recognise my own thoughts. I lean closer still, staring into my own eyes.

'Get a grip,' I tell myself. 'She's just a girl. Use her to find the book. That's it. Take care of Jimmy.'

I nod at myself, like it's a done deal, but I'm not convinced. She feels more than just a girl. God, I've turned into Mister Split-personality. I growl at myself and head out the door.

Jimmy, I say in my head. And then, for good measure, I say it again. I force myself to picture him smiling, making me smile in return and then picture him after the burn, the pain clear on his face, his body rigid, even if he's trying hard to stay quiet. That's what will happen if I don't stay focused. Fuck, it's not hard! It shouldn't be anyway. It never has been before.

And yet, I still find myself looking for her in the group of kids that crowd that area. I see her blue hair over the other side and go to make my way over before I stop myself again. I have to think about my approach – how I'm going to be when I'm around her. Because if I don't have a plan, then I'm just me and I can't do that if I know I'm going to leave as soon as I've got the book. I can't leave myself open like that.

And then it hits me. Like the frigging lightning bolt people talk about.

What if we don't leave?

That thought has me sucking in a breath so deep it's like my lungs are the size of the Grand Canyon. What if what Kat and Fox were hoping for is possible? What if, when we get this book and it turns out to be the last thing Gep wants, we get to stay here?

I get to stay here.

With her?

What if I *could* go out with her, like Jimmy said?

Could that be possible? Or will Gep have us moving again, away from the scene of the crime. Or maybe it won't matter. As long as he has it, maybe we won't have to move, and he'll do what he wants to do with all the stuff we've stolen, and it'll all be good.

My heart's thumping so hard as I push my way through the crowd it's a wonder it doesn't drown out everyone's conversation. I'm so focused on the flashes of blue that I get through the moving puzzle of students I don't even notice Alex and Rory and a few of the other guys sitting at one of the benches.

'Hey, Penn!'

I stop and turn, trying to ignore the flash of anger that grips me around the throat at their interruption.

'Hey.'

I walk over, trying not to look like it's the last thing I want to be doing. It wouldn't be smart to piss this lot off on the second day here. I sit down at the edge of the bench and lean back against the wall. I still have a view of the general area where Selti is but being that much lower, I'm not getting glimpses of her anymore. I try to focus on what the guys are saying.

'There's practice tomorrow.' Alex is leaning back, looking at me. 'But we thought we might try and get some time on the court this afternoon. Try and get ready for regionals. Are you in?'

I'm at war with myself. It'd be smart to go with them but after how Jimmy was this morning, I just want to get home and make sure he's okay. He wins, like he always does. I shake my head.

'Nah. I've got things I've got to do at home this arv. My dad would crack it. You know, chores, moving in stuff.'

Rory snorts. 'Parents suck.'

'What about your mum? Would she let you come?' Alex is leaning forward, forearms resting on his legs.

'She died when I was three.'

'Shit, man, sorry.'

I shrug.

'No big deal. It was a long time ago.'

He nods but there's an uncomfortable silence and I look away. For some reason, thoughts of my mum hurt today. I wonder what she'd say about the life I lead now. The stealing, the lying... I know she was with Gep for a bit under two years before she died but maybe she didn't know. Maybe Gep was different back then. I shut my eyes for a second, not wanting to think about how disappointed she'd be. And when I open them, Selti is there, standing only three metres away from me, talking to another girl. But she keeps looking at me.

My heart leaps into my mouth and I can feel its beat right

through my body. I go to say hi but her eyes flick to the guys around me and she gives me that half smile she seems to be really good at before turning away and melting back into the crowd.

I stand up before my brain even registers what I'm doing.

'Hey,' Alex says, grabbing me on the arm. 'I'm sorry, man. I didn't mean to upset you or anything.'

I shake my head.

'No, it's all good. Just…' I point towards the crowd and he smirks at me.

'You're not still chasing after the blue haired weirdo, are you?'

He must think he's being funny or witty or something, so I force a laugh out of my mouth. The other guys join in. And for a second, I hate myself more than I ever have before.

'What?' Rory punches me. 'You got a thing for Selti?'

He makes it seem like it's the most stupid, pathetic thing on the face of the planet. Yes, I want to tell him. So much that the word seems to be filling up my mouth, making it hard to breathe. But that's stupid. I don't know her.

So I swallow the word down.

'Nah. Just knocked her over earlier, that's all. That's why Alex thinks I've got a thing for her. But she's just some lame chick; not really my type. I was … going to get a drink.'

He raises his eyebrows at me, like he doesn't believe me, so I shove past him and head over to the drinking fountain, like I was always going in that direction. I don't want to give them even the smallest hint about what's going on in my head. I can't let them in. Not just because of how I want them to see me, but for Selti too. I don't want to give them any more ammunition on her. Which sounds shit because again, I don't even know her. But there you go. None of this makes sense.

I don't see her again that break.

Even though I look.

CHAPTER 11

By the time the last bell of the day signals our freedom from school, I've decided on a course of action. Mainly because Gep's going to want something from me – good information, a possible lead…something – and I know he's not going to give me much leeway this time. Not after the last town.

So…I'm going to try and be friends with Selti and use the contact with her to get more information. I can do that. And if I'm careful, I can keep it from the guys and still have them as my back up plan. Easy.

When I say it in my head like that, it sounds reasonable. With a hippy mum and a professor for a dad, chances are good they'll have the book or at least know something about it. And if they don't lead me to what I need, then I'll look at the role players. And then the guy who owns the sawmill. And Jimmy will be okay. And so will Selti.

But when I catch sight of her and my heart trips over itself in its hurry to respond to the fact that she's close, I know there's nothing reasonable about it. I'm screwed.

She stops short when she sees me and her lips part in a way that makes me want to stroke them with my finger. Then she snaps them shut in a tight line and looks down at the ground as she moves past me. I frown.

'What, are you ignoring me now?'

She keeps walking and I'm clueless. Absolutely no frigging idea about what's happening here.

'Selti?'

She stops again and turns around to face me. She looks angry, her face stiff and hard, like it's been set in plaster.

'Don't talk to me, okay? Just shut up and leave me alone.'

I raise my eyebrows, looking for an explanation, but she turns around again and starts to stride off, her blue hair flapping behind her like it's having the last word. I hurry to catch up to her, not sure if it's the smart thing to do, but then, not much of what I've done in the last few days has been very smart.

'Hey, wait up.'

She doesn't and so I grab her arm and stop her.

'I don't understand what's going on? I thought we were starting again. I know I was a jerk about your hair but…you know…I apologised for that.'

She smirks at me and then stares at my hand until I get the hint and drop it from her arm.

'Yes, you did. I just didn't realise that the first Penn I met, the one in English, was actually the real you and the apology was fake. That you truly are a jerk and I made a mistake believing you were sorry.'

She mashes her lips shut again, tight against each other, like she's trying to keep any more words from spewing out. All I can do is look at her because my brain's having a hard time keeping up.

'What?'

Not eloquent, but pretty much explains where I am. She sighs and shakes her head like she's running out of patience.

'I heard you, talking to the guys at lunchtime.'

It's sad that I'm still really confused. I can't think of anything I said to them that would have got her upset like this. She must see the cluelessness in my face because she snorts.

'How I'm just some lame chick.'

Her words make it all click into place and I really want to kick myself – if I could, I'd boot myself a good one. I run my fingers through my hair and leave my hands up there.

'Are you kidding? That was nothing. Something to say to the guys to get them off my back.'

'Yeah, right. And I really would be lame if I fell for that.'

'No, truly! It was.'

She's quiet for a moment – just a second that makes me feel like there's still some hope – even though her eyes have narrowed.

'Get them off your back about what?'

I grimace. I really don't want to say it, but she's standing there looking at me, waiting for an answer, which I know I have to give. I roll my eyes. Talk about frigging awkward.

'They think I have a thing for you.'

'Oh,' she says and her face goes that really awesome shade of pink again.

I almost move my hand to her cheek to see how hot it is but have enough sense to keep it on top of my head.

'Oh,' she says again. 'Well, okay then.'

It's her turn to look confused now. I'm glad I'm not the only one it's happening to this afternoon. Makes me feel slightly more intelligent than a minute ago.

'That's why I said it. So they'd shut up and stop being jerks.'

Her eyes flick to mine, only for a moment, before she's looking at the ground. When she doesn't say anything else, I drop my hands to my side.

'What do you think then? Can we still be friends?'

She looks back up at me, her eyes staying on mine for a bit longer this time.

'You want to be friends with me?'

'Sure. Why wouldn't I want to be?'

She puts her hands on her hips. Her tough stance, I'm coming to realise. Like armour.

'I'm not stupid. I've lived with those guys most of my life. I know they think I'm…weird. Are you sure you want to do that to your reputation?'

I laugh. 'I don't care what sort of reputation I've got.'

And the stupid thing is, at this precise moment, standing there with her, I mean it. For the first time ever, I don't care. Even if it means I don't get the book.

God, what the hell am I thinking?

But I want this. I want to be friends with Selti. I want to be normal and not have to make every friendship based on whether I can get something for Gep or not. I want to be selfish. And maybe for the moment, I can be. At least until I know where the book is.

She's smiling at me now, a small one, like she's embarrassed or shy or something.

'Well, I guess that means we're friends then.'

I smile back at her.

'I guess it does.'

And I don't know where this is going to lead me. All I know is that for now, it feels right.

CHAPTER 12

I'm so busy thinking about Selti's smile – the big one that fills up her whole face – that I walk in the front door like I don't have a care in the world. Stupid. It's been a long time since I haven't kept my guard up.

As I make my way to the kitchen, grinning for Christ's sake – you'd think I'd know better – Gep looks up from where he's reading something at the table. When he narrows his eyes at me, I know I'm in trouble, and the smile slips from my face without any further prompting.

'You're in a good mood.' It's not really a statement – more a confrontation.

I move over to the fridge and stare into it, not really looking at what's in there but needing something else to do rather than look at Gep.

'Did you hear me?'

My hand grips the door fridge tighter and I shut my eyes for a second, imagining us away from here. Me and Jimmy, some-where safe.

'I'm just in a normal mood. Nothing different. Where's everyone else?'

I'm hoping, with every cell of my being, that he's going to let it go – be distracted by my lame, see-right-through-it question, but it mustn't be my day. He taps the table beside him.

'They're down the back at the creek. I told them all to go there so we'd have a chance to talk by ourselves. Come and sit.'

I know there's no point trying to get out of it. When Gep's like this, he gets what he wants, one way or the other. I walk over, hands in fists by my side, and slide the chair over a bit so I'm not so close to him. The crappy, cheap laminate on the table is starting to come off and I pick at it with my nail, feeling the sharpness of the edge, waiting for him to start.

'How's school going?'

I shrug.

'Same as all the other schools.'

He nods. I can see him out the corner of my eye, trying to act concerned, like a real parent. I don't know why he even bothers. Maybe he thinks he can still fool me, like he could when I was little. When I wanted him to like me and be proud of me…when I loved him, sort of… before the power really changed him and he became the sadistic bastard he is now.

'We've had to do what we're doing, you know that, right? It's never been an option to stop. Never been an option to give you boys a normal life. I've needed to get the things we've collected so I can make sure you boys are safe.'

This is a new one. Haven't heard this before. I hold myself still, wondering where he's going with it. Because it's not just small talk. It never is with Gep.

'And if I have one regret about all of this, it's that I haven't been able to give you boys the normal life you all deserve. The type of life your mum would've wanted you to have.'

The muscles in my stomach go tight, clenching, like my hands want to around Gep's neck. I can't believe he's brought her into this but I know he's looking for a rise from me and I refuse to give it to him.

'Did I ever tell you how I met your mum?'

I shake my head, enough so he knows I'm answering him. But I don't want to hear it. I don't want his words to dirty the memory of the only good time in my life. There's no choice here, though. To leave now is only going to make him angry and I don't know if I can deal with the repercussions of that this afternoon.

'It was at a butterfly enclosure. She had both of you boys with her, you were only small, just old enough to sit up on your own, and she'd spread this blanket out and you were all sitting on it.'

A small smile touches his lips like the memory's a good one. Which is probably more disturbing than if he'd just told me matter-of-factly. How could my mum love this man? Was he so different back then, before the power got to him, that she thought he was someone good enough for her? For us?

'Jimmy was sitting on your mother's lap and you were sitting next to her. And you were covered in butterflies. I'd never seen anything like it. They were all over your body, your face, your hair, and yet they weren't worrying you. You were sitting there totally still, watching the butterflies, like you already knew if you moved, they'd leave, or you'd hurt them. There was something about you, even then. And your mum – she was this tiny, little thing with long, blond hair – she was giggling…she had the most amazing laugh…like bubbles that got under your skin and made you feel lighter.'

He smiles again and then gives his head a small shake.

'I tried, you know. I tried to keep her away from the drugs.'

Drugs! What the fuck? I jerk back in my chair, trying not to let him see my reaction. But it's too late. He knows he's shocked me. But he's lying. I know it. He must be! That wasn't my mum…

'It's a shock, I know. But I've never told you about it before because I wanted you to be able to have good memories of your mum. She was such a special woman and I loved her. Very much. You have to know that. But she was so fragile. So…damaged.'

I clench my hands around the seat of the chair, like I'm trying to make my fingers meet through the hard wood. I need to hang on to something otherwise I'm not sure what I'll do.

'So why the fuck are you telling me now?'

He puts his hand on my upper arm and my heart quickens, waiting for the burn, not trusting his touch. The fake, fatherly concern is still on his face, like he means everything he says.

'I tried to be as good a father as I could to you boys. I tried to do that for her. She didn't know who your father was – someone she slept with when she was high, so I felt like it was something I could do for her even though she was gone.' He sighs. 'I don't want to be your enemy, Penn. We're family. Even though I wasn't your real dad, I always felt like I was meant to be in your life. Like your mum picked me to take care of you. Who knows where you'd be now if I hadn't been in your life? In and out of foster homes maybe. You and Jimmy probably would've been separated.'

I fight the nausea that's threatening to rise, burning my throat. He wants me to be thankful for the life he's given us? The burns and the anger and the constant moving and the fear and the life of crime? Fucking bastard!

'I know you're thinking about leaving when you turn eighteen.'

He shakes his head as I try and keep my face neutral – give nothing away – it seems like I've been doing that for most of my life.

'There's no need to try and hide it. I know you have. I know you want to take Jimmy and get as far away from me as possible. And I understand that. There're times when I really wish I could've been a better father but I did what I had to do to keep you safe. And I know the power…corrupts me, sometimes. But I want you to know something. I care about you. About all of you. And I want us to stay together, like a family.'

I look down at the table, at the small corner of chipboard

that's been laid bare by my picking. It's that little bit of wood, scared by the glue used to stick the laminate to it, but still there, still hanging on, that makes me decide I'm not hiding anymore. I'm sick of it.

'We've never been a family. You've used us the whole time. Used us to get the power you've always wanted. To do all your dirty work. If you cared about us then you would've given us a different life, no matter what.'

He's nodding, like he agrees with me.

'I know. But I've had to do this to keep you safe.'

It's the third time he's said that this afternoon. I don't trust him but I can't work out yet why he's lying to me. He always seems to be one step in front of me, like he knows everything I'm going to say and has a story to cover his own arse.

'That's bullshit. The only thing we've needed to be kept safe from is you.'

I know I'm pushing him and I figure I must be a sucker for punishment. Maybe there's some sick part of me that actually enjoys the burn. Maybe I'm a sadist at heart. But he doesn't react like I think he will. He just picks up the book he was looking at. It's only then I realise it's a photo album.

'There are things I'm going to tell you this afternoon I was hoping to never have to tell you. I was hoping I could keep it all under control and let you boys go when you were old enough – just let you get on with your own life – but it's not working out like that.'

My skin's cold, like I've stepped out of the water on a windy winter's day. I can hear the frustration in Gep's voice, but under that, almost hidden, I'm sure I can hear something else too. Something I didn't think I'd ever hear. I can hear fear. And that scares me more than anything else. I stand up so suddenly the chair flips over, landing with a loud clatter on the floor. Gep grabs my arm before I can move.

'Let me go. I don't want to hear any more of this crap. You're just trying to bullshit me again, like you always do.'

But I can hear the waver of uncertainty in my voice and I know he can too.

'Please, Penn. You have to listen. It's the only way we can keep Jimmy safe.'

I shut my eyes and stand there, feeling his hand on my skin. It feels like a chain. But he knows my kryptonite. He knows I'll do anything for Jimmy. I turn and pull the chair back up, sitting on it backwards so I have something physical between us. My face is hard when I sit down. It's the only way I can keep myself together.

Gep takes a deep breath and looks at me.

'You understand I have powers?'

I nod, not giving anything away. But I'm not stupid. I worked out long ago that the things Gep does aren't normal.

'I'm a Sorcerer, Penn. That's what we call ourselves.'

I snort.

'What is this? A Disney movie?'

He smiles like I'm trying to be funny. I'm not.

'When I first met your mother, I was a moderate level Sorcerer. I had some innate talent my mentor had helped me develop but I'd never really done anything with it. Only dabbling. But I was drawn to her. Your mum. I can't describe it. I *needed* to be with her. And she felt it too. As soon as we met. And being around her made me stronger as a Sorcerer. My power felt like it doubled.'

He stops to check I'm still listening, and I am, but my head is spinning. Sorcerer, mentor, power… Jesus! How can this be my life?

'The power got too much for me. It made me greedy. You don't understand how…consuming it can be. Sometimes it feels like it's the only thing I can think about. That nothing else matters, even though I know that's not true. It's hard to pull back.'

Well, this part feels true at least. So then why is he still doing it? Why, if he knows that, doesn't he just stop using it, for God's sake? Asking us to be conduits to get more power, over and over? We're obviously not as important as the next fix. And neither was Mum, despite the fact he says he loved her. But I don't say that. Not now. He gives me a look so filled with pain that if I hadn't been living with him for most of my life, I might actually believe.

'It didn't matter how much I had though, it was never enough. I had to have more. And it would take over sometimes, like I had no control over it, and I'd have times when I was…not who I really am. When it'd make me angry and vengeful. Like it still does sometimes now. That's why your mother started doing drugs again. To cope with it.'

'So you fucking drove her to drugs? You're the reason she's dead?'

There's a rage burning in me, hot and white, like the burn's happening already. Except I'm in control of this one. Sort of. Enough that I want to hear the rest of the story. Then I might kill him.

Gep nods.

'Yes. She was doing drugs occasionally before she met me but I'm the reason she started getting into them heavily. I'm not the reason she's dead though.'

'What, was that just a convenient accident, was it?' The sarcasm's hard to miss but then I'm not trying to hide it.

'Your mother's death was never convenient. Never. And it was never what I wanted. But that's not what I'm trying to tell you. I'm trying to tell you it wasn't an accident.'

I'm watching him. Perfectly still. Like I'm paralysed. Like even my blood's stopped pumping.

'What?'

'It wasn't an accident. I'd summoned a spirit a few months

before and I was in control. I had him. But he…he told me your mother was going to die. That she was to be the sacrifice of me getting stronger. I couldn't believe what I was hearing. It didn't make sense. And all I could think was that he'd be a part of it, so I destroyed him. And we thought that was the end of it. But we had a picture of the four of us – your mother, you, Jimmy and me – and it got me scared. Because she was fading. In the picture, your mother was fading. Like her essence was going.'

'A picture was fading?'

He nods.

'And they got her, Penn. They killed her. That's why I make us move so often. That's why I'm collecting the stuff we need. That's why I'm trying to make you boys as tough as I can. So I can keep you safe.'

I shake my head. None of this makes any sense.

'I know it's a lot to take in,' he says in a perfectly reasonable voice, like he's acknowledging the sky is blue. 'But I need you to believe me.'

'Why? Fuck! You tell me all this…strange shit and now you tell me I have to believe you. Jesus!'

I look away, staring at the table, trying to get my thoughts straight. Then a horrible thought flicks into my head.

'Why are you telling me this now?'

He sighs, like he's in pain.

'Because of this.'

He opens the photo album and pushes it in front of me. It's a happy family snap. Taken at the beach, the sky a vibrant blue, the sand so white it looks fake. It's of us – me, Jimmy, Gep and only the barest outline of my mother. It's as if her image has been faded by the sun – just in this part of the picture…nowhere else. Just like Gep said.

'That's you,' he says, pointing to the toddler she's holding in her arms. In comparison to her, my colours are strong and vibrant. Gep's finger slides over to the other side of the photo to him, looking only slightly younger than he does now. And to the toddler in his arms. Jimmy.

But my breathing stops as I look at it and it's as if all the blood in my body has drained to my feet in a split second, leaving me dizzy and sick. Because the image of Jimmy, the person I care about most in the world – the one person I can't even contemplate anything happening to – is starting to fade.

CHAPTER 13

I don't even remember standing but suddenly I am. I move back from the table, trying to get some distance between me and the picture. Gep is wrong. Jimmy is fine. This is bullshit. Except my brain doesn't want to listen to me. It's too busy believing all of this might be true.

But it can't be. I won't let it be.

'You can't go,' Gep says. 'I need your help. We have to keep Jimmy safe. We have to save him.'

That stops me. But when I look at him, all I can see is the person who's used his power on me until I've passed out. The person who seemed to enjoy my pain. The person who I've tried to protect my brother from all of these years. The person who's brought all of this into our life. It's his fault. Everything.

All I see is my enemy.

'Who the fuck do you think are? Going on about loving us and wanting to protect us and trying to keep my mum alive. It's because of you she's dead! You're a psycho! Jesus, you've made us all do the ritual over and over. I was fucking eight when you first made me do it! Inviting fucking spirits into our life that you're now telling me killed my mum! And you've made us criminals. I fucking *steal* shit for you! What do you think my mum would say about that? She'd kill you for what you've done to us.'

His face goes ugly with a scowl which, in a strange way makes me feel like I'm on more solid ground. This is the Gep I'm used to.

'Don't you tell me what your mother would think! I knew her better than anyone! She was my life companion. The only one who could make my sorcery reach the levels it did. She was my muse! And I've done everything – *everything* – to keep you boys safe!'

But I'm not going to listen to this anymore. I can't. Because none of it makes any sense and if I stand here and think about it, I'll be lost. I turn and start to run, slamming the door open, not caring that the handle makes a hole in the wall.

'Don't you fucking walk away from me! Penn! Get back here.'

But I don't even break stride. For my own sanity, I can't. I just run, not thinking about where I'm going or what I'm going to do. I just need to get away. I'm not sure how long I run for, and I guess, if anyone saw me, they'd have serious questions about my mental stability, but my body finally forces me to stop at a playground that's definitely seen better days. I lean forward, trying to gasp in enough air to stop me from passing out and press the heel of my hand into the stitch that's cramping the muscles under my ribs until I feel it start to fade.

I fall onto one of the swings – it squeaks under me and the rusty chain leaves orange marks on my hands – and try to fit my legs into a position that feels half comfortable. These things are obviously not made for someone my size.

It's only now I'm sitting – now I'm away from the house and from Gep and from the things he's said – that I let myself think. Think about all of it. The photo and Mum and the drugs and the spirit and his explanation for it all…

I still can't understand how any of it can be possible. How can a person die just because their photo's fading? This is real life, for

God sake. And yet, I know Gep's power. I've seen it. Felt it. It makes sense that he's a sorcerer, as much as I feel like an idiot for even thinking the word. And I know there are spirits. I've had them in me, taking me over. Is it such a stretch to think Mum died because of something to do with all of this…?

Yes, I decide. It's too much. Because that would make me more a part of it than I want to be. I've only ever got into this because Gep's forced me to. It's not something I want in my life. And it's definitely not going to be something I'll have anything to do with when I get the hell out of here.

With Jimmy.

Who's going to be fine!

Which makes me wonder where he is now. What sort of brother am I that apart from the half-hearted question I asked to get Gep off my back, I haven't even thought about whether he's okay or not? I just believed what Gep said.

I stand, panicked, thinking about the fading picture, and for a split second, until my mind actually kicks in, I wonder if I'm too late. What if I've already lost him? Which is stupid. Of course it is. It has to be.

He'll be down at the creek with Kat and Fox, like Gep said. Except why would Gep allow that? Maybe he wouldn't have told me what he did if Jimmy was there. Although maybe he was lying and Jimmy was there and Gep wanted him to think he was dying. Christ! I can't find any sense in my whirlwind of thoughts.

Gep's mind works in ways I can't even begin to understand. And I'm sick of trying to double guess him, sick of trying to stay ahead of his games, sick of trying to make sure we're safe…sick of all of it.

And then, like a balloon with a hole, the urgency rushes out of me and I deflate until I'm flat. I don't want to see Jimmy or Fox or Kat. And I definitely don't want to see Gep. I want to disappear. Pretend I'm not Penn, Jimmy's brother, or Fox or Kat's. Unhook my brain from all the memories and responsibilities and start fresh. Do whatever the hell I want. Scrub any sense of Gep from my soul and be no one.

I am empty. And he's made me that way.

I stuff my hands into my pocket and make my way down to the river that flows past the edge of the park. The water's flowing pretty fast and I push the toe of my shoe against the moss on a rock at the edge, marking my presence, even though I don't know why. Maybe to prove to myself I'm still real. Still here. I wonder where the water flows to. Where I'd come out if I threw myself in and let it take me away…

I squat down, scooping up a handful of the soft dirt and leaf litter and let it fall through my fingers. The smell of the earth is good – real. About the only thing in my life that is. Although that's not true. Jimmy is real.

But our life isn't.

It's then that I notice a flash of colour out of the corner of my eye, further upstream where the river twists around in a sharp curve. I think maybe it's a bird, but as I look closer, I realise it's not.

It's Selti.

I stand back up, moving over closer to the tree next to me and lean against its trunk, feeling the sharpness of its bark against my fingertips. She hasn't noticed me yet, half hidden as I am in the shadows of the trees. I watch her, like some sort of weirdo perve, noticing the way her hair falls forward as she bends to pick up something at the water's edge, and then the graceful way she pushes it back behind her ear, the smile on her face as she looks at what she's found.

My heart's thumping and I push my fist against my chest, like that's going to bring it under control. I'm breathing through my mouth to get enough air to keep up with it. I don't understand how just seeing her can create this sort of reaction in me. It can't be normal.

Not that I really care. It's like being able to watch her is my reward for having to put up with all the shit with Gep this afternoon. Which must make me truly weird. Gep has finally pushed me over the edge.

She slips her shoes off and wades into the water. It must be cold because she hesitates before taking a few more steps. The stream's flowing around her calves as she bends forward to pick up something out of the water.

And then, like it's in slow motion, she stumbles and falls forward. I lose sight of her for a second – long enough for my heart to squeeze so tightly it's actually painful – and then she's up again, floundering against the water, trying to get back to the bank. But it must be deeper than I thought because it's not working for her. The rush of water is pulling her along, bringing her down closer to me, holding her captive no matter how much she tries to break free.

And without giving it any thought, I launch myself into the water as well.

CHAPTER 14

The coldness of the water has me gasping for breath as soon as I surface. It's seeping into my bones faster than I would've believed possible but all I can think about is Selti. I swing my head, trying to spot her. Nothing. I can't see anything. And then, suddenly, I do. Just a snatch of blue – enough that I know it's her. I strike out, swimming as best I can fully clothed, including the only pair of shoes I own. Not that I could care less.

She's being dragged away from me and I go at an angle, trying to catch up with her. I can hear her spluttering and then, she's in front of me and I grab her. But she's flaying about so much she takes me down with her and I get a mouthful of water before I go under. I stretch for the surface, the water too deep for me to be able to use the bottom. And finally, I break through the surface and manage to grab a quick breath before I'm under again.

I kick out, trying to get us closer to the edge so I can at least get a foothold to bring us in. At least she's stopped struggling...enough that I'm not being dragged back under anyway.

'I've got you.'

I'm choking on water and only just manage to get the words

out but she notices – she clings to me and I get her in a hold that means I can keep her head above water. Thank God Gep taught us how to swim – about the only worthwhile thing he's ever done.

My whole body feels drained by the time we make it to the bank and I collapse onto the grass and dirt, not caring that I'm probably going to get filthy. Selti is next to me, still coughing up water. She's shivering, and I have this really stupid urge to offer her my jacket, even though I'm as wet as she is.

'Are you okay?'

She nods, her blue hair hanging like clumps of discoloured seaweed down her back.

'I think so. Thanks.'

She says it like she's confused and I look at her, waiting, not sure what she's confused about.

'Lucky you were here.'

I nod. 'Can't you swim?'

She goes red and looks away from me.

'Not very well.'

'What the hell were you doing going in the water then? Especially when it's flowing that fast!'

I can hear the anger in my voice, even if I'm not really sure why I'm so pissed off. Whether it's because I'm wet and half drowned? Or if it's a left over from how angry I was at Gep?

Or maybe it's because I couldn't stand it if anything happened to her...

I don't want to even think about that last one. It's stupid. I hardly know her. So why then, does the thought of her drowning fill me with panic? A thick panic which crams into my throat, making it hard to breath.

Her face goes tight and one eyebrow goes up, like I've offended her. Which I guess I probably have.

'I didn't realise you were my keeper. It might surprise you, but I can do whatever the hell I want. I don't need your permission.'

'Not if you drown while doing it. That's stupid.'

I watch her face going even tighter, if that's possible, and curse myself. What is it about her that makes me blurt out the most idiotic, insulting things I can think of? I'm usually good at being whoever a person wants me to be – good at picking what I need to show them for them to like me. Why can't I do that with her? God, it's like she's short-circuiting all the wiring in my brain!

I take a breath and let it out in a soft laugh, running my fingers through my hair, feeling the water trickle down my back as I do.

'Sorry, that came out really bad. I think my brain's waterlogged.'

She stares at me for a second and I can see her soften, just a bit...enough that she stays here. Beside me.

'It's okay. You're probably right anyway. It was stupid to go into the water when it's running so fast. I didn't expect it to be so...strong.'

'Yeah, sometimes it can be a bit deceptive.'

Her hand is only millimetres from mine on the ground. Close enough that if I moved my little finger I'd touch her. It's so distracting I'm having difficulty thinking about anything else. And then she moves it, sitting up slightly, and the spell's broken.

'It's funny that you were in the right place at the right time though. Good. But weird. Don't you think?'

I shrug, heart thumping, even though I don't have anything to feel guilty about. I mean, I was watching her but it *was* a total coincidence I was here, in this park.

'Lucky for you my dad pissed me off enough I had to get out of the house. I just went for a bit of a run and this was where I ended up.'

She looks like she's going to ask questions about that. And I don't want to go there. Not yet. That's way too high up the freaky, what-sort-of-family-do-you-come-from list. I lean back on my elbows.

'What were you doing in the water anyway?'

She purses her lips, like she doesn't want to answer me. Like she has her own secrets. I stay silent, watching her, and she sighs.

'I guess I do owe you an explanation since I almost drowned you.'

She holds out her hand. In her palm lies a stone. It's pretty – mostly white, although it's flecked with blues and oranges. But it's just a rock.

'You almost drowned yourself because of a rock?'

Her cheeks colour again.

'It's not just a rock,' she says and then she laughs. It makes my stomach cramp up and I push my legs out, trying to stop it. 'Well, I guess it is, but it's perfect for what I need.'

'What do you need it for?'

'It's…I just need it for something.'

I narrow my eyes, trying to ignore the words filling my mouth, trying not to press her, trying to let her keep her secrets like I'm keeping mine. But there's obviously something she doesn't want to share with me and that makes me want to know it all the more. Which is frigging psycho. I'm getting as bad as Gep!

I struggle not to say anything…really, I do. But I reckon it's only thirty seconds before the words force their way out of my mouth.

'So what's the something? Do you collect rocks? Whole amateur geologist thing going on?'

I try to make it sound light, so she can't hear the desperation in my voice. Why the hell do I care so much anyway?

She still doesn't say anything though. She stares at the rock, twisting it round and round in her hands.

'Come on, I thought we were friends. And I did just save your life.'

She looks up at me finally and then rolls her eyes.

'Okay, but you've got to promise not to go all weird, okay? Because that's how most of the kids at school are.'

Now I'm really interested. Hook, line and sinker. I'm a dead fish basically.

'No weirdness. Gotcha.'

She takes a deep breath and then lets it out in whoosh, the words coming with it.

'I'm a Wicca.'

I'm stunned speechless. This is totally the last thing I expected her to say. All I can picture is Gep, making us be a conduit, harnessing the power that takes us over. Using his power to hurt us. To hurt Jimmy. I don't know how to get my brain into action, so I sit there like an idiot, saying nothing. At least my mouth isn't hanging open though – one small victory.

'Well, are you going to say something?'

She's not twisting the rock anymore. She's holding it tightly in her hands; the skin on her fingers t0urning white where she's pressing them into the hardness of the stone.

'Um, okay.' I struggle for something to say that doesn't give away my own secrets. Well, mine, Jimmy, Fox and Kat's. 'Like, do you mean you're a witch?'

She screws up her nose, the freckles on it all scrunching up together in a way that makes me want to kiss them smooth.

'I hate that word. It makes me think of the witch from the Wizard of Oz – green with the big nose and that really horrible laugh and she had those horrible flying monkeys. I used to have nightmares about them. And it sounds…I don't know…evil.'

'What, you're not going to turn me into a toad then?'

She pushes me and I fall onto one elbow, laughing with her. It feels good, like our laughs join together somehow. In harmony. Jesus, I've turned into a love sick girl with a huge crush. How is this the first time this has ever happened? It's not like I haven't been attracted to another girl before. There'd be something seriously wrong with me if there hadn't, given the number of girls I've come in contact with! But this is different. Scary different. Probably because this is the first one that feels like it's important. This is the first time I really want it.

'Don't tempt me.'

'What do you use the rock for? Something big if you wanted it that much?'

She starts to twist the stone again, round and round.

'It's for a ritual Mum and I do.'

Ritual. That word has me pulling away in my head but that's not fair. Not everyone is as twisted as Gep. And I can hear the reluctance in her voice still. Hear her waiting for me to get weird, like she was worried about.

'Your mum's a Wicca too?'

'Yep.'

She's watching me, like she's waiting for something. I don't know what she expects me to do though.

'What?'

She shrugs.

'You seem to be taking this really calmly.'

It's on the tip of my tongue to tell her I've lived with something like this for most of my life but I can't. It's not just my secret. And it's a something I've kept hidden for as long as I can remember, so it's probably more of a habit than anything else.

'Yeah, I'm a pretty laid back guy, you know.'

She laughs.

'Yeah, that was my first thought about you, especially with how you reacted to my hair. Really laid back.'

I laugh with her again but I can feel my face getting hot.

'So, is your dad into it too?'

'No. He doesn't practice but he's a professor in Sociology, so it really fascinates him. That's why our house is full of things about it – artefacts, books, research. It's how my mum and dad first met.'

My stomach lurches at her words. It reminds me I still have a job to do. And if Gep is telling me the truth, which my brain is still struggling to comprehend, I need to get the book.

I need to save my brother's life.

CHAPTER 15

That thought pushes me to my feet – urging me to do something now, now, now, because how could I forget about Jimmy and how could I not even check on him to see if he was okay and what if Gep is telling the truth, even partially. Even if I don't know what to do. Find the book? Although, truly, how can that help? Does Gep even care what happens to Jimmy? How can I trust him to not use this whole Jimmy thing just to make sure I get the book and then he'll do whatever the hell he wants anyway? What if he's making the whole thing up?

My thoughts go round and round, creating a twisting, turning mess of confusion and frustration that I can't find the end of to start the unravelling process.

Selti is looking up at me, her brow furrowed like she can't work out what I'm thinking. Welcome to my world. Instead I stick out my hand to her.

'Come on, we'd better get home before we die of hyper-thermia.'

She takes my hand, her fingers wrapping around mine, and the heat from that contact – the instant warmth of her skin on mine – is awesome and terrifying all at the same time. But I hang on, pulling her up next to me, and then don't want to let go. She's looking at me, her brown eyes serious, and for a moment, I'm convinced I'm not the only one who's feeling the weirdness of this connection between us. But then she's dropping her hand from mine and, once more, I'm not sure of anything.

'Well,' she says, 'thanks again for saving me.'

I stick my hands in my pockets – wrong move – the material squelches under my fingers and when I pull them back out, the lining comes with them and I have to push them back in again, like a total dork. She watches me, not saying anything. I can guess what she's thinking though.

And as much as the urgency is still racing under my skin to do something for Jimmy, I don't want to leave her either. I'm torn – my chest, my brain, my heart ripping like a piece of paper, excruciatingly slow, down, down, leaving jagged, raw edges. And yet the decision should be easy.

Jimmy. Always Jimmy.

But it doesn't feel easy this time.

'I'll walk you home.'

The words are out of my mouth before I have a chance to think about them. And yet it seems right. A chance to look for the book. Of course.

'No. That's okay. You should get home and get dry too.'

My blood pressure stutters for a moment at her rejection. I try to do a laid back, I'm-cool smile – trying to not let her see how desperate I feel. Pathetic. And I'm not sure I succeed anyway. It doesn't really feel like it fits on my face somehow, which is not a problem I've ever had before – it's part of my tool set – something I call on to get the information I need. So why does it feel so weird now?

'Nah, I'd feel better walking you home. Just in case there's another river somewhere between here and your house.

Wouldn't want you getting distracted by another perfect rock and getting swept away to God knows where. I'd never forgive myself.'

She gives a small laugh and then shakes her head, her wet hair moving over her shoulders.

'Fine, whatever. It's your health. Just let me get my shoes.'

We walk back to where she initially fell in and there are her shoes, dry and warm, because, of course, she was smart enough to take hers off before she went in. Unlike me, who didn't stop to think about anything except her safety. My shoes squelch with every step I take, loud in the quietness of the late afternoon. It was worth it though. Even if I have absolutely no idea what I'm going to wear to school tomorrow since they're my only pair of runners.

The cool air teases over me as we walk home and I struggle not to shiver. Really, it'd be better if I went home. Smarter. But I'm here walking beside her anyway, just because I want to do. Even if we're not saying anything to each other…it's like my brain has gone on strike, leaving me a tongue-tied idiot.

We get to a set of white gates with a driveway that disappears into a tangle of trees and bushes on either side and Selti turns to look at me.

'Well, this is it. Thanks for walking me home.'

I peer down the driveway, trying to see anything that even resembles a house. But all I see is bush.

'Are you sure?'

She laughs and my chest constricts, trying its best to stop my heart.

'I think I know my own home. We're on eight acres – believe me, our house is in there.'

I smile at her and then feel a wave of awkwardness wash over me, making me shuffle from foot to foot like I've never spoken to a girl before. Which I have. Plenty of times. Just never one I've felt like this about.

'Okay then. Well, I guess I'll…you know…see you tomorrow.'

She nods back at me but neither of us go to leave. We stand there, looking at each other. And then suddenly she's moving forward and grabbing my hand, pulling me down slightly so I'm equal to her height. The feel of her lips on my cheek is so unexpected I almost jerk backwards. I manage not to, thank God.

When she steps back, her face is pink and her eyes are bright.

'Thanks. For saving my life, I mean.'

My face feels as red as hers.

'No worries. Anytime. Although probably not a good idea to make a habit of it, in case I'm not around.'

And we stand there again, looking at each other. My brain feels like it's a total stranger to me. I have no idea what I should do – how to end this or what to say to her now.

It's only the sound of a car coming up behind us that stops it becoming so awkward we'll never be able to come back from it.

I turn and watch a white car come up slowly and stop beside us, the passenger window coming down. There are two people inside – a man and a woman. The woman looks so much like Selti, except for her hair, which is a dark blond, that I know without even being told this is her mum. And I'm guessing the guy is her dad.

Selti steps up closer to the car and her mum frowns at her.

'You're all wet! Why are you all wet?'

Selti gives her a half smile, half grimace.

'Yeah, I fell into the river. This is Penn. He's new at school. He saved me from drowning, basically.'

Her dad leans forward in his seat to look past Selti's mum and give me the once over. It only takes a few seconds and then he's smiling at me. What can I say – I'm good at inspiring parental confidence. That's a mask that's easy to put on.

'Well then, looks like we're in your debt.'

I shrug and smile back at him. Selti's mum isn't smiling but she's not glaring at me either, so at least that's something. It's somewhere in the middle, like I've confused her. Not a reaction I'm used to. And truly, I don't like it. It's like she can see the real me. The one who would be in no way good enough for her daughter. I want to look away, move away, before she really works me out.

'How come you were near the river?' It sounds like she's asking Selti, but she's still looking at me when she asks the question.

'I found the stone,' Selti says, her voice excited, and she reaches out her hand to show her mum.

At least that stops her mum from staring at me. She reaches out to take the rock and rolls it on her palm before smiling at her daughter.

'Yes, you're right. It's perfect.'

Selti smiles at her – a big one that lights up her face. A small shiver of jealousy catches me before I can prepare myself. I want to be the one to make her smile like that.

'Well, we'd better get you inside and warm,' her father's saying. 'Can we give you a lift home, Penn?'

I take a step back.

'No, that's fine. It's not far. I'm all good.'

'You sure? It's no hassle, especially after saving our daughter.'

I shake my head. The last thing I need is for these people to drive me home. I don't want Selti anywhere near Gep. And I don't need Gep asking questions. Selti and her mum are looking at me again, and if I wasn't so freaked out over the idea of them going to our house, I'd probably have smiled. They have the exact same expression on their face – questioning, like they can't quite work me out yet. Which is not a bad thing. Her parents would probably ban her from coming anywhere near me if they knew the truth.

'So, I'll see you tomorrow?'

Selti nods at me.

'Sure. See you tomorrow.'

And as I turn to start walking home, I know that thought is going to keep me going for the rest of the night. Which is kinda scary...but nice, all at the same time.

CHAPTER 16

As I walk into the house, I debate whether to go straight to the shower and try and get rid of some of the goose bumps that've taken up permanent residence on my skin or to disappear into my room and pretend I'm not here. Because, now I'm home, I want to see Jimmy, check he's okay…but what if he's not? What if I walk in there and I can see a change in him? See him dying, like Gep believes he is? I feel sick at the thought, overwhelmed by what that would mean. Overwhelmed by the thought I might not be able to do anything for him. Coward. That's what I am.

But my squeaking shoes are a dead giveaway and the choice is ripped away from me.

'Penn?' Gep's voice comes from the kitchen. 'Is that you?'

I take a few seconds to respond – enough time to figure out there's no point in trying to avoid him. It's not like I can stay away from him forever. I don't want to go in there though. I don't know if I can face him yet. I haven't had enough time to think. But then, maybe I never will.

'Yep.'

'Come in here, will you?'

I sigh, not ready to deal with the consequences of defying him, and shut my eyes for a moment before walking towards the kitchen.

They're all sitting at the table – Gep, Fox, Kat and Jimmy – like one happy family. And Gep is helping Jimmy with his dinner. I can't remember the last time he did that. It's my job. Always has been. *I* look after Jimmy. Seeing Gep sitting there throws me, like I've fallen into an alternate universe on my way home. Jesus, is there something in the water here that's changing all of us? Not that I really think Gep's changed. More like he's manipulating us for something I can't work out yet.

I look at Jimmy, searching his face. He looks…fine. Like Jimmy. Not like he's fading…dying like Mum. Gep is wrong. Another lie. And the constriction that's wound its way around my chest eases, just a bit.

'Hey, you okay?'

Jimmy nods, his hair falling forward into his face as he tries to control his movements. Gep pushes the hair back in a way that looks almost…affectionate. Kind, even. And Jimmy smiles at him! What the fuck's going on? What's his game? I want to get out of here before it does my head in.

'Okay, well, I'm going to have a shower.'

I indicate down the hallway and start to turn before Gep's voice stops me.

'Why are you wet?'

I stop and look him in the eye.

'I fell in the river saving a dog.'

Seconds tick by as he looks at me; assessing me – assessing my words. He licks his lips, like he's trying to taste a lie in the air and my heart jolts, waiting, on guard. Especially with him being so close to Jimmy. Sometimes, he can catch us out on lies. I don't know how, but then I don't know how he does most of the things he does. The trick is to tell enough of the truth that it seems to confuse him.

He nods. 'Okay, go and have a shower and then we need to talk.'

I don't bother to respond before turning again. But I can feel four sets of eyes on me as I go and I know I've missed something. Something big. And the thought that I've failed Jimmy somehow crashes into me, sideswiping me so it feels like my head's reeling. And I don't know what to do now. He's been with Gep, under his control, while I was with Selti. While I was running away. And I don't know how to beat Gep – how to keep my brother safe. How can I do that when he always seems to be one step in front of me and I don't know the path? I'm walking blind. Lost in a maze all of Gep's making.

I shut my eyes in the shower, letting the warm water take the numbness from my bones and try to think; try to get something happening in this head of mine that feels as empty as Gep's soul. Because even if I can't work out what Gep's up to I need to have a plan. Something. There's no way I want to walk back into the kitchen without some sort of idea.

First, all this crap about Mum and then the photo and then Jimmy... fading. And now he's being Mr Nice Guy, feeding Jimmy, getting Jimmy to smile for Christ sake! When Jimmy should hate him. Like me. But maybe it's only me that can see Gep for what he is. My guts are churning with anxiety. It's crap. All of it. The things he said are lies. They need to be. Mum didn't do drugs and Jimmy's not going to die...he's doing it to scare me for some reason. Keep me in line.

Except he already has a way to do that.

I shake my head and turn off the shower, standing there for a minute and letting the water drip off me. I need to talk to one of the boys. Alone.

Wrapping the towel around my waist, I open the door a bit, leaning my head out.

'Fox, I left my towel in my room. Grab it for me, would you?'

'God, what am I, your slave?'

But I hear the chair drag back on the lino anyway. As he comes down the hallway, I wave him over. He sighs and rolls his eyes.

'What?'

'What's going on? All this good father crap...what's that about?'

He shrugs.

'I don't know. He left and when he came back this afternoon, he was just like that. Happy and everything. Who knows what goes on in his head? Enjoy it while it lasts.'

I shake my head. I can't afford to do that.

'Yell out that you can't find my towel.'

'What?'

I sigh. 'Just do it.'

He rolls his eyes again but does as I say.

'It's on the bed,' I yell back. That should give us a few more minutes. 'Why's he giving Jimmy his dinner?'

With anyone else, the question wouldn't make a lot of sense, but Fox knows what I mean.

He shrugs again, his eyes on the ground. 'I don't know. Who knows why Gep does any of his crap? All I know is I started helping Jimmy with his dinner and then Gep came and took over. And he's been cracking jokes and stuff. Kat's lapping it up, like Gep's a new man or something. A real dad. Moron.'

I ignore that. Kat's probably the most optimistic of all of us. Always has been so I don't take his reactions into account. It's usually what he wants to believe rather than the truth.

'Do you know what he wants to talk about?'

'Nuh.'

'Jesus, man, give me something to work with.'

'What do you want me to tell you? Gep's a manipulative, sadistic bastard and who knows what game he's playing? You know that already. Christ, if you can't work out what's going on, what makes you think I can?'

I sigh and shake my head. He's right. How can I argue with that?

'Sure. Okay. I'll be out in a minute.'

Fox turns and walks away, not hesitating. Just going back in so he's there to try and work out what game Gep's playing now. Sometimes it's better to be there when it all comes undone – the fall out seems to be less than what you cop if you come in on the tail end. And that's our father figure – not someone who's taught us how to be good, decent people but instead, skilled at working out how to get hit by the least amount of shit. Awesome!

I walk to the room with my towel on and pull the first dry things out of my drawers, not giving a damn if they match or not. I want to get this over and done with. I stop for a minute just before the entrance to the kitchen and take a deep breath.

And then I step into the room.

Gep looks up at me.

'What was that breath for? Courage?'

I don't know how to answer him. Once again, he's put me off balance. And so I don't say anything. Gep sighs.

'Listen, Penn, boys, I know I haven't been a good Dad to you. And I realise I haven't given you a real good life.'

I almost snort at that. Talk about frigging understatement of the year. But I want to see where this is going, so I manage to rein it in.

'I want to change that,' Gep says, putting the fork he's using for Jimmy down on the plate and folding his hands together on the table. 'I want to be the Dad I should've been all along. I want you to have a good life. I promise you I'll do everything I can to make sure of that.'

None of us say anything. We all look at each other with blank faces. This is new. Sure, he's apologised before, but it's never been as big as this. And it's never included a promise.

Kat is the first one to break, a smile spreading over his face. How did I know he would be?

'You mean it? You want us to be happy?'

Gep smiles back at him. It looks like a real smile…like he means it. But then, he's the master at this. I don't know how many times over the years I've been sucked in by his words. By the hope he offers. But it's always been a sick hope, full of twisted, dark manoeuvres that hid behind the fake sunshine sweetness. And you don't notice until it's too late.

'Every word.'

He's looking at me now. Steady. Like he wants me to believe him. I stare back at him.

'I know you don't trust me,' he says finally. 'I know I have to prove myself to you. But it's worth it. You know it is.'

I know he's talking about the whole Jimmy's-photo-fading thing and my stomach tightens like someone's tugging at it from the back. I stand up straighter – it's a load of crap…it has to be. There's nothing wrong with Jimmy. But I can't stop my eyes from flicking over to him anyway.

When I look back at Gep, he has a smirk on his face. A small one. Enough that I know it's there. But I don't know what it means and truly, I don't care. I'm tired of it. Tired of wondering what he wants and what every single one of his words mean. Why couldn't we have normal parents… like Selti's? They seemed okay. Concerned about her, friendly…normal.

Gep's waiting for me to say something. But he can wait all day as far as I'm concerned.

He sighs.

'Anyway, the first thing I'm going to do to prove I mean what I say is that Jimmy's going to go to school. Tomorrow.'

I suck in a breath. He's got me. Even though I swear to myself, every time he reverts to nice guy mode, that I won't react, I can't help it.

'You mean it?'

He nods – slow – like he's a frigging king bestowing a favour on one of his lowly muck-covered peasants.

'Awesome!' Jimmy's eyes are wide and bright. He looks happy.

And while I'm happy that he's happy, that he's getting to do this, I wonder what the price is going to be. I know Gep. There's always a price. I just hope it's going to be something we're willing to pay.

CHAPTER 17

The admin lady doesn't look happy this time. Her face has this grim set to it – like the two lines on either side of her nose are trying to bury themselves deeper into her face.

'I'm afraid we don't have any teacher aides available to assist your brother with his schooling. This really is something we need to know ahead of time so funding can be organised.'

I can feel the anger building in me, like a fire smouldering in my guts, and I fight to keep it down. It just pisses me off when they talk about Jimmy as if he's not here – or that he can't hear or understand what they're saying. That he's an idiot.

Jimmy pushes his hand against my arm, like he knows what's going on for me, and looks up at the woman from his wheelchair.

'I understand that me coming here could be difficult,' he says, speaking a bit slower than normal, trying to make his words clear, 'but we've done this before. If you put me in classes with Penn, he writes for both of us and I have a really good memory.'

She looks startled for a moment that he's spoken and actually made sense – even if it's a bit of slurry.

'Well certainly,' she says, 'but for exams and the like. We have no one to assist you with this.'

Jimmy smiles at her and I can see her softening a bit – Jesus, he could win anyone over!

'I usually use a computer to do them. The exams get loaded onto it and I get a bit of extra time to complete them. That's what I've done in the past.'

She watches him for a moment, her eyes narrowed as if she's trying to work out whether she should chuck us all out or whether it'd be easier to let Jimmy in and make it someone else's problem.

'Fine,' she says, sighing like we've made her life so much harder. 'But I'll have to speak to the principal about this. And we still haven't had the opportunity to talk to your father yet. Especially in light of this new development.'

She looks at me, pointedly, eyebrows raised, like this is all my fault.

'Well, he's been looking after Jimmy for the last week because he hasn't been well either. That's why he didn't start the same day as us. And that's left Dad feeling really low...you know, with having cancer and everything. He hasn't quite recovered yet.'

Jimmy doesn't even react to that. We've made up too many stories together over the years for him to even flinch over something as minor as giving Gep cancer.

'Yes, well, he still needs to come in.'

'I'll let him know,' I say and she nods at me.

'I suppose you boys better get along to class then.'

I grab the handles of Jimmy's chair and get us out of there before she thinks of anything else that means Jimmy won't be able to come to school. I'm in such a hurry to get us out that I almost run into Selti, walking on the path beside the building. She's with another girl I haven't seen before – tall and lanky – taller even than Selti but scrunched up like she's trying not to draw attention to herself.

'Oh, hey!' Selti says and there's a smile on her face, like she's happy to see me. And then she looks at Jimmy and I can see confusion replace the smile.

'Hey. This is my brother, Jimmy. Jimmy, Selti.'

I hold my breath as I wait to see what her reaction's going to be. It's important. I really want her – need her – to be cool with Jimmy. Otherwise...well, otherwise, she's not the person I thought she was.

The smile's back on her face again, even if she still looks confused.

'Hey. Nice to meet you. You guys are twins?'

Jimmy nods.

'Yeah, but I'm the better looking one.'

She laughs and it seems genuine. I let out the breath.

'I can see that.'

'Hey!' I say, but I don't really care because she's smiling at me now.

I grin back at her, my lungs feeling like they're collapsing into a heap at the bottom of my chest. I want to touch her, take her hand, feel the taste of her lips with my tongue...

'So you're Selti,' Jimmy says, sending a sideways look to me. 'The one Penn's been talking about.'

My face goes hot – instant sunburn hot – and I want to punch his arm but I know that'll only make it worse. He can be such a shit sometimes – makes me question why I actually want to protect him. Selti's grin gets wider.

'You've been talking about me?'

'No! Well, yeah, I mean, I had to explain why I was wet and everything.' My voice trails off and it sounds totally lame...so frigging smooth – not! She chuckles.

'It's okay. I've been talking about you to Mum and Dad too.'

I grin at her.

'You have?'

'Sure. You know, I had to explain why I was wet and everything.'

I laugh along with her. It feels good. Nice. Normal. Not that I've ever really been that, but this is what I imagine it'd feel like.

'This is Emily,' she says and I smile at the girl next to her, who nods her head but only glances at me before looking at the ground, her cheeks going red. The break in the conversation is awkward and I'm not sure how to come back from it. Not with Selti standing there and messing up what should be pretty normal brain activity anyway.

'Well,' Selti says, 'I guess we'd better get to English before we're late.'

I latch onto it like a lifesaver thrown to a drowning man.

'Yeah. Jimmy's in all my classes so he's doing English with us.'

'What are you guys doing in class?' he asks and Selti answers him, telling him all about the book report. I'm happy to watch her, listen to her voice, watch the way she tucks her blue hair behind her ear in a way I'd love to do. And I watch the way she turns to Emily, checking she's included in the conversation with Jimmy. She's a good friend – a good person – but I think I knew that anyway.

We sit second row from the front – Jimmy on one side of me at the edge of the room with Selti on the other side of me. I feel cushioned between the two people I want to be next to most in the world. Weird. I don't know her…not really…but that doesn't stop it feeling right.

Alex and Rory walk in, laughing about something, and stop when they see me sitting there already, their eyes shifting to Jimmy, widening like I knew they would before they look back at me.

'Hey, this is Jimmy, my brother. Jimmy, this is Alex and Rory.'

Alex and Rory look at him again but they don't say anything. Probably don't know how to act. I know not everyone has had a lot do to with people with a disability and I try not to let it shit me off when they don't act like he's a person. But it does anyway.

'He wants to try out for the basketball team too.'

They look at me in shock – actually it looks more like panic – and I shake my head and roll my eyes. Jimmy laughs like I've told the best joke in the world.

'Yeah,' he says, 'I usually play defence but you know…wherever you can fit me in.'

They still haven't spoken and they're looking at Jimmy like he's an alien. It's beginning to really piss me off now. But Jimmy knows how to handle it – he always does. He's a better person than I'll ever be.

'I know it's a shock to see twins,' he says, smiling at them. 'But don't worry, it's actually pretty normal. Penn tells me the basketball team is one of the best he's ever played on.'

Alex gets it together before Rory does.

'Yeah, we're pretty good. We've made it to the finals again this year. And your brother's not a bad addition to the team.'

'He learnt everything from me,' Jimmy says and they grin with him.

He's won them over, quicker than I ever could. They sit in front of us and I can see them turning slightly during the lesson, watching Jimmy out of the corner of their eye. Or maybe they're watching me and Selti. I don't really care anymore. I don't care what they think. And I don't care about the book. Well…not at the moment anyway. Not with Jimmy sitting here beside me, looking like he's enjoying himself. Enjoying himself and not fading.

Not that I'm stupid enough to think Gep's going to let us forget it, even with his new found parent of the year act. But right at this moment, it seems…unimportant.

Mr Mac's pretty cool with Jimmy, which shouldn't surprise me, but sometimes it's the people who you expect to be okay who react in the worst way. Our maths teacher in the next class looks like she's almost about to have a fit when I introduce Jimmy and she keeps shooting us dirty looks the whole lesson, which have me scowling and Jimmy grinning. Like I said, better person…

At lunch time, I push Jimmy out into the covered area and look for Selti, but Rory and Alex corner me before I see her. They're casual about it but I can tell by the looks passing between them that they're going to be smart arses. I tense, waiting for whatever it is, waiting to see if it's about Jimmy…

'So,' Alex says, leaning against the wall like he's some mobster wannabe, 'you and the blue haired freak, huh?'

I shrug, struggling not to pull my fingers into a fist.

'She did some witchcraft voodoo shit on you and now you're her slave?' Rory chuckles, thinking he's funny.

'Voodoo and witchcraft aren't the same thing, you moron.'

Rory's face crumples in on itself for a moment, like he didn't expect me to answer and now I've confused him.

'Is there practice this arv? Can I come and watch you guys play?' Jimmy is looking up at them, his face innocent. Diverting. Protecting me. Even though I don't need it.

'Nah,' Alex is the first to recover, 'Wednesdays and Fridays.'

And then Jimmy is off, asking them both questions about their techniques and their plays so they forget about Selti. Frigging attention spans of gnats. Not that I'm ungrateful but jeez…

I see Selti then, over the other side on the concrete. She's sitting with Emily and another girl I haven't met and they're laughing; her face alight with it. She twirls her hair with her finger, twisting it in a way that keeps me starring, mesmerized in a way that if I stopped to think about it would make me look like a total dork. It's only when Alex punches me on the arm that I turn back to them.

'Christ, lover boy, you've got it bad. Don't say we didn't warn you. She's into some freaky shit, man.'

I want to punch him…so hard his nose will crumple on his face, blood pouring down his chin, and for a moment, I take the luxury of curling my fingers into a fist, before smiling at him. It's the hardest smile I have ever done in my life.

'So, has Jimmy got you to agree to let him play yet?'

Alex laughs. I think that's what makes me relax a little. He's going to leave it alone. So I don't notice right away when a group of kids start to form in a circle just off the edge of the cement. It's only when they start chanting 'fight, fight' that I actually look up.

'Hey,' Rory is standing on his toes trying to see over everyone, 'isn't that your little brother? Fox or something?'

I react without thinking – pushing my way through the crowd – not caring if I'm pissing anyone off. This is Jimmy's first day back at school for Christ sake! If Fox gets in a fight and gets suspended, Gep will take it out on Jimmy. That's what he always does. Fox knows that! What the hell is he thinking?

I get to the front of the circle just as the other kid lands a good one on Fox's face, and manage to get myself between them before Fox can land one back. His face is bright red when he looks up at me and he pulls his hand out of my grip.

'Get out of the way, Penn.'

'Don't be a dickhead. You'll get suspended. And then you know what'll happen.'

'I don't care.'

'Fox...'

'Get out of my way!'

But before I can do anything else, the teacher is here, breaking the crowd up as she pushes through them to get to us.

'Right, what's going on here?'

'This kid started it,' I say, before Fox can say anything. 'He punched my brother. Fox didn't do anything.'

She frowns at me like I've done something to personally insult her and then looks at Fox and the other kid.

'Is that right?'

Fox shrugs and the other kid scowls at the ground. But it's hard to miss the mark on Fox's face that's already coming up into a bruise. The teacher sighs and shakes her head.

'Right, Mr Butler, you can come with me to the Principal's office. Mr...'

Reed.'

'Well, Mr Reed, you can take your brother down to the school nurse. And I do not want to see this happening again. Is that understood?'

'Yes, Ma'am.'

Fox gives a half-hearted nod and I want to slap him. Is he forgetting everything today about putting on a good act? Christ, I'm usually the stupid one!

The teacher leaves with the other boy and I move to go to the school nurse but when I look around, Fox isn't following. He's walking off in the other direction. I shake my head and sprint over to where Jimmy's still with Alex and Rory.

'I better go after him,' I say and Jimmy nods at me. 'Can you guys take Jimmy to the next class if I'm not back?'

'Yeah, sure,' Alex says, like it's no big deal, and I wonder if I've been too hard on him. Maybe he's not so bad.

'Don't let him go home,' Jimmy says and I can hear the fear in his voice, even if it's not clear to everyone else. We both know what'll happen if he goes home. I nod and turn to race after Fox again. I see him just as he's about to leave the school grounds, bag slung over his shoulder.

'Fox! Hey, wait up!'

But he doesn't even slow down and I have to really sprint to catch up. I fall into step beside him, even though that means we're both out of the grounds now. But I can feel the anger pouring off him like it's acid on my skin.

'What the hell happened back there?'

'Nothing.'

'Fox, come on. Something happened.'

'Just forget about it.'

'No, I won't forget about it. You're my brother.'

He snorts. 'Yeah, right.'

I do stop him then, grabbing his arm and turning him to face me.

'What's that mean?'

He slaps my hand away.

'Nothing.'

'It's not nothing. Tell me.'

His eyes meet mine. They're hard, angry. And I realise I've never seen him this heated before. Not that I can remember anyway. But maybe I haven't been paying attention, just focused on Jimmy.

'Don't say I'm your brother. I'm not. You think I don't know that you'd take off with Jimmy if you had the chance? Leave Kat and me with Gep? I've heard you say it. So don't act like you suddenly care!'

My stomach feels like it's somewhere down around my knees. Because he's right but it seems like such an arsehole thing when he says it out loud. And I don't want to be that person. But if it was between him and Jimmy – I'd pick Jimmy every time. I don't know what to say so I just look at him instead.

He nods, narrowing his eyes before he starts walking again, leaving me standing there.

'Fox, come on. You know I have to protect Jimmy. He can't do it himself.'

He stops and turns back around.

'You want to know what that fight was about?'

I don't know that I do now but I nod anyway.

'They called Jimmy a retard. Said that because I had a retard brother, I must be one too.'

My jaw tightens and I struggle to relax it. I don't want to be mad at Fox.

'So?'

'So I'm sick of it. I'm sick of all of it – moving all the time and not having friends and knowing you and Jimmy have each other and I have no one. No one! God, I reckon Kat would even choose to stay with Gep than come with me.'

I don't answer, mainly because I still don't know the words to make this better.

'This is fucked,' he says. 'I'm going. I'm going to go and find somewhere to live and get a job and… I don't know…be normal. Find a family of my own. Someone who wants me to be around. Get a life.'

But all I can imagine is him on the streets, being bashed up by someone bigger than him and dying, lying in the gutter somewhere bleeding to death until the only colour that's left in him is his red hair. And that socks me in the gut in a way I've never felt before.

'Don't Fox. Stay. It's stupid to leave, man.'

'Why? Why should I stay?'

I take a deep breath.

'Because I promise Jimmy and I won't leave without you.'

He looks at me, his grey eyes narrowed, assessing me like I've seen Gep do a million times before.

'You mean that?'

'I said it, didn't I?'

'Swear it. On Jimmy's life.'

I jerk back, his words reminding me of the picture…Jimmy's picture…fading.

'I'm not swearing it on his life!'

His jaw gets hard.

'Then you don't really mean it. You're just jerking with me.'

I shake my head and glare at him but he glares right back.

'Fuck! Alright, I swear it on Jimmy's life. We won't leave without you.'

He's quiet for a second and then he nods. 'Alright then.'

And before I can say anything else, he turns and starts walking back to school, leaving me standing there.

I can't help wondering though, if I should've left him go. Whether it actually would have been the nicer thing to do.

CHAPTER 18

Gep doesn't even notice Fox's eye – or if he does, he doesn't say anything. Which makes me hopeful and suspicious all at the same time. I don't want to get my hopes up because I've been sucked in so many times in the past but…maybe he meant what he said about changing. About trying to be a better father. Or then again, maybe not. I watch him moving around the kitchen, cooking steak. For us. I can't even remember the last time that happened. It's so weird, none of us are talking. We're just watching Gep. Wary that he's going to turn around and attack at any moment. Whack us with the steak maybe? Poison us? Who knows…?

This new Gep is making me feel like I don't know where I fit in my life anymore. And I don't like it.

He swings around with the tongs in his hand and Fox flinches in the seat beside me. I shove my knee up against his and he shoots me a look that's half grateful, half pissed off. I ignore it.

'So, my boys, how's it going with finding the book?'

We're all quiet, none of us wanting to speak first. It's usually not safe to.

'Kat, any leads?'

'Um, not really. I mean, I thought I had a good one, but it didn't work out. I've got others though, and I'm going to check them out more but I haven't had a chance yet and I think they might be the right ones this time and...yeah.'

Kat's hands are pressed together on the table, his knuckles white under the force of the hold. He's staring at the table but the rest of us are watching Gep.

'Well, as long as you're still looking.' We wait for the rage...the power... the abuse...to start. But it doesn't and my heart's beating in my chest so hard it feels like it's trying to use my ribs to climb up to my throat. I don't know what to do here – how to react.

Kat's looking at me like I should know the answers but I shrug at him and he looks away again. The look of hope in his eyes is enough to make me wish Gep really has changed. Fox shakes his head like he doesn't trust it. I guess Kat's the most hopeful one of the bunch of us. The most naïve maybe.

Gep dishes up the steak and we're all still watching him. Everyone is quiet. Small talk is hard to make when you're waiting for the mood swing to smack you in the head. He puts the plates in front of us and I cut Jimmy's into small pieces. Gep sits down at the head of the table and smiles. It actually looks real. Makes his eyes crinkle at the sides and everything. He looks like a person you could trust. I grip the cutlery tight and try to look like none of it's fazing me. Maybe that's his plan. Psych us out until we break.

He looks at all of us and spears a piece of steak with his fork. I see Fox flinch again.

'So,' Gep waves the fork around like it's a baton, 'how was school today, Jimmy?'

'Good.'

Gep waits for more but when it's obvious he's not going to get it, he puts down his fork. I put mine down too and grip the side of the table. Ready to leap up if I need to, the muscles in my legs tight. Waiting.

'Is that it? Did you make any friends? What subjects did you do?' He sighs and runs his fingers through his hair. 'I'm trying here boys but I need you to help me be a good Dad. Okay?'

Kat nods like his head's about to fall off. He wants this so bad. It's sad to think I used to be like that. I want Kat to get it – even if I don't trust Gep, I want him to be changed so Kat has a chance at a life we all wanted.

Fox is scowling at his plate and Jimmy is leaning back in his chair, taking it all in, although there's a ghost of a smile on his face too. A small hope maybe, that all of this is true. Maybe I'm the only cynical one here. My face is blank – it's the look I've perfected – but inside my stomach is churning so much I wonder if I'm going to throw up. I want to leave but I can't. Not after what I'd said to Fox earlier. Because now I have to protect him too. Him and Jimmy. Even if I don't want to, I said I would. And I guess that probably includes Kat now too. Jesus, how the hell did I get to this place…responsible for bloody everyone?

So, I stay and try not to say anything that's going to set Gep off.

'School was good,' Jimmy says. 'It was nice to be back. The English assignment is one we've done before but that's okay. And I met a few kids.'

I hold my breath, waiting for him to say something about Selti, but I should've known better. Jimmy would never sell me out like that. Still, my heart takes a while to slow back down.

Gep nods and smiles at him. He looks at Kat then, and asks him about his day. And, of course, Kat goes on and on and on. Which is okay because it means the rest of us can pretend not to be there. I try to give Jimmy a hand with his dinner but by the third mouthful, he's pushing the fork away.

'You have to eat. Do you want something else?' I say to him under my breath, hoping Gep doesn't overhear. Because I know where he's going to go with it. It's the place where I already am – the photo, the fading – and even though I know it's a load of shit, it doesn't stop the panic that's starting to build in my chest, like someone's poured cement into my lungs.

'I'm just tired. Think I'll go to bed.'

It's quiet at the table and I'm trying really hard not to turn around and look at Gep, although I can feel his eyes boring into the back of my head. His voice echoes around the room.

'Kat and Fox, can you help Jimmy get to bed?'

I shut my eyes for a second.

'I can do it.'

'No,' Gep says in a voice that sounds like he's trying to be nice. 'Fox and Kat will be happy to do it.'

I can see Fox roll his eyes but both of them get up without saying anything else. Jimmy looks at me as Fox grabs the back of his wheelchair. I can see he's worried about why Gep doesn't want me to help; why he wants to keep me here – I only have to look in his eyes to know that – but I can see how tired he is too. His face is pale and there are dark circles under his eyes, so I nod at him, giving him a small smile that's probably not going to make him feel much better.

It's only when they've gone into the bathroom that I turn back to Gep. The sorrow in his eyes is not what I want to see. Anger, hatred – something I'm used to. Something I know how to deal with. I glare at him, daring him to say something even though I've got nothing to threaten him with. He doesn't take the hint anyway.

'It's starting,' he says. 'That's how your mother was. Tired all the time. Not wanting to eat.'

'He's had a big day. After being shut up in a frigging house for so long, it just took it out of him going to school today.'

'You know it's not that – '

'Shut the hell up. I don't want to hear it.' I'm gritting my teeth, trying to keep my voice low so Jimmy can't hear us. The bathroom's not really that sound proof. Actually, the paper thin walls don't offer any sort of sound proofing.

Gep is glaring at me now and I'm shocked by how much I was counting on him staying the 'nice' Gep. Jesus, only forty-five minutes of his act and I'm already buying into it. I'm as bad as Kat!

'Telling me to shut up is not going to change what's happening. Get your head out of your fucking arse otherwise you may as well sign his death warrant now. I need your help with this. I know you have it in you. And that book will show us what we've got to do. It, along with the other things you boys have collected for me. That's why I needed them, as an insurance policy.'

I don't know what the hell he's talking about. All I know is I want to hit him. So badly my hands are aching because I'm holding my fist tight, the nails digging into my skin. But that's probably going to make things worse.

'I don't believe you.'

'How do you explain the photo then?'

I snort.

'You're the sorcerer. You tell me. Some kind of cheap trick.'

'It's not a trick. Jesus, Penn, you have to listen to me. He's going to die unless we find that book. Like your mum. We need to get it and get it soon. It's the last piece in the puzzle. The last thing we need to bring it all together. It's vital. Vital!'

I shift in my chair, uncomfortable suddenly, like his words have made my legs twitch and my stomach roll. I don't know what to say. I know we have to get the book – like we always have to get whatever it is Gep wants, just because he wants them. He's never given us a reason before. Never told us why. And I guess I've never really questioned it. I've never really wanted to know. But now he's telling me we need it to save Jimmy? That that's been the reason for all of it – the insurance policy. To even think about acknowledging that in my head…it seems like I'm giving into his pathetic lies.

'We'll find your stupid book. Just shut up about Jimmy. He's not dying.'

I get up from the table, shoving the chair back in so it bounces off the edge before settling back. As I leave, Gep doesn't say anything else. And I'm not sure if that's good or bad.

CHAPTER 19

*I*t's Friday afternoon before I really get the chance to talk to Selti again on our own...without Jimmy looking on with a knowing grin or Alex and Rory whispering and nudging each other like they're frigging ten year old girls or Emily standing there, looking at me but never meeting my eyes.

She's at the office when I go in to finally give them Gep's signed papers for Jimmy attending school, along with a hand written note to give them, to stop them questioning me about him – that sort of thing usually works for a while. At least until we leave the town.

She's standing with her back towards me at the front counter and the sight of her makes my stomach turn itself inside out. Her hair is up in this messy bun thing and there's little wisps escaping against her neck. All I can think about is kissing her skin, right beneath her hair line, so when she finally does turn around, I know I have this moronic look on my face.

She smiles at me though and all I can do is smile back.

'Hey.'

'Hey right back at you. Where's Jimmy this morning?'

I point with my thumb out the door.

'He's with Kat and Fox. I had to bring this stuff in for my dad.'

She nods and we stand there, looking at each other, still smiling, like a pair of weirdos. Is it stupid that I could look at her all day? Surely this isn't normal?

'I'd better go then.'

It's only when she's past me that I get the courage to do it.

'Hey, Selti?'

She stops and raises her eyebrows at me. My heart's pounding and I'm sure if this place wasn't air conditioned, I'd be sweating like I'd spent an hour in a sauna. I swallow…it's hard. Feels like there's a big lump in my throat for it to get past.

'What are you doing tonight?'

'Not much. Homework probably. I think Mum and Dad are going to a dinner for Dad's work. Why?'

'I was wondering if…you know…you'd you like to do something? With me?'

She looks startled for a moment, like I've told her I'm an alien, and I know, in that moment, she's going to say no. She's going to say no and I'm going to look like an idiot and she won't want to ever talk to me again and I won't even have that to look forward to.

'You want to do something with me?'

I nod. Waiting. Holding myself tight.

'Okay.'

'Okay?'

'Yeah.' She smiles and it looks like a real one. Like she's said yes because she wants to and not because she thinks I'm lame and doesn't want to be nasty. 'What are we going to do?'

I hadn't really thought that far. Stupid! But I was so sure she'd say no, I haven't got any sort of plan. Nothing. Zip. Zero. Zilch.

Not that I'm about to let her know that.

'Leave it with me. Then it can be a surprise.'

'Okay.' Her skin is pink now and I want to run my hand over her cheek, caress her skin, have her lean into my touch…Christ, she's watching me, and I wonder what sort of expression I've got on my face.

'Okay then. Well, I'll pick you up at six?'

'Okay.'

We stare at each other for a moment more and then laugh.

'Okay, well, I'll see you then.'

And then she's out the door and I can see her do this sort of skipping thing down the path, which makes my heart want to explode with happiness. I give the papers to the admin lady and then push the door open so hard it bounces off the wall behind it and nearly slams back into me again. And I must have this dopey grin on my face when I come out because Fox scowls at me.

'What's up with you?'

I whack him on the shoulder.

'Fox, my man, the world is a great place.'

He steps away from me.

'Whatever. Frigging idiot.'

I laugh and Jimmy's looking at me with a knowing expression on his face. He must have seen Selti come out. He grins at me and I grin back, knowing he has a pretty good idea of why I'm acting like a loon without me having to say it out loud.

Kat, as usual, is pretty clueless but I guess he's just happy that we're happy. And the good mood lasts all day. Despite Alex and Rory bitching at each other like an old married couple and despite the fact that I don't really get a chance to talk much to Selti. None of that seems to matter. I'm buzzing. And then all the boys come and watch the basketball practice, even Fox, and we walk home together like none of us want to let the good feeling go. Kat chats all the way home, walking up on the gutter and jumping back down, running backwards – acting like a goof ball. It's nice. It feels what I imagine kids with a normal life feel like.

Even going up the stairs to the house – carrying Jimmy while Fox and Kat manoeuvre the wheelchair – and seeing Gep there, waiting for us, isn't enough to dampen my buzz.

It even makes me stupid enough to smile back at him when he smiles at me.

'Someone's had a good day. What's happened?'

The grin slips from my face – not too fast because then he'd know I was hiding something. And I'm determined to keep him in the dark about Selti for as long as I can. I put Jimmy down in his chair, helping him to adjust himself so he's comfortable, spending more time than it normally takes to come up with a good lie.

'Just...uh...managed to get in a lot of my shots at basketball practice. And I've got a good lead on the book. I'll follow it up tonight.'

'Tonight?'

'Yeah.' I look behind him and it's only then I notice the chicken guts on the board in the kitchen. I look back at him and he's watching me, like he's daring me to call him out on it. And I am so fucking up for it. He's not going to spoil tonight. 'No. No way. It's not even the second Friday. It's not happening. You're not getting one of us to do it. This is shit!'

For a second – one fleeting moment – I see the old Gep in his face, see his hand come up and I tense, waiting for his touch and the burn that usually comes with it. But then it's like he takes hold of himself again and takes a deep breath.

'We have to. I need it. I need information, I mean. Information about...you know.'

He looks at Jimmy and I want to punch him. Does he think Jimmy's stupid? That he won't pick up on it? And it's crap about wanting information. That's not what he wants. He wants the frigging high he gets from the power. And once more, we're the pawns. Giving us a new life – what a crock!

'Bull.'

'What's bull?' Jimmy's pushing his chair forward slightly, looking at me.

I glare at Gep.

'Nothing. It's nothing. Just Gep trying to get us to do his dirty work.'

He doesn't believe me – I can see it in his face but he leaves it. For now. I know the next time we're alone, there's going to be a million questions because I'd do the same thing.

'You're not going out tonight.' Gep's hands are on his hips, watching me.

'You said we need the book. That it was really important. Well, this is the best lead we've had so far. I'm going out.'

Every part of my body feels like it's quivering with tension. This is the part when I feel the burn – the part when standing up for what I want never pays off.

Ever.

Kat steps up beside me.

'I'll do it if you want. Let Penn go out and see if he can find the book and I'll be the conduit.'

'No! No one needs to do it.' I'm not looking at Kat. Only at Gep.

He gives me a long, measured look. One that tells me I've done this. Forced Kat to do it. Naïve Kat who's only been the conduit twice before and both times, he cried afterwards. Sobbed so much his shoulders heaved and his eyes were swollen. Sobbed even in his sleep. I know because I lay there in the dark, listening to him, not knowing what to do. And hating Gep more than I thought was possible.

And I know, as he gives a small nod of his head, that he hasn't changed. The power is still more important than anything in his life. Including us, despite what he says.

'Okay, Kat. You'll be the conduit.'

I sigh, a ragged one, and drag my fingers through my hair. I want to go to Selti – so bad the thought of not going is actually painful – but I can't let Gep do this to Kat. Not while I'm not here.

'No. I'll do it. Then I'll go out.'

'No, you'll go and find the book.' Gep turns away from us, going over the bench to the chicken, like that's the end of it.

'Stop it. I'll be your frigging conduit.'

'No. Kat will be the conduit. And you will go and find the book that'll help us to save your brother.'

'What?' Jimmy's voice squeaks as the word rushes out of him. 'Save me from what?'

I want to punch Gep, right in the guts. Watch him double over with pain and not be able to get enough air into his lungs. But I turn to Jimmy instead.

'It's nothing. Just Gep being psycho. He thinks you're in danger and that we need the book to keep you safe.'

'Danger from what?'

I can't find the words. How do I tell him Gep thinks he's going to die like our mum? That his frigging picture is fading like hers apparently did? That I might lose him too.

'From dying,' Gep says and there's an edge to his voice. I can't work out what it means. 'I'm trying to stop you from dying, Jimmy. From the life force being sucked out of you, like the spirits did to your mother. I'm trying to save you, son.'

And that makes me want to punch him even more. Punch and kick and scream until he stops. Or leaves. Not just the fact that he told Jimmy but that he's called him son. Claiming him like he has a right to it when, if it wasn't for him, we wouldn't be in this position. Him and his frigging unending desire for power. He's the one that should be dying. Jimmy looks from Gep to me with wide eyes.

'What does he mean?'

I kneel down beside him, my hand on his arm, keeping it down. Panic makes control worse for him and I know he hates that.

'Jimmy, trust me, man. I'm not going to let anything happen to you, okay. Okay?'

He nods, scanning my face like he's looking for the lie.

'I'm going to find the book and Gep will do what he has to do. But it's bullshit. You're not dying so don't even think about it. You're not sick, are you?'

He shakes his head, movements jerky.

'But I'm tired, Penn. Really tired.'

My stomach clenches, sucking in on itself, but I keep it from showing on my face. All the practice with Gep has come in handy.

'That's because you've been back at school again this week, man. Using your brain again, making friends. And you haven't been out for a while. Of course it's going to wear you out.'

He's looking at me like he really, really wants to believe me.

'You've got to trust me. I'm not going to let anything happen to you. You know that.'

He nods but I can see he's still scared. I massage his arm for a moment, trying to keep my fingers from digging in too hard. But my anger for Gep is so hot I feel like it's going to melt my bones. I give Jimmy one last smile and then stand up and go over to Gep. He turns before I get to him.

'If you ever pull that fucking shit again, I will kill you.'

He sneers at me.

'Stop trying to be a big man. Because while you're busy doing that, I'm trying to save him. He has the right to know. Now go and find the fucking book.'

I'm so mad but all I can do is slam the door on the way out.

CHAPTER 20

*I*t takes the whole fifteen minute walk to Selti's place before I feel like I'm capable of human thought again, rather than just thoughts about how I want to end it for Gep – all of them violent and very, very satisfying. It's not until I get to their front gate that I realise I have absolutely no frigging idea what we're going to do for the date. Moron!

I stand there, hand on the metal strands of the fence, trying to decide whether to go in or not. Because I don't want her to think I don't care about this. Like it's nothing. But finally, the thought of not seeing her outweighs the thought of having to tell her that I'm lame and haven't put any planning into it at all. I'm hoping maybe she'll go for the sympathy vote.

But my heart's thumping as I knock on her door and I'm holding my breath as she opens it. She smiles at me and I smile back but there must be something wrong with it because she immediately frowns.

'What's wrong?'

'Nothing.' I run my fingers through my hair and slouch against the door frame. 'I mean, nothing really. I had a major fight with my dad and I had this plan for a great date for us but I sort of left without getting anything organised.'

'Oh.' That's all she says and I don't know what that means.

'I'm sorry. I wanted to have it all organised and have a great time with you but...I'm sorry.'

She smiles then and the tight feeling around my chest loosens a little. Enough that I can breathe again. She leans against the other side of the door frame, like it's just the two of us holding the house up.

'What were your plans?'

'I was going to get some food and a blanket and take you down to the creek where I saved you from drowning so we could have a picnic under the stars.'

She smiles. 'I like that idea.'

'You do?'

She nods and then stands up straight, holding the door open wider.

'Come on, we can still do it.'

I follow her into the house. It's nice. Rich without being over the top. Polished wooden floors with these rugs you sink into when you walk on them and the most amazing artefacts in different corners, all lit by their own individual lights. It's a bit like a museum but more like a home. Gep would have a field day here probably.

Selti turns and gives me a smile over her shoulder and every-thing in me clenches tight. How does one of her smiles do that to me? It shouldn't be possible. But I don't want it to stop.

I follow her through to the kitchen, which is all white marble. Really modern compared to the rest of the house but it doesn't seem out of place. What I wouldn't give to be able to live somewhere like this rather than the shitty rental places Gep's always settling for. Just once. It'd be nice to feel like I'm living somewhere...solid.

The only colour in the kitchen is a painting, attached to the wall above the bench. It's a landscape full of blues and greens and pinks and I go closer to check it out. That's when I notice her name signed to it.

I turn to her. 'Holy shit. Did you do this?'

She looks at me, then the picture, before her eyes slide past me again to look at the bench.

'Yeah. Mum and Dad insisted on hanging it.'

'No wonder. It's really good.'

Her eyes met mine and stay there this time, even though they look like they want to slide away again.

'Thanks.'

'Is that what you want to do? After school? Be an artist?'

She shrugs and then nods and then shrugs a second time.

'I guess. I'd love to but…you know. It's a bit of a dream. I probably need to do something that'd make me actual money.'

She laughs but there's a stiffness to it, like she's forcing it.

'Nothing wrong with having dreams.' I should know.

"Maybe.' She smiles at me. 'What are your dreams?'

It's my turn to shrug. 'I don't really know yet. I'm still waiting for inspiration to hit.'

Except I do know. I'm just not about to tell her how lame they are. Get Jimmy away from Gep. Have a real life. That's it.

She gestures to a stool under the island bench and I sit down, leaning my elbows against the counter top, happy to watch her as she whirls around the kitchen, getting things out of the fridge and the cupboard. I wonder if there'll be any food left for her family by the time she's finished…there seems to be food spread all over the bench. She frowns.

'Do you think that'll be enough?'

I laugh.

'Well, I don't know. Is it just you and me or are you planning to invite the rest of the basketball team as well?'

Her face colours and I feel like a jerk. Here she is trying to help with the date I should've planned and I'm making smart arse comments. I want to get up and wrap her in my arms to make her feel better. I don't, of course. I lay my hands flat on the bench instead. It's cool under my fingers.

'Should I put some back?'

I shake my head.

'It looks great – better than what I would've managed to get.'

She goes over to a cupboard in the hallway and grabs a picnic basket out. An honest to God picnic basket. I thought only people in the movies had them. When I think about the plastic bag I would've used to put stuff in, I'm sort of happy I didn't actually follow through on the idea. Although that makes me feel shit too. She deserves to be treated like a frigging queen.

'I'm sorry this is the lamest date you've probably ever been on.'

She laughs and shakes her head, squeezing her mouth shut like there's something she was going to say but decided not to.

'What?'

Her eyes meet mine for a second before darting back down to the food. But she still doesn't say anything and my curiosity ramps up about one thousand per cent.

'Come on, Selti. What were you going to say?'

She rolls her eyes at me and then sighs. 'This is the *only* date I've ever been on. My very first.'

I'm sure my mouth drops open. Only slightly but enough that she'd see it.

'What do you mean? How can this be your first date? Are all the other guys at school stupid?'

She blushes again and ducks her head, hiding behind her hair while her hands move over the food on the bench like they need something to do.

'You've seen what it's like. I've lived here my whole life but...' she stops for a second, like she's trying to work out what to say. Or maybe she doesn't want to say it at all. 'I'm different. Our family is different. And they don't really cope well with different.

Even if someone has been…interested on going on a date, they don't really want me to be me. They want me to be the same as them. I know that. You probably fit in better in the week you've been here than I ever will.'

I want to tell her it's all make believe – that me fitting in isn't real. It's just what I have to do in every town we move to – be who they want me to be; take on a role. That I'm as much an outsider as she is, or I feel like it anyway. But I don't. Because that would take a bigger explanation than I can give. Even though I'd love to tell her the truth. Just to have someone else know what's happening and understand why I do the things I do – to have someone else, apart from Jimmy, know who I really.

'Well, I still think they're stupid.'

She smiles at me, a shy one, before she packs everything in for the picnic. I grab the basket from the counter. It's only when I turn that I notice the wall behind me is one huge bookshelf. And there's not one space free. It's totally full of books. Crammed in. I let out a low whistle and put the basket back down while I go over, running my fingers over the spines, feeling the indents of the titles and the different textures of the covers. I know, without knowing how, that the book Gep wants is here. I can feel it. Somehow. Faint, like a mozzie buzzing at the ceiling. You can hear it – you know it's there – but you can't see it. All I know is that the book Gep thinks will save Jimmy is within reach and my skin prickles at the thought that I'll have to steal it.

From Selti.

Shit.

I hear her come up behind me.

'My parents are pretty much bower birds when it comes to books. I think every book they've ever owned is still here.'

'It's nice. To have this, I mean. We have bugger all stuff from our childhood or my parents' childhood.'

'Is your mum…not with you? I mean, you always talk about your dad but you don't mention your mum.'

'Mum died when we were three. It was the same accident that put Jimmy in the wheelchair.'

'Wow. That must have been really hard.'

I shrug like it doesn't mean anything.

'It was a long time ago.'

I don't want to talk about it. Just for a few hours, I want it to be about me and Selti. Not about Mum or Gep or even about Jimmy, which makes me a totally shitty brother. But it doesn't seem like a lot to ask. Just a few hours where I get what I want. Especially now I know the book is here.

'Come on,' I say, turning and grabbing the basket again. 'The stars await us.'

I give her a bow and she laughs, the sound reverberating through my soul. She picks up the blanket she grabbed from the cupboard too and links her arm through mine. It feels good. Really good.

'Well then, we'd better not keep them waiting.'

She does most of the talking as we walk to the river in the softly fading daylight. I'm happy to let her do it. I like hearing about her life and about what she thinks and what annoys her or makes her happy. My brain is storing all of it away, every piece of information she feeds me, each one a small bit of treasure that's making me richer with each passing moment.

When we get there, the water is starting to darken, flowing along like it has its own business to attend to and couldn't care less what we're doing. It's quiet – peacefully quiet not spooky quiet. Like it's just me and Selti in the world. No one else to worry about or think about or try and work out what game they're playing.

It's nice.

She spreads out the blanket and I put the basket on top before we sit down. I'm as close as I can be without actually touching her, even though that's what I want to be doing. With her hand gone from my arm, I feel…heavier, even though that doesn't make sense. Selti opens the basket and takes out an electric lantern. It casts a soft glow around us. Just us. Surrounding us in our own world. She starts to unload the food and even though I'm really not interested in eating, I grab some grapes from the plate she's set up so she doesn't feel bad.

'So, you've let me go on and on, what about you?

'What about me?'

She nudges me with her elbow.

'Come on, don't do the strong silent type. I don't know. Where were you living before you came here, what do you like doing…anything?'

I laugh.

'That's me – the strong silent type.' I run my hands through my hair. 'Anything, huh?'

She nods.

'Okay. I hate broccoli – like really hate it, makes me gag. I don't understand how people can eat it – the texture of it is just wrong. I love anything with chocolate, can't stand it when people are up themselves, pretty much will listen to any music, I'm a Capricorn and before here, we weren't anywhere long enough for it to matter.'

'So that's you in a nutshell, huh?'

'Yep, that's me.'

'Do you move all the time?'

There's something in her voice when she asks that question… something that makes me think maybe she wouldn't want me to move. But maybe that's just wishful thinking.

'Pretty often. This is my thirtieth school since grade one.'

'Thirtieth! Not thirteenth?'

I shake my head. 'Nuh. Thirtieth. Three – zero.'

'God, you weren't joking when you said you hadn't been anywhere long enough for it to matter. We've never lived anywhere else. One primary school, one high school. With the same kids mostly.' She pulls her hair over her shoulder and twists the end as she looks out over the river. 'Is your family planning to stay here for a while or will you be gone to your thirty-first soon?'

I swallow – it's hard against the big frigging lump that's suddenly formed in my throat, like a golf ball has wedged itself in there.

'I hope we'll be staying.'

My voice is husky and she looks back at me, her face serious, eyes searching my face like she's trying to find all the answers there. She looks away again then, down to the food, and I'm disappointed but only for a second, because she brings a piece of chocolate up towards me.

'You said you like chocolate.'

I grin at her before opening my mouth. She grins back at me, moving it towards my lips, so slowly I want to grab her hand, but suddenly, she's moving fast, back towards her. She grins at me as she puts it in her own mouth.

'Hey!' I grab her arm, even though it's too late, and lose balance as she pulls herself backwards. And then she's lying on the rug and I'm over the top of her, holding myself up on my elbows.

My heart loses balance too, tripping in my chest for a second, as she looks up at me, eyes serious again. My whole body feels alive, every cell clenching like it can't believe I'm about to do this. And I can't believe I am either. I lower myself down, closer to her – closer to her lips – watching her while I do. Like she's watching me.

My lips touch hers – the lightest of touches – enough that I can feel their softness. I come back up, just the smallest distance, to look at her again. To check she's okay with it, that I haven't overstepped the mark – ruined things before they've even started…

And then, her hand is around the back of my neck, pulling me down, closing her eyes, and I can't help myself this time.

My tongue flicks along the edge of her lips and I can taste the chocolate she's eaten. She tangles her fingers into the hair at the nape of my neck and I'm kissing her, tasting her, wanting her like I've never wanted anything in my life. I kiss the edge of her lips, following the line down to her jaw, her neck, tasting her skin. She wraps her other hand around my back, following the line of my vertebrae down to the edge of my jeans.

I know I should stop – there's a voice in my head telling me to do. But I can't. Or I don't want to. I can't decide what it is. I just want her.

But then suddenly, she's pulling away from me. Pushing me up and away. I let her, even though I know I could push against her if I wanted to. But that's not what I want. I don't want to force myself on her. I want her to want me.

And she is gasping, pushing away from underneath me. As much as I'd like to think it was my awesome technique, I don't think her breathlessness is from our kissing.

'Oh my God. Penn!'

She's shaking, hand up to her mouth, pointing at me.

And when I look down, I know why. My skin – my arms, my hands – are glowing blue.

CHAPTER 21

*H*oly shit!

I sit back on my heels, holding my hands out in front of me, shaking as much a Selti is. They're glowing with a dim fluorescent blue, like I'm holding a glow stick in my hands, even though I'm not.

I flick my hands, like it's something I can throw away from me – shaking, flicking, like I've got a nervous tick or something. Crap. Crap! I try rubbing them on my shirt, my pants; rubbing one hand against the other; rubbing until my skin feels tender. Nothing works. Nothing!

Holy shit! Holy shit!

What the hell is this? What does it mean?

Selti reaches up to touch my face, her eyes still really wide. Freaked out. Like me. I'm amazed she can stand to be close to me and it's nearly impossible not to jerk away from her touch. Her fingers are cool though, like ice on a burn.

'It's all of you, Penn, not just your hands,' she says. 'What is it?'

'I don't know. I don't know! Jesus! I'm blue.'

'Like my hair.'

And at that moment, it comes back to me, clicking into place like an engine that suddenly fits together. That night when I was the conduit and the spirit talked about the blue claiming its power. I'd thought it was about Selti – a reference to her hair – but maybe it wasn't. Maybe it was about some sort of spirit claiming me or something.

Fuck!

I spring up and race down to the water, flicking it up, splashing it all over me, trying to wash it off my skin. It's not working either but it's the only thing I can think to do. My movements are jerky, panicked, and it feels like my jaw is about to break I'm clenching it that hard.

Selti comes and kneels next to me.

'What are you doing?'

I don't know what to say to her – how to explain any of this. But I can't get my brain to think around the panic – can't find a lie that would explain this away.

'I think a spirit has claimed me. That's why I'm blue because it's claimed me and I have to get rid of it. Before it does something to me. Possesses me or something.'

'Penn…' she reaches out to me.

'No! Don't touch me! I can't…I don't know what it'll do.'

'Penn,' she says again. 'Look at me.'

I don't stop trying to wash it off but I do look at her.

'There's no spirit.' She sounds like she thinks I'm crazy.

'No, you don't understand – '

She reaches out and touches my face before I can stop her.

'I can see spirits, Penn. That's one of the things I can do. And there's no spirit around you. Nothing's claimed you.'

I stop, staring at her.

'You can see spirits? You know about them?'

She nods.

'And there's nothing…nothing claiming me?'

She shakes her head.

'Why am I blue then?'

'I don't know.'

I sit back on the edge of the river, looking at my hands, dripping wet but still definitely glowing.

'Fuck!'

We sit there for a moment in silence, looking at my hands.

'Why did you think it was a spirit?'

I swallow hard, trying to get some moisture into my suddenly dry mouth.

'No reason. I mean, I just panicked.'

She looks at me in a way that says she knows I'm full of shit and I sigh.

'My dad…he knows all about spirits. He calls them sometimes, asks them questions and stuff.'

'Why?'

This is getting too close to having to tell her the whole truth. And I don't want to do that because she might hate me. Be disgusted enough with the life I've led that she'll tell me to get stuffed and want nothing more to do with me and my freaky history. And I've only found her. I don't want to lose her. Not yet. I know I probably will, but not yet.

'I don't know why. Because he's an idiot. You'll have to ask him.'

I sound angry but I can't help myself. Because I *know*, without any shadow of a doubt, that this is something to do with Gep. It has to be.

She reaches out her hands and takes one of mine between them. The words to tell her not to touch me, not to risk it, rise up in my throat, but I'm selfish enough not to say them. Because her touch is helping me. Calming me.

'Your skin's really hot.'

I nod. I don't know what else to say. She closes her eyes, like she's trying to think about something.

'It feels like strength. Like power.'

I suck in a breath and hold it, watching her until she opens her eyes, blinking like she's coming out of a dream.

'What do you mean?'

She shakes her head.

'I don't really know. It just feels…you feel…stronger. Can you feel it?'

I stop for a moment and close my eyes like she did. Not being able to see the glow helps me to feel a bit less panicked.

I don't know if it's because Selti said it – maybe I'm easily influenced – but I think she's right. I do feel different. I feel… bigger…wider…full of energy.

Open.

Like my whole body is filled with some sort of strength. As if I've changed somehow. Spiderman bitten by the frigging spider.

But no, that's not true. I don't feel weird. Instead, I feel more like me than I ever have in my life.

Complete.

I open my eyes. Christ. What does this mean? And why now? What do I do with it?

I stand up and Selti stands up next to me, looking at me with such a serious expression on her face I'm sure she's going to tell me she doesn't want see me anymore – sorry, weirdo freak, but this is all too strange for me. See ya.

I hold my breath, waiting for it, steeling myself. But all she does is step forward and kiss me again. A light one. One where I can only just feel the slight pressure of her lips on mine before she's pulling back so she can look me in the eyes. And it's like she's really looking at me.

For the first time ever, someone sees me.

My soul is soaring. This is what I've been waiting for without even knowing it. I feel real.

'Hello Penn.' That's all she says.

But it's all I need.

I kiss her again then. It is full of everything I have to give. Full of me. I cradle her head with my hand, under her hair, letting it fall over my skin, and pull her closer with my other hand in the small of her back. Every part of the front of her body is touching mine and yet it still doesn't feel like enough. I breathe her in, tasting her, wanting her.

When we stop, she actually collapses a bit in my arms. As if she's swooning, like you see in the old movies they've made us watch at school sometimes. I grab at her, lifting her up again.

'Hey? You okay?'

She puts her hand against my arm and smiles at me.

'Yeah, just a bit light headed for a second.'

I grin back at her – hearing that does great things for my ego – and lead her back to the blanket. She collapses and I sit beside her, moving around so I am supporting her with my chest. She is in my arms. And it feels good.

Even if my arms are blue.

Shit.

'What am I going to do? I can't go to school like this. I can't go home like this! I don't even know what it is!'

'Do you want to come back to my house? Maybe my mum will know something.'

That thought sends my panic into hyper drive again. I can't. She'll think I'm a freak! What is she finds out what Gep does? What if she stops Selti seeing me because of it? What if she tells me I'm evil or something?

'No. I'll work it out.'

She turns slightly so she can see me.

'*We'll* work it out.'

I squeeze her gently, hoping that tells her how I feel.

'Yeah, we'll work it out. But if I could go back to my normal skin colour while we do, that'd be great.'

And just like that, the glowing stops.

CHAPTER 22

She stands beside the front door, hand on my arm, and smiles at me. I could stay here forever. Except for Jimmy – and I guess Kat and Fox now – I have no reason to go home. Only her mum and dad might have something to say about that.

I can't believe it's only tonight that we've kissed. Only tonight that I felt this connection with her – like I've known her my whole life. Which should be scary. But it's not. It feels real and solid, like I've finally found myself, which sounds corny and soppy but makes absolute sense.

She strokes her fingers down my arm, making my hairs stand on end. In fact, it has an effect on my whole body. All I can think about is her touch.

'Are you okay?'

I nod.

'Do you think it's going to come back? The glow?'

My heart thumps at the thought, so much so it feels like it's actually hurting in my chest.

'I don't know. God, I don't even know what it was. How am I going to stop it if it comes back?'

'I'll do some reading tonight. See if I can find anything about it. You never know…and then we'll have a better idea.'

'But what am I going to do if it comes back tonight?'

'Well, it hasn't come back yet and it's been two hours. And we've kissed again, so it can't be that.' She blushes, ducking her head slightly, and I want to kiss her again but not here…at her parent's front door. What if they see us? What if they think I'm crap for their daughter and warn her off me? Jesus, what's happened to me that that thought causes actual physical pain, deep in my guts?

I touch her hair instead, moving it gently over her shoulder.

'No, it can't be the kiss. Which makes me really happy.'

She smiles, bringing her hand up to mine.

'Me too.'

'Can I see you tomorrow?'

'If you want to.' She sounds unsure, like she can't believe I'd really want to. Which goes to show she doesn't understand how I feel about her. Probably a good thing otherwise she might wonder whether she should really be around me. Stalker alert.

'I want to.' I manage to keep most of the desperation out of my voice. Cool. Sort of, anyway.

'Why don't you come over about ten then, and if I haven't found anything, we can look together?'

'Will your parents be okay with that?'

I watch her carefully, waiting for any sort of pause that means I should be concerned but she shakes her head straight away.

'You saved me, remember? I think they've been waiting to see more of you actually. They keep asking how you are.'

I feel myself get hot with the thought that they think I'm a good person. And then wonder what they'd think of me if they knew I was planning to steal from them. Even though it's for Jimmy – to save him, protect him. Even then, I'm still taking it from them. And who knows what Gep is planning to do with it after he saves Jimmy. Because I'm not stupid enough to believe he's got nothing to gain from all of this stuff.

'Okay. Well then. I guess I'll see you tomorrow.'

I shuffle awkwardly, feeling like a real idiot, not knowing how to end this. Not when it's something I've never done before. She steps forward and plants a soft kiss on my lips before stepping back with a small smile.

'See you tomorrow.'

I can't help smiling as I go down the steps. It stays there until I'm about half way home. That's when I start to check myself, over and over, looking for any sort of indication that the glow is coming back. Or that it was there in the first place. God, how screwed up is this? Checking myself to see if I'm some sort of human glow stick? I still can't wrap my head around the fact that it happened in the first place. And then it went again. Just like that!

It can't be normal – definitely not – except I feel fine. Great actually. Strong and…real. Like it's some sort of punctuation point in my life. Penn, before and after the glow!

It still hasn't come back when I go up the stairs at home. I take a deep breath before I go in, unsure what's waiting for me on the other side. Especially if they've done the ceremony.

It's quiet when I go in. And except for the lights being on, I wouldn't think anyone was at home. I go through to the back – to the kitchen – and they're all sitting there, around the table. Like the world's been on hold since I left. Jimmy looks like he's about to fall asleep but his eyes widen when he sees me, like he's trying to tell me something without words. I've got no frigging idea what he's trying to say but it sets all the cells in my body buzzing. Alert.

Kat looks up and smiles. It looks like one of relief.

'Hey, Penn. You're back.'

Gep shoots me a look that says he's still angry with me – situation normal then; I know how to deal with this Gep.

'I expected you home earlier.'

'Sorry. Didn't know I was on curfew.'

I know I'm pushing him but at the moment, I don't care. Not after what he said to Jimmy.

He narrows his eyes, looking at me.

'What's wrong with you?'

My heart does a somersault, sure I'm going to look down and be frigging glowing again. But I look normal. I think I do anyway. I frown at him.

'What do you mean?'

He comes closer, like he's going to smell me or something. Weird. I take a step back and he narrows his eyes at me. Looking at me. Staring. Then he shuts his eyes and takes a big breath in, holding it for a second before a smile touches the corners of his lips. And I feel scared for a second. Really scared. Even though I don't know why.

He opens his eyes again.

'Did you get the book?'

I shake my head. 'I know where it is though. I just couldn't get it tonight.'

'You don't have the book on you?'

I frown at him, still jittery; my blood feeling like it's full of popping candy.

'No. Why? What's your problem?'

He stands up to his full height and looks at me again. Seconds go by and still he doesn't say anything, only watches me, like he's trying to read my mind. Finally, he looks away, smirking. I don't know what it means.

'I don't have a problem.' He moves over to the kitchen bench. It's only then I notice the chicken entrails are still there. They haven't done the ceremony.

I try and look calm.

'What's going on?'

'We decided to wait for you,' Gep says. 'Since you were only going to be a few hours. To have all of us here is going to make it much more effective.'

I can feel the adrenalin pumping around my body, filling me with nervous anticipation.

'Sure. Let's get on with it then. I can be the conduit now.'

Gep gives me a smile. One that says we're in deep shit.

'Well, here's the thing. I've been thinking about it since you've been gone. Thinking about what you said. That there's nothing wrong with Jimmy. That he's just tired from school. And that he has the right to know everything.'

I go still, muscles tensed. Waiting. 'I didn't say that last part. You did.'

He shrugs. 'Whatever. It's still true.'

I go to say something else but Jimmy interrupts.

'He's right, Penn. I want to know if there's something going on.'

I turn to him. 'There's nothing going on.'

'I've told him everything,' Gep says. 'While you were out, looking for the book, I showed him the picture. I explained to him what happened to his mum and what I think is happening to him now.'

I glare at him, hands clenched. How can he do that to me over and over? Get one up, just when I think we're okay.

'Do you believe that's what happened to Mum?' The fear is easy to hear in Jimmy's voice.

'No. It's bullshit. How does that make any sense? It's a fucking photo.' Except my glowing this afternoon didn't make any sense either...

Fox clears his throat, like he's been waiting for this moment.

'It's weird though, Penn. Scary weird. What if we lose Jimmy?'

'We're not going to fucking lose Jimmy!' My voice is harsher than I want it to be and he looks down at the table, not meeting my eyes. And I want to say sorry to him but I can't because that would make him more of a target with Gep too. If Gep knew that I'd sworn to protect him and Kat…

'You're right. We're not going to lose Jimmy.' Gep picks up the chicken guts. 'That's why we're going to do the ceremony. To get answers.'

'Fine. Let's get this over with then.'

I go to move towards the bench but he puts his hand out, stopping me.

'No, actually, I don't think you're the right one to do this. Not today. Not now.'

I don't know what the hell he means by that but I can feel my mouth tighten.

'Leave Kat out of it. I'll do it.'

'I wasn't going to get Kat to be the conduit. I think we need some strong answers. You have to understand that. And since it's about Jimmy, I think we need him to do it.'

'What? Fuck off!' The words explode out of me. 'You are not making him the conduit!'

'I want to do it, Penn.'

I turn to Jimmy. His eyes are firm, willing me to go with him. But I can't. I won't allow it. If Gep's right…if…then he doesn't have the energy to do this.

'No. I'm not going to let you.'

Jimmy's mouth goes into a thin line.

'You can't tell me what to do. It's my choice.'

Christ. I've handled this wrong. I take a deep breath, trying really hard not to roll my eyes.

'I'm not trying to tell you what to do. I'm just…worried about you. You said you were tired. It's going to take a lot out of you. Let me do it.'

He shakes his head. 'I need to know. I need to feel it. Understand it myself.'

'You don't need to be the conduit to do that. I'll do it. Then you'll know.' And then you'll be safe. But I don't say that. I'm not that stupid.

'I do, Penn. I need to do this. Please.'

He wants to do it bad. I can see it in his face. He's my brother. The good one of our duo, the one who suffered brain injury while I came out of the accident scot free. Not even a scratch. And he's scared. There's no way I can say no. Even though I know I should.

It's hard to be still. I'm tapping my fingers, pacing the floor, muscles tensed as I watch Gep do what he does best. Fox and Kat are sitting on the couches, watching us, eyes wide like they're scared shitless too but don't know what to do. Jimmy looks calm, although I'm pretty sure it's just a cover because his arms and legs are really tight. It's been a long time since he's had to be the conduit. Years. That's why I do it so often...to protect him.

Gep's not even looking at him. He's helped Jimmy hold the chicken and put it in the pan. I can see the sticky mess all over Jimmy's fingers and just want to grab a cloth and rub it off him, before it contaminates him somehow. But I don't. I watch Gep over at the fire, still talking to himself like the weird psycho he is. Watching him, I can barely contain the desperate need to go over and knock the pan out of his hands before he gets anywhere near my brother.

But I promised Jimmy.

So I start to pace again.

And then Gep's bringing the pan back, holding it in front of

Jimmy who's looking at it like it's poison. Finally, a response I know is true.

'Don't do it,' I say.

But when he looks up at me, he looks trapped.

'I need to.'

I hear a noise from behind me and turn. Kat's fist is shoved into his mouth, trying to stop the sobs that want to come out. It's because it's Jimmy. None of us want to see him do this.

'Come and help him to put it in his mouth.' Gep's voice is buoyant; fanatical, like he's loving every second of this.

I shake my head. No fucking way. But then Jimmy is looking at me again and I know what he wants and I know that as much as I feel like I'm going to throw up, I'll do it for him. I drag myself over, my heart being torn in two – I want to do what he's asking of me – especially when he doesn't ask me to do very much – but it's waring with my need to keep him safe, safe, safe. Like I've always done.

I can feel the sweat on my forehead and I know it's not from the heat of the stove.

And then my hand is reaching down and I'm pulling a piece of the entrails away. I hesitate, holding it between my fingers, feeling the juice run down my wrist, and Jimmy nods, arms reaching out like he's trying to move himself closer to me. I push it into his mouth, feeling his jaw stiffen as his mind struggles to keep up with what his body needs. And then...and then, he is swallowing it and I know it will only be seconds.

He stiffens, jerking like he's having a seizure and I reach out to hold him in his chair, not caring that I'm getting the chicken juices all over his clothes. It's only when his body relaxes and he opens his eyes again that I know the spirit's there. Largely because Jimmy's eyes aren't green anymore. They're a muddy shade of brown. And when he talks, his words aren't even slightly slurred. A smile twists his face.

'Ah, I can feel the energy in the room.'

Gep puffs out his chest like he's been paid the best compliment. He steps forward, closer to Jimmy. Closer to the…thing.

'Tell me about the fading. Will we lose him like we lost his mother?'

The thing in Jimmy laughs.

'Of course you will. But you know that. It's what you want.'

I turn to Gep, anger sparking in me like the flicking of a lighter, watching his reaction, seeing if it's true.

'No,' he says. 'I don't want that. I don't.'

The thing in Jimmy makes him lean forward. He's looking at Gep. 'Power has always been more important to you than anything else, Sorcerer. It is what drives you. Do not pretend that it is any different.'

'No.' Gep hesitates, like he's struggling with himself. 'Not anything. I want it, I want the power, but I didn't want to lose Marceline.'

He doesn't say anything about Jimmy but it doesn't matter. I'm waiting to see what the thing says.

'You can't ask for the power – use the power – without consequences. You know that.'

'But that's not what I wanted,' Gep says. 'I wasn't prepared for that. I didn't want to lose her.'

'And yet, Sorcerer, you continued to use the power. Even when she was dying – fading from you. But then, she was weak already. Just like this boy. He is easily used.'

My heart feels like it's going to explode in my chest, taking out all my other organs with it. It's going to use him up, until there's nothing left. Use him until it kills him. It's going to kill him! Fuck. Fuck! Not my brother. Not Jimmy!

I grab the arm of the wheelchair, turning it more towards me so Jimmy…the thing in him…has to look at me.

'Get it out, Jimmy! Push it out!'

The thing in Jimmy smiles at me again. I hate it. Every part of my body, every single cell, is quivering with anger.

'Oh, but I like him very much. He has a clean energy, a clean spirit. I am enjoying using him.'

I turn to Gep.

'Get it the fuck out of him!'

But Gep is shaking his head, looking numb. Looking scared. Scared!

I grab Jimmy's arms, getting down to his height.

'Push it out, Jimmy! You can do it.'

'You are wrong. He is too weak for that.' Jimmy's eyes are still brown. I don't even know if Jimmy is still there!

That's when I panic. I don't know how I do it. I'm not even really sure what I do. But I...push myself into him. Push my energy. That's the only way I can describe it. And like I got the spirit out of me the last time I was a conduit, I push it out of him. I'm not sure how long it takes. It might be seconds or minutes or even hours. I don't really care. All I care about, as I lean into the arm rests of the chair, panting like I've run a sprint, is that Jimmy's eyes are green again. And he's safe.

For now.

When I have enough energy to stand up, Gep's glaring at me. It's not what I expect. Stupid. Why do I keep on getting surprised? But what he said during the ceremony – I thought maybe he felt bad. Maybe he'd be happy I managed to get it out of Jimmy.

I stand there, not moving, not sure what to do or what to say. Not sure why he's angry. He steps in closer to me.

'How long?'

I have no idea what he's talking about. Absolutely no clue.

'What?'

'How long have you had fucking sorcerer's powers?'

'What are you talking about?'

'I thought I smelt it on you – felt it in you – before, in the kitchen, although I wasn't sure. But you kept it from me. Hid it. How? And why? Why, when we could have worked together?'

'You're fucking crazy.'

He's yelling at me now. 'That's the only way you would've been able to do that. Fourteen years I've looked after you, tried to help you develop your power and now I find you've hidden it from me. Hidden it when I could've used your help! So how fucking long?'

I shake my head. I've had enough. This is crap. Jimmy being taken over by the frigging spirit – not being able to find his way back – and now this. And that he thought, all along, that I'd have powers. Like that's the only reason he's kept me around.

I step into him, finger in his chest.

'I haven't been hiding anything, you fucking psycho.'

And when he swings his fist, connecting with my cheekbone, he takes me by surprise again.

CHAPTER 24

Gep is gone. I don't know where. I don't even know if he'll be back, but knowing my luck, he won't stay away.

He left as soon as he landed the punch, leaving us all in a stunned paralysis for a couple of minutes. Then Fox came over to help me up off the floor. And while Kat got me an ice pack for my cheek, I forced Jimmy to have something to eat. He didn't want to but I was so scared about how weak he was, I didn't give him a choice. But it took him ages to eat even a fraction of the food on this plate. I wanted to ask him about what happened…what it felt like…but I was too scared to. Scared that whatever it was in him might have caused damage that I can't fix or push out or protect him from. Scared that I'd failed to protect him.

I helped him to bed and went and sat on the back steps, icepack against my skin, wondering what the hell was going on. It felt like my whole world as I knew it – even if it was a sucky world – had been turned upside down and shaken up, like a kid's snow globe.

What the hell was happening? What did Gep mean about me having powers? Did it have something to do with the blue glow?

And how do I deal with what the spirit said about Mum and Jimmy? God!

Kat and Fox came out at one stage but I didn't want to talk. Mainly because none of it made sense to me so what was I going to tell them? All I knew was that, for the moment, Jimmy was safe. He was alive. They disappeared after about five minutes of me not talking. And I sat there until the night was well and truly entrenched before crawling into bed myself for a few hours of restless sleep.

When I wake up, Kat's sitting on his bed, looking at me. I grunt and shut my eyes again.

'Penn…' He sounds scared.

'What?'

'Do you think Gep's coming back?'

I open my eyes again. 'Isn't he back yet?'

Kat shakes his head, eyes wide.

'What do you think it means? Has he gone? Has he left us, do you reckon? What'll we do if he's left for good? I mean, for money and food and rent and stuff? And going to school – what if they need a note signed or something? Do you think he *has* left us? Do you think we'll have to be split up? Live in foster care? I don't want to do that! I like it here, with you guys!'

I want to say I hope Gep has left for good, but I know how much a family means to Kat. Even a shit family. And I can hear the panic in his voice. I sigh and sit up.

'No, I don't think so. He didn't take the car and all his stuff's still here. He probably took off to…I don't know…think or something. I bet he'll be back today.'

He nods, like he's not really listening to me but is already thinking about what else he's going to say.

'What did he mean, about you having powers? Are you like him?'

'I'll never be like him. And I don't know, Kat. I don't know what he meant. All I wanted to do was make sure Jimmy was safe.'

'Yeah,' he says, and I can already hear the relief in his voice. 'Yeah, that's what I said to Fox last night.'

'Is Jimmy awake?'

Kat shakes his head.

'What time is it?'

'Just after seven.'

I groan again and flop back down on the pillow. Kat's quiet for the moment but I know it won't last long. He won't be able to help himself.

'Did you find the book?'

'Yeah, I think so.'

'Will it help Jimmy, like Gep said?'

'Jesus, Kat, I don't know. I don't know anything. I hope so.'

I count to twenty before he asks the next question.

'Do you think Gep's going to be…nice again when he comes home? You know how he's trying to be a good Dad. Do you think he'll be like that again or do you think he'll be…like he used to?'

'You're asking the wrong person. I never trusted in that anyway.'

I look over at him and he looks devastated. I'm an arsehole. Jesus, how hard would it be to lie?

'I think he'll be good to you, mate. It's me that seems to bring out the worst in him.'

'How's your cheek?'

'Sore.'

'Yeah, it's all black and yellow.'

I touch it gently with my fingers. But it doesn't matter how gentle I am, it still throbs, each pump of my heart pulsating pain through it. I wonder if I should go to Selti's today, looking like this. Stupid question. Of course I'm going. I want to see her. Need to. And I need to find the book as well. Especially after last night. I can't leave Jimmy so vulnerable again.

I drag my legs over the edge of the bed and sit up, feeling like shit. Heavy and tired. And sitting up only makes my cheek throb more. I drag my hand through my hair.

'I need a shower.'

Kat nods and watches every movement I make as I get my stuff together. I have to get away. His neediness is doing my head in. Which sounds crappy but there it is. I'm not his dad. And I'm barely feeling alive myself let alone making him feel like everything's good. I don't say anything else as I go out. Mainly because I don't know what else to say.

The shower helps me to feel slightly more human. I dry myself off, looking in the rust spotted mirror. Kat's right. It is black. Black and blue and yellow, stretching from the bottom of my cheek up to my eye. Attractive. But worth it since it made Jimmy safe.

Fox is sitting at the kitchen table when I walk out, pulling apart a piece of toast rather than eating it. He looks up and watches me as I put a piece of bread in the toaster, not saying anything until I sit down, which is nice after Kat.

'He's not back yet. And Jimmy's still asleep.'

I nod.

'Why do you think he hit you last night rather than using the burn?'

I look up at him. It's something I hadn't even thought about. Gep should have used the burn. That's what he would have done in the past. When I don't say anything, Fox shrugs.

'I think it's because he's scared of you now.'

I snort. 'Yeah right. Because he's been so scared of me in the past.'

He looks at me for a moment, like he's trying to work out whether he should say something or not. Secrets. I'm sick of them. I'm almost ready to stand up and go when he finally decides to speak.

'You didn't have your powers then.'

I roll my eyes.

'God, since when have you started to believe what Gep says? I don't have powers. I pushed it out of Jimmy the same way I did it for me. That's all.'

Fox shakes his head.

'I felt it. I felt you use them. It felt like it does when Gep uses his. He's right. You've got powers.'

I stare at him, trying to take all of this in, squeezing my hands on my thighs like it's the only thing keeping me grounded.

'You can feel them? The powers?'

He nods.

'Since when?'

He shrugs.

'I've always been able to do it.'

'How come you never told me that?'

'You never asked.'

He's right.

I can't sit there anymore. I get up and start pacing, the floor creaking in time with each step, trying to sort this out somehow in my head. The spirit and what it said and Jimmy feeling weak and what Fox can do and how I, apparently, have powers. Like Gep.

Fuck.

I have powers. Was that what the blue glow was about? Gep said I felt different when I got home? But what the hell does that mean? And how do I control them? What do I do with them? I stop, looking at Fox.

'Are you scared of me now?'

He snorts like I'm an idiot. 'No.'

'Why? I mean, if I'm like Gep…'

'I said you had *powers* like him, not that *you* were like him.' He shrugs. 'You care about other people. About us. You're different to Gep.'

I don't know what to say to that. To the idea that he has such faith in me. Faith that I'm a good person. It creates a warm glow in my guts. Pathetic but nice.

'What do you think I should do?'

He shrugs again but I can see he's been thinking about something. It's in the way he won't look me in the eyes.

'Come on. Spit it out.'

He sighs and looks at me.

'You're not going to like it. But I think you need to work with Gep. Get him to help you control whatever it is you can do.'

I'm shaking my head before he stops.

'No way. I'm not working with him. He'll only show me what he wants to show me anyway. Only the things that'll help him. Feeding him the power he always wants.'

'He might help to keep Jimmy safe.'

I hesitate, but just for a second.

'Nuh, don't trust him. He says all this shit about wanting to protect him and helping him and then look what he did last night. Made him the frigging conduit.' I don't say anything about Jimmy wanting to do it. Gep could have said no. He should have if he really wanted to protect Jimmy. 'And besides, remember what the spirit said? About him wanting the power more than anything. About him using them even when my mum was fading.'

Fox finally nods. 'Okay, but you need to do something. I don't know – maybe the book Gep wants will help.'

That's my focus. Get the book. Even if I don't trust Gep to put himself first, he keeps saying the book will help Jimmy. So I'll get the book.

'You have to do something about your powers though. About controlling them.'

I can hear the fear in his voice. Not big. But there. Just below the surface, seeping into his words.

'Why are you so worried about it?'

He picks up a piece of toast again and pulls it in two.

'You know how I said I felt your powers last night?'

I nod.

'Well, yours were strong. Big. Bigger than Gep's. And they felt…I don't know…wild, I guess. Like a lion stalking something, wanting to feed.'

I don't know whether to be scared or impressed. Wild, huh? I scrub my face with my hands.

'God, I don't know what to do. I didn't ask for any of this crap.' I lean on the back of the chair, staring at the table, hoping my brain's going to come up with some magical solution. Nothing. No surprise really. 'Maybe you're right. Maybe the book will help me too, since Gep wants it so bad. It's probably the best place to start anyway. I'm pretty sure I felt it there, in Selti's parents' bookcase.'

'Will you get it today?'

'Yeah, if I get a chance.'

'What about the other stuff? Do you think it might help?'

I frown at him. 'What other stuff?'

He rolls his eyes, which is fair enough. I think the punch has affected my brain as well as my cheek.

'The other stuff we've stolen for him.'

A seed of hope plants itself in my gut, trying to find space between the guilt and the rage and the worry. The other stuff. God, why hadn't I thought of that? Stupid! Gep said the book was the last bit of the puzzle, so maybe…if what Fox said about my powers is true…maybe, I can use it. Now. To help Jimmy somehow. Make him stronger or something.

'Do you know where he keeps them?'

Fox shrugs. 'Gep always carries his own stuff in. But I guess in his room.'

I'm walking to Gep's room before Fox is even out of the chair, but I can hear him following me. The door's shut but not locked. Not that we ever go in there. It's not worth the pain that'd follow. I look back at Fox, hand on the knob.

'Are you sure he's not back?'

Fox nods. 'I can't feel his power.'

I nod back and turn the handle. Slowly. Just in case.

It's empty, the filtered light coming through the curtains in the window showing a room in total order. Bed made with frigging hospital corners, not a single wrinkle in the covers, pillow placed neatly. And the things on the top of the chest of drawers are lined up with military precision. Even his shoes are lined up beside the wall like he's waiting for an inspection. I'm almost afraid to walk in – afraid to touch anything – just in case he notices.

'Control freak much.' Fox's voice is soft, like he can't talk too loud in here and I only nod back.

'You look in the cupboard. I'll look in the drawers.'

I pull out the drawers slowly, careful not to disturb the contents. Careful not to leave any evidence that we've been here. But it's only clothes. Nothing we've stolen. Nothing that gives off the feeling the book did at Selti's. I look over at Fox.

'Anything.'

He steps back from the cupboard and shakes his head. 'Just clothes and his suitcase. And it's empty.'

I sigh and link my fingers on my head, trying to think. They need to be somewhere in the house. We haven't been anywhere else that he could've stashed them. I get down on my hands and knees beside the bed and lift the covers slowly, careful not to mess anything up. There's nothing under there except slightly dusty floorboards. It's only when I start to lower the covers back down that I notice a glint of something, up towards the head of the bed. I bring out my phone, shining the light on a small, silver key, attached to the springs by a piece of string.

I untie it and hold it up to Fox. 'What do you think this is for?'

'Don't know. I haven't seen anything that's got a lock.'

'Yeah, me neither.' I frown, trying to think like Gep. Not that I want to but if it helps… 'The car?'

'Maybe. That's something he'd do. Ready for a quick getaway.'

The garage is dark and I flick the switch, flooding it with light, and head to the back of the car, using the button to pop the boot. It's empty and I can feel the disappointment swell in my gut, squashing the hope. Fox leans against the car.

'Up in the roof maybe?'

I shake my head. 'I've never seen him do that in the other houses. I think we'd notice. Did you see him do it here?'

'No.'

'Christ. He can't make anything easy, can he?'

And then I see it. Right at the edge, hidden slightly in the shadows. A small space. Enough to get your fingers in. I reach down, tugging at it, lifting the section of boot floor. It's filled with the spare wheel and I'm almost about to lower it back down when I notice it, over to the side where the tools should be. A black metal box. With a lock.

I grin at Fox and he smiles back before reaching down to pull it out. Not surprisingly, the key fits and when we open it, there's everything we've stolen in the last couple of years – a blue stone with white streaks through it, a stone bowl with symbols all around the inside, a small drum that looks like someone spent a long time making it, a bronze cross that's so full of swirls and patterns it's almost hard to look at, an old bone, shaped like a hammer, and a knife with intricate carving on the black handle sit among the other things.

The knife was the last thing I'd stolen for Gep, from the house of an old woman whose husband had collected this stuff. She was nice to me – paid me for mowing her lawn and plied me with the best homemade biscuits I'd ever had. She even showed me the collection, making me feel like I was a half decent person, and offered to give me something from it. But what went down after that was reason Jimmy wasn't allowed to go to school when we first got here. I should have thrown it – pretended I wasn't able to find it, like I was going to when I took it from her house. Probably would've if I'd known Gep would take it out on Jimmy.

There's no buzz, like I got from the book, but when I run my hand over the top of everything, the stone feels…warm. Which is crazy because when I pick it up, it's cool against my skin.

'Your power spiked.' Fox takes a step away and looks at me, eyes narrowed, like he's trying to see me properly.

I throw the stone in the air and catch it again.

'Yep, this feels different.'

'Do you think it'll help Jimmy?'

My momentary enjoyment at finding this stuff crashes to the ground.

'I don't know. I don't know what to do with it. Maybe.' I think of Selti and the rock she nearly drowned to get and, for a moment, I wonder if it would be worth asking her. Stupid thought really. I can't tell her about all this shit. Even if she'd believe me, who'd want to get mixed up in this? 'I'll give it to him – Gep won't notice it's gone – just in case. It's something anyway and hopefully I'll get the book today. Although that might be hard if her parents are around.'

And when all I want to do when I'm around Selti is talk to her and look at her and touch her…kiss her…

'Don't get side-tracked.' Fox is looking at me like he knows exactly what I was thinking. 'It's important Jimmy's safe.'

Guilt makes me respond harsher than I need to.

'Don't tell me how important it is. He's my brother. And I'm the one who always keeps him safe. Always.'

I don't give him time to respond. I turn, knowing he'll pack everything else up, and go to his and Jimmy's room, hesitating at the partially closed door, not sure if I want to see how weak Jimmy's looking. Not when he's been through so much already. And I still remain untouched. Strong. Stronger than ever, if Fox is right. Our life is frigging messed up.

I take a deep breath and open the door. He's lying flat on his back, mouth open, one hand out to the side, the other over his head. His back is all screwed up and I know he's going to hurt when he wakes up, his muscles tense from sleeping in a bed that doesn't support him. None of his equipment is the stuff he should have – all of this shit furniture and even his wheelchair make it harder for him. When we move out, he'll have the best of everything…fitted to him properly.

I sigh. I can't put it off anymore and go over to shake him awake.

'Jimmy, hey man, wake up.'

He stirs and opens his eyes. Identical to mine except for the pain in them.

'You look like shit.'

I laugh. 'Yeah, and you look so frigging hot yourself.'

'Does it hurt?'

I shrug. 'I'll live. How are you feeling?'

He closes his eyes. 'Sore. And tired.'

My anger at Gep roars up again, like someone's thrown alcohol on the fire.

'I can't believe he did that to you. Not when he thinks…' The words dry up in my mouth.

He opens his eyes again. 'Not when he thinks I could be dying.'

'You're not. Don't be stupid.'

He sighs. 'I told him I wanted to do it anyway. It's my fault as much as his.'

'It's not. He should have said no.'

A tired smile settles on his face.

'Like you did. Always trying to make sure I'm okay. You're a good brother, Penn.'

I don't like the way he's talking. Like he's trying to make me feel better. Like he's already decided that maybe Gep is right about the fading…

'It was different last night, when the spirit was in me. Even though it's been a long time, I still remember what it felt like. And it was different.'

I take a deep breath. I can't hide from this anymore…not if Jimmy wants to talk about it.

'Different how?'

'It scared me last night, when that spirit was in me. I couldn't move   it's like it was taking all of me up. Like there was no room left for me in my body anymore and I was only hanging on by a thread. Like I couldn't fight back.'

'It's because you're tired. Because of school and stuff.'

He goes on like I haven't even spoken. 'And then, you did that thing. Pushed it out of me. Made it go.' He shakes his head.

I sit down on the edge of his bed, heart thumping even though I don't know why. Except this feels different to normal. I feel different. But I don't know if it's enough. And it needs to be. Has to be.

'Fox and I were thinking that, if Gep's so sure we need the book, maybe something else that we've taken for him…well, maybe it will help.'

'Help me?'

My eyes flick up to his and back down to the rock in my hand.

'Yeah.' I feel terrible even saying it. Like acknowledging it somehow makes it more real. I hold up the stone, showing him, and he reaches out for it. There's part of me that hopes something amazing will happen when he touches it – that he'll leap out of bed or something, full of energy again – even though I know he won't. And it doesn't do anything. Of course. It just sits there in his palm.

'A rock?'

'Yeah.' I sigh. 'It's stupid but I was thinking…you know… worth a shot. I don't know how any of this works. I don't even know how I pushed that thing out of you last night!'

He looks at me like he knows me better than anyone. Which is probably true.

'Does that scare you?'

'A bit.' I take a deep breath and race the words out before I can change my mind. 'Fox reckons he can feel power and he says that when I did that to you he could feel power in me. And that it's bigger than Gep's.'

Jimmy lets out a barking laugh.

'I could have told you that. I've known that since our accident.'

I stare at him for a moment, confused.

'The accident?'

'Yeah, you know. The car accident. When we were kids.'

'I know which accident you mean. But how do you remember anything from it? And what do you mean you know I had power? We were only little kids. And Fox was only talking about seeing my power last night. Not before that.'

I can't remember anything about the accident – at all. Except waking up outside the car with Jimmy beside me, his body all broken and blood all over his head, just before the rescue crews got there.

'You did this thing, in the accident. Don't you remember?'

'What thing? And how come you've never told me about this before?'

'I don't know. Guess I thought you remembered but didn't want to talk about it. Like it was something you wanted to pretend didn't happen.'

'Just tell me.'

He rolls his eyes.

'I can remember laying there and I could see you but my head was so sore. Like it was being crushed. The tree the car had run into was laying on me, pushing the metal bits of the wreck onto me, crushing me. And I started to cry.'

I want to tell him to stop; tell him he doesn't need to tell me, but part of me really wants to know.

'And then you looked down at me...you were still in your booster seat and looked okay...and said, 'Don't cry, Jimmy', and then you shut your eyes and the next thing I know, it was all moving off me, like something was grabbing it but there wasn't anything. It was just you. And then you came and unbuckled me and carried me out. And then I don't remember anything else.'

I stare at him, in shock. God. It can't be real. How could that be real?

'I moved it? What, with my mind?'

He nods at me, like he's sure about what he's telling me. But if that's the case, how the hell don't I remember any of it?

'You don't think…you don't think you were dreaming? Like the head wound was making you hallucinate or something.'

He shakes his head.

'No, man. You saved me.'

'I saved you?'

'Yep. And you've been trying to do it ever since, like last night, with the spirit.'

And I know, without any doubt, that it's up to me to save him again. To prove the spirit wrong. To make sure he's strong again. Because I can't lose him, not if there's something I can do.

I have to get the book.

CHAPTER 25

The smile slips from Selti's face the moment she opens the door and sees me. Sees my face. Her hand reaches up to touch my cheek and it's only when I flinch back that she stops, hand hovering in the air like a honeybird waiting to land on a flower.

'God, what happened to you?'

I don't want to tell her. I don't want her to be drawn into this.

'I slipped and fell. In the shower. Last night.'

She watches me for a moment and I get the feeling she's going to call me out on the lie but, finally, she just holds the door open more.

'Do you want to come in?'

I nod, wanting more than anything to touch her as I go past, but she's giving off this weird vibe and I don't know if I should or not. So I don't. I stand in the hallway while she shuts the door and turns.

'Do you want a coke?' Her smile looks tight. Controlled.

'Sure.'

I follow her through to the kitchen, still clueless, and watch silently as she gets the bottle out of the fridge and pours it into two glasses, pushing one towards me. I take a sip, the bubbles cold against my tongue, and smile at her.

'Thanks.'

She nods and then plays with her glass; her fingers tracing the moisture on the outside.

'Is everything okay?'

She looks up at me then. 'I don't know. Is it?'

And I know I'm in deep shit. She knows I'm lying. She must. That's the only thing that makes any sense. But I don't want to tell her the truth – she doesn't deserve to be dragged into it. And really, I don't want to talk about my shit life. I want to have this… her…to just me. She must see the panic on my face though, because she sighs and looks sad for a moment. Enough that my heart hitches in my chest. I don't want to make her look like that but can't tell her. I can't!

'Don't lie to me, Penn. Please.'

'What…?'

She raises one eyebrow at me.

'Did you really fall in the shower?'

Shit, I was right. And I so didn't want to be! My hand goes to my cheek in reflex and I wince. God, maybe Gep broke a bone. Not that it matters. But I can't pull her into this. Not when all I want to do is get out of it.

'Yes, I fell in the shower.'

But even I'm not convinced by that. Why is it that when I'm with her, the mask is really hard to keep up?

She looks at me, waiting. I try to resist. It's for her own good. It is! She looks down at the bench, dragging her eyes from mine and I think that maybe, I've convinced her.

'I think maybe you should go.'

'What? No, wait!' I sigh, dragging my hand through my hair. Shit. I don't want to go. I need to get the book. For Jimmy. But more than anything, I don't want this to be over. For me. And I know I don't have a choice. I guess if I want her to trust me, I need to trust her. I take a deep breath. 'I didn't fall in the shower. My dad punched me. Last night. Actually, he's not my dad. He's my step dad.'

She comes around the bench and I turn so I'm facing her. Her hand reaches up to touch my cheek and this time, I don't flinch. Her touch is gentle, her skin is cool against mine, and wet slightly, from the glass.

'Does it hurt?'

'Yes.' Her closeness is making it hard to breath. She stands on her tiptoes to reach up and kiss the bruise and for a moment, I do stop breathing.

'Why did he punch you?'

There's no way I'm getting into that with her. All the mumbo jumbo powers and spirits crap, even if she is a Wiccan. Even if she can see spirits, like she said. I'm sure she and her mum don't do what Gep does – the fact that he uses the power, is corrupted by it. And that he's made us a part of the…evilness. Besides, it's all too weird. Too much.

So I shake my head instead. It's a relief when she doesn't ask any more questions. She just brings her lips up to mine this time and kisses me softly, like a breath out, and my body thrums with need for her, likes it's attuning itself to her rhythm. Matching hers.

I'm about to pull her closer when the sound of the front door opening stops me.

'Hey, honey, we're back.'

Her dad. And two sets of footsteps, so probably her mum as well. I go to take a step back, put some distance between us, but Selti takes my hand, keeping me there, and smiles at me before answering them.

'We're in the kitchen.'

I don't know what to do – how I should act. I've never been in this situation. Never pretended to be someone's boyfriend, in all the lives I've made up, all the different people I've pretended to be, I've never done this. Not that I'm pretending now but still…I hold myself stiff, waiting to see their reaction. Waiting for them to tell me to get away from their daughter and the hell out of their house. Waiting for them to see that I'm not good enough…

Her parents are both smiling when they walk in and it doesn't disappear when they see me, which throws me. Makes me more awkward than I already am. Although her mum's smile does dial down a bit. Or maybe I'm just reading more into it than I should.

'Penn, nice to see you again.'

Her dad says it before he sees our hands and then he looks at Selti, eyebrows raised and she shrugs at him, a smile on her face. I want to pull my hand away and yet, I don't want to. I want the whole world to know she's chosen to be with me, as corny as that sounds, and my fingers tighten around hers. If Selti's good with it, I don't care what they think. Well, I'm trying not to anyway.

'What happened to your face?'

Her mum's voice sounds concerned, not accusing, but I don't know what to tell her. Tongue tied, when usually the bullshit flows so easily.

'They got a bit rough at basketball training yesterday.' It's a good lie and I'm glad Selti managed to do it when I couldn't. It sounds more plausible coming from her anyway. I nod, supporting her. Glad I can trust her not to tell the truth. Not to tell them how crappy my life actually is.

Her mum winces. 'I don't understand boys and sport.'

'Just a bit of fun, huh, Penn?' Her dad's grinning at me and I smile back, as much as I can with an aching cheek.

'Yeah.'

Her mum cocks her head, looking at me for a moment, and I don't know what to do – where to look, how to stand, except that I drop my hand from Selti's. It's weird – like she's examining me. Selti and her dad are quiet, waiting for her, like they do this all the time…

She frowns and, for a second, I think she's going to tell me to leave. My stomach clenches, a fist holding it tight, waiting for the words.

'Honey, you okay?' Selti's dad is smiling at her and she looks at him, like she's coming out of a trance. The relief of not being scrutinised like an ant under a magnifying glass is intense.

She laughs. 'Yes, sorry. All good.' She turns back to me. 'Sorry, Penn, sometimes I get carried away in my own thoughts.'

I smile back at her, even though I don't want to. 'No worries.'

'You're a strong person but you need to look after yourself, okay?'

The words seem ordinary – after all, my face looks like it's been slammed by a brick – but the way she says it, the force of her words, makes me take a step back. Like she's seeing more than I know.

'Sure.'

There's silence again, one that makes me feel self-conscious, as if my body's too big for their house. Thank God the empty air is filled by her dad.

'What are you kids planning for today?'

I look to Selti for an answer. I've become a mindless moron.

'We haven't got any plans yet. We'll probably hang out here.'

There's no way I'm ready for that. Geeze, I can't even keep up the pretence for five frigging minutes let alone for a day! But I don't say anything. If she wants to hang out here, I'll work out a way to do it. For her.

'Great.' Her father comes and puts his arm around my shoulders. 'Bring your drinks out to the patio then. We can get to know each other.'

There's a moment of panic that starts in the bottom of my guts and shoots through my organs, infecting all of them, making them cramp and ache. Shit.

Selti groans. 'God, Dad, don't do this. Penn doesn't need the third degree.'

But he's already steering me away and I grab the drink as we head out the back.

'I won't give him the third degree. Just…getting to know him a bit. Guy to guy. That's alright, Penn, isn't it?'

No.

But there's no way I can say that, so all I do is nod. I turn back to glance at Selti. She mouths 'sorry' to me but she's probably as powerless as me to stop it. I smile. Well, it's half a grimace but I can't help that.

I sit opposite him at a rectangular wooden table – the kind which is solid and has been looked after. Like someone cares about the place they live in. That's what I'm going to get for Jimmy when we move. Something solid and looked after. Something that's really his.

As I put the drink down, I notice I'm facing the bookshelf. The one I'm sure has the book. I have to stop myself from getting up and going over. Not now. Wait. The chance will come. But Selti's dad must see the tenseness in me because he laughs.

'It's okay, Penn, I promise. It's not a third degree. No lie detector test to be seen.' I try to smile at him, try to laugh back… try to keep my eyes from going to the books. It must work because he settles back in his seat. 'So, I believe you haven't been in town long.'

He's been asking about us then. I hope it's only Selti he's been asking and no one else in the community. That's always when things start to get messed up, when people ask questions, wanting to meet Gep, wanting to provide support and make us a part of the community. Include us. That's when Gep makes us move again…

'Yeah, only a couple of weeks.'

Short answers. Not too short that he gets suspicious but no extra information offered. That's the best way to not get caught up in the lies.

'Tell me about your family.'

I try not to grimace. Body language tells people much more than you say.

'There's my dad and my brothers – Jimmy, Fox and Kat.'

'Fox and Kat? They're interesting names.'

I shrug. 'Nicknames. They don't like their real names, so we've just always called them that.'

He nods. 'Try having Albert as a name, especially as a teenager. You can call me Alby.'

'Thanks.' I probably won't call him anything but it's nice that he's being friendly.

'And what does your dad do?'

'Nothing.' Except for being a spirit-calling psycho. Not really what I want to tell the father of the girl I like. 'Not at the moment anyway. He's been really sick. Cancer. He's just spending time getting over it. That's why we moved here. Get away from cities and hospitals and get into the fresh air and stuff.'

'Oh. Well, that's no good. I'm glad he's getting better though. Is there anything we can do to help?'

'No.' I've said it too quickly, like I'm trying to hide something. 'I mean, he doesn't really like people to know. He's pretty private.'

'I can understand that.'

There's silence for a moment – an awkward one where neither of us know what to say to a pretty much complete stranger.

I nod towards the book case. The one I can't keep my eyes off. I'm glad he can't see the hammering in my chest. It'd be a dead giveaway that something was off or weird about me.

'You guys obviously like to read.'

He half turns to look over his shoulder and then turns back to me with a smile.

'Yes, you could say that. I'm a bit of a collector. Do you like to read?'

I nod. It's the truth, even if I don't get a chance to do it very often. There's not much point in having a library card if you're never there long enough to actually finish a book and take it back. And somehow, it seems wrong to steal from a library.

'Yeah. I prefer non-fiction though.'

He grins at me again.

'Would you like to have a look at them?'

'Sure.' I try and get the right level of enthusiasm – keen but not desperate, which is what I'm closer to feeling.

We walk back inside. Selti and her mum aren't anywhere to be seen but that's probably a good thing. No distractions. Find the book. Save Jimmy. Be with Selti. It's like a dot point in my head.

The bookcase climbs its way up to the ceiling and takes up the whole back wall. I should despair at the number of books it holds but I don't have to. I can feel it. Feel the…weight, the pressure… of the book we need. Like it's taking up more space than it actually is. I know it's there. On the far right. Third shelf up.

'Most of them are ones I've collected during my studies. Some more interesting than others. Any area you're particularly interested in?'

I hesitate. It's too much to tell him that straight up. And it might sound like I'm using Selti – like I know about them and I'm only doing it to get something. Which is true, even when it's not.

'Nah. Pretty much interested in all different types of subjects.'

I run my finger over the spines of the books on the shelf above where the one I need is. He comes over next to me and picks out the first one in that row.

'This one is all about a tribe in the amazon who up until ten years ago had never had contact with the outside world.'

I nod. 'Sounds interesting.' And it does. One I'd probably be happy to read if I had the time. But it's not going to help Jimmy.

I put my finger on the row below. I feel it thrumming almost, like it can feel my energy and is calling to me. Maybe there's something in what Fox said. I can see it. Brown leather. A gold symbol on the spine. No name. Just like Gep said. But it's not until I touch it that I know for certain. It gives me a jolt, like the grounding out of static electricity, except it feels good. I pull it out.

There's nothing on the front to tell me what it's about. Nothing except the gold symbol Gep told us to look for – a circle which looks like a cake cut into eight pieces. I have no idea what it means but I run my hand over the lines, tracing them.

'This one looks interesting.'

He glances at it.

'You have good taste. That's a really old book. I found it in England when we went there on holidays a few years ago. Actually, Ellen found it. Selti's mum. She convinced me to buy it – not that I took that much convincing but it was pretty expensive.' He grins at me, like a kid being given a second scoop of ice-cream and I laugh, like I feel he expects me to.

'What's it about?'

My heart's pounding so hard in my chest I'm sure it's going to give me away – he'll hear it and know how important it is and grab it off me.

'It's about the occult actually. Spirits, their link to this world, suppositions on things like the transference of energy, both positive and negative. Really interesting stuff. Well, I think so anyway.'

'It sounds it.' I pause and take a deep breath, trying to find the right words. This is too vital to stuff up. 'Any chance I might be able to take it home and read it? I promise I'll look after it.'

Much better than having to steal it. Imagine not having to do that anymore; being able to change that about me. Imagine not having to move because we haven't done anything illegal. To be able to stay here.

With Selti.

But he's shaking his head and the hope of being able to

change, building in my chest, sinks to my guts, making them heavy.

'Sorry, Penn, not that one, mate. It's too old. Irreplaceable. You're more than welcome to read it here though.'

That's something at least. Maybe Gep doesn't need it. Maybe there's something in it I can use to help Jimmy, without needing Gep. And the more I think about it, the more I like that idea. Maybe this whole power thing's not so bad, not if I can protect Jimmy on my own and cut out Gep as the middle-man.

'Great. Thanks.'

I open the front cover. The pages are yellowed with age and the sides are starting to turn a darker brown. The edges feel crisp under my fingers. It makes me feel really young. New. Like I know nothing.

'Oh, you want to start it now?'

I look up, startled, and feel my face go red.

'Sorry. It looks really interesting. But I don't need to.' Yes, I do. Right now! But I can't tell him that because then I'd have to tell him why. And that's definitely not a conversation I want to have.

'No, no. Go right ahead. I like a young person with an enquiring mind.'

Brownie points for me then. I open it again and start to read but it's awkward. I can feel his eyes, watching me, gauging me. When I glance up at him, he grins again and looks away, pulling another book from the shelf and opening it himself.

'Tell me again what happened to your face?'

He's caught me unprepared. I struggle for a moment to remember Selti's lie. The pause is too long and I jabber words out before I can even think what I'm saying.

'I fell down.'

His eyes come back up to look at me.

'I thought it happened at basketball.'

Shit.

'Yeah, that's right. One of the boys pushed into me when I was going up for a shot and when I fell, I hit my cheek.'

It's his turn to stop now, the silence feels sticky between us, like any moment, it's going to trap me and he's going to send me as far away from his daughter as possible. Panic stirs in my guts, a whirlpool waiting to happen.

'Oh. It's a wonder you didn't lose consciousness or get concussion.'

I try for a grin. It feels sort of convincing. I guess I've had lots of practice.

'Yeah, I think it's my thick skull.'

He smiles and I feel the panic slow down a little.

'And Selti tells me you're a twin. Identical?'

'Yeah. Jimmy.'

'I'm a twin myself.'

I didn't expect that. It's…nice. To have something so personal in common with him.

'Cool.'

'Herbert. My mum had a really old fashioned taste in names.'

I feel a hand on my shoulder and know, without even needing to turn, that it's Selti. I mean, obviously, she's probably the only one who would touch me in this house, but it's as if I just… feel her. Her dad looks at us and winks.

'Anyway, Penn, you're probably sick of me by now. I'll let you young people have some time.'

Selti leads me over to the couch. We can see her mum and dad in the kitchen, moving together, chatting. It's nice but it makes my heart ache. For a second, I wonder what my life would've been like if Mum had never met Gep…

'Was it terrible?'

I look at Selti, startled for a moment. It's like she's read my thoughts. And then realise she's talking about her dad. I shake my head.

'No. He's pretty cool actually.'

She smiles and leans back against the couch.

'I did some reading this morning. About…you know… the glow.'

I glance at her parents but they aren't paying any attention to us. I don't think they are, anyway.

'And did you find out anything?'

'I think so. My mum,' she hesitates, like she's about to tell me a secret, 'my mum can see auras.' She rushes the words like she can't wait to get them out of her mouth but she's worried what will happen once they are out. She shouldn't have worried – they make absolutely no sense to me.

'Auras?'

'Yeah. You know, the energy field that surrounds all living things.'

She must see the confused look on my face because she sighs.

'It doesn't matter, you'll just have to believe me. Anyway, the book I read said sometimes, when a huge change happens in the body – a big shift in its energy, like really big, bigger than most people ever get – people's auras have been known to make them glow. Usually it's only the eyes, but I guess it could happen to the rest of the body.'

'Right. So, what was the big shift and why was I blue?'

She shrugs. 'I don't know yet. It could have something to do with…no, don't worry. It's stupid.'

I take her hand and smile at her.

'No way. You can't do that. You have to tell me now.'

She rolls her eyes. 'Okay. It could have something to do with power, like I said the other night. Something to do with a shift in energy.' She takes my hand, like she's worried I'm about to take off. 'I don't want you to think I'm crazy or anything. I mean, I know I'm a Wiccan but I don't think everyone is magic. Truly, I don't. And it might not have anything to do with it. Right?'

I nod. That's all I can do. Because my mind's too busy to come up with words to say out loud. All I can think is that she knows.

She knows and she's going to hate me and want to get away from me because the power Gep has is nothing like the power she has. She's good. And I'm not. Not with all the things Gep's being doing. I can't be. So I don't want to tell her she's right. Not that I have to say anything because her mum and dad come over then, plates in hand.

'We've made some lunch. If you want to stay?'

And even though my heart's still racing as much as my head is, I can't say no. Especially if I want another chance to look at the book before I leave. I have to stay. For Jimmy.

And for me.

CHAPTER 26

The sky is still shades of pink and orange when our house comes into sight. I stop for a second and take a deep breath, readying myself for the fact that Gep might have come home during the day. I feel like I'm at war in my own head. I don't want to go in just in case he is back. My cheek throbs, in total agreement with that idea. But I need to see Jimmy. See how he is. See if he's improved during the day – if the rock's done something…anything – or if he's fading further. I shake my head. I can't think like that.

The stuff I managed to read in the book after lunch was interesting but it didn't really mean anything to me. Stuff about transfer of power and paranormal energy…which sounds like what Gep was banging on about but I don't know what to do with it – how to use it in a way that's going to help Jimmy. How to do anything with my powers, actually, except the thing where I've pushed the spirit out.

It's totally shitty that I probably still need Gep. And Jimmy still needs him.

Fox is sitting on the front steps when I come up to the house, scrunched up in a ball almost, trying to fit on the stairs. I feel bad that I only notice now how tall he's getting. Like I haven't even been paying enough attention to know that about him. It looks like he's been waiting for me and I get a sick feeling in my guts. Enough that I want to turn and run, ignore him, not listen to what he has to say. But none of this is his fault. I stop at the bottom of the stairs.

'Hey.'

'Hey.' He stands up, stretching himself, before his eyes meet mine. 'He's back.'

I feel my face scrunch up almost of its own accord. 'Right.'

He doesn't move out of the way to let me by though, so there must be something else. I wait for it. Sometimes I wish he was a talker like Kat. Get it over and done with. He picks the paint off the railing of the steps for a moment and I have to force myself not to hit his hand away.

'I can't feel him anymore.'

'What?'

'Gep. His power. I can't feel him anymore.'

My brain scrambles to make sense of that. It fails. Nothing new there, especially when it comes to Gep.

'What does that mean?'

He shrugs. 'I don't know. But I thought I'd better tell you before you go in.'

God, I hate changes. Even Gep as an evil, sadistic bastard is better than a changing Gep. A Gep where I don't know what to expect. One that catches me out and makes it harder to protect Jimmy.

'Okay. Thanks.'

He nods and then turns to go in.

'How's Jimmy?'

He looks back at me. 'Still in his room. Said he didn't have the strength to come out. I made him have some lunch though.'

I'm hot and cold all at the same time. It sweeps through my body. But Gep can't be right. No way....

Fox doesn't wait for my reply. He turns again and walks into the house and I follow him to the kitchen. My whole body is tight. Wound up.

Gep's sitting at the table with Kat. He looks up, watching me. I watch him right back. I don't want to be the first one to talk. I need to know what I'm facing before I give him anything.

'You're home.'

I nod. He looks older somehow – like the creases in his skin have become deeper. Crevices instead of grooves. Like he's aged for the first time I can remember. I don't know if that's good or bad. After the stuff I read today in the book, I'm guessing it's probably not good. Or maybe it is. Maybe that means he'll be gone from our lives forever... Except what does that mean for Jimmy?

'Have you found the book?'

I nod again, giving nothing.

'And?' He raises his eyebrows.

'Where have you been?'

'It doesn't matter where I've been.'

His voice is controlled but I'm waiting for the explosion. What is it about me that I have to keep going at him, like picking at a scab?

'It matters when you punched me before you left, and we didn't know where you were or if you were coming back. We didn't know anything.'

He sneers at me. 'It's touching that you missed me.'

'Kat missed you.'

He glances at Kat who's looking down at his hands and his face softens slightly. Huh! Maybe he really does care about him. More than he cares for the rest of us anyway. Not that that makes any difference to me. I've gone way past trusting him or wanting his approval or love.

'I had to go away and think about how we're going to deal with...all of this.'

'All of what?'

He doesn't answer me. Except by glaring. I guess that's some sort of communication. He's kidding himself if he thinks I can understand him though.

'All of what?'

He puts his hands on the table. They're balled into fists.

'Your power.'

'What's there to understand?'

He stares at me for a moment without talking. I'm pushing it but this time, I want to. I want this all out in the open. All the shit out in the daylight so I know what the hell I'm dealing with.

'How long have you known you had it?'

I debate for a second whether I should lie to him but there's no point really. Not when I need his help to understand all this.

'Only in the last week.'

'What brought it on?'

I shrug. I want it all out in the open but there's no way I'm telling him about Selti. Or our kiss. There are some limits still.

'It just sort of happened. When I had to get the spirit out of Jimmy to save him, it kicked in. That's when I really felt it. Before, it was…there but not there.'

It takes a moment but he finally nods.

'Why didn't you tell me? Come to me?'

I can't believe he's asked me that.

'Well, firstly, I didn't really know what it was. And second, why would I?

It's there for him to hear – how much I hate him. Not that he doesn't already know that. He ignores it. First time for everything I guess.

'But you found the book?'

It's my turn to hesitate, trying to figure out how I can give him the least information possible without making it obvious.

'Yes. I found it.'

'And?'

'It's pretty well protected. I managed to read some of it today. But I don't know if I can get it.'

'There's no choice. You have to get it.'

'But – '

He bangs his hand on the table. We all jump.

'There are no fucking buts! We need it. Jimmy needs it.'

I glare at him, my heart angry and scared and all screwed up.

'Yeah, well you weren't thinking about Jimmy when you made him be the conduit last night.'

'I know.' He takes a deep breath, like he's trying to control himself. 'I know. I shouldn't have. If I'd known you had your power, I wouldn't have done it.'

'Why? Why does my power make anything different?'

He looks me in the eyes, his face serious.

'Because for some reason, mine's gone. Or I can't access it anyway. I need you to use yours to save Jimmy.'

CHAPTER 27

*J*immy's still sleeping the next morning when I get up. I watch him from the doorway of their bedroom for a moment. He looks pale. And thinner. And less… there. He was asleep last night when I went in to see him after being grilled by Gep. And I didn't want to wake him then, not when he looked like he needed it. But the fact that he's still asleep now…

The panic bubbles in my stomach, like vinegar being poured on bi carb. Building and building until I feel like if I open my mouth, it's going to bubble out and I'll have no control. A panic volcano that'll overwhelm me, burying me.

Gep's right. As much as my mind doesn't want to admit it could even be a possibility. I have to get the book. Even though it might mean I never get to see Selti again because her parents aren't stupid. They'll know, if the book goes missing, that it was me. Or pretty strongly suspect it anyway. I don't know what I was thinking trying to have both her and Jimmy. That's not my life. Jimmy is my life. And I need to get the book. Get it and take it so Gep can save Jimmy.

I walk quietly into his room, the floor boards protesting

under my feet, but even that's not enough to wake him. I lean down over his bed, the light from the gap in the curtains enough to see the movement of his eyes under his eyelids. Rapid. Like he's in agony. Like he's trying to wake up but can't.

I shake his shoulder.

'Jimmy. Wake up.'

He groans but his eyes stay shut.

The shake this time is harder.

'Jimmy. Wake up! Hey, Jimmy, man!'

Both my hands are on him before he finally opens his eyes. Only a crack. But I can see him.

'What time is it?'

'It's nearly nine thirty. You need to have some breakfast, get some energy into you. Man, you slept the whole night. I could hear you snoring from our room. Don't know how Fox got any sleep.'

I'm babbling but can't stop. Trying to make everything normal even when it feels anything but.

'I don't think I have enough energy to get up today. Maybe I should stay here and see if it helps.' His words slur, blending into each other.

The breath in my airways solidifies, chocking me, and I gasp in fresh air, pushing down the volcano. He's never wanted to stay in bed for two days running. Ever. Even when his body has been so stiff he's almost crying for me to help him.

'You have to get up.'

'I can't Penn. I'm tired. Really tired. I need to sleep. Maybe I've got a virus or something.'

'Yeah, that's it, a virus. Just rest then, and you'll be good tomorrow.'

He opens his eyes all the way then and looks at me. It looks like it's taking him a lot of effort.

'Do you think it's the spirit that was in me the other day? Do you think it did something?'

I'm shaking my head before he's even finished.

'No. No way. I got it out. Pushed it out. There's nothing in you.'

He nods. Trusting me. The panic bubbles higher.

'Do you think Gep's right then? Do you think I'm like Mum? That I'm going to fade away?'

I can hear the fear in his voice.

'Don't listen to Gep. He's a fucking psycho. Just trying to scare you, like he does all the time. Don't worry, I'll look after you. Don't I always?'

His hand shakes when he reaches over to grab mine. But his grip is hard, biting into my skin.

'I know. You always do. I know you'll keep me safe.'

'Course.' I massage his fingers, helping him to relax, trying to think what I can do – how to help him, like I apparently did in the car. But there's no floating him out of here. 'Where's the stone I gave you? The blue one?'

He jerks his head and I take it from under the pillow. I can feel the warmth of it again, like it's radiating energy, against the actual coolness of the stone. I put it against Jimmy's arm, holding it there.

'What does it feel like to you?'

'What do you mean? It feels like a stone.'

'Yeah but cold or warm?'

'Cold. Why?'

I nod without answering him. Okay then, if I can feel it and he can't, I figure there must definitely be something about it – something magical. And Fox did say my power spiked when we were in the garage with it. I hold it in my hand, staring at it, willing it to do something. Anything.

And of course, what I get is absolutely nothing. It just sits there in my hand.

Shit. Why can't any of this be easy?

'What are you doing?'

Jimmy's looking at me but closes his eyes after he asks the question, like he doesn't have enough energy to keep them open anymore. Like he hasn't slept the whole night…or the best part of the day before… And that's when it hits me. Energy. That's what he needs. And maybe that's what I can give. Some of my energy.

I look at the stone again. It's like it's waiting for me to do something. I shut my eyes, trying to think about the power in me…how I felt when I was with Selti, when I was the human glow stick…

'What are you doing?'

'Shut up,' I say. 'I'm trying to concentrate.'

He huffs but doesn't say anything else. I focus again, trying to…latch on to the power. Trying to push it somehow. Liked I pushed the spirit out of Jimmy. I squeeze the stone tighter, and I feel it. A trickle of power leaving me, like water dripping off my fingertips. I squeeze my eyes shut tighter, but it doesn't make any difference. It continues to trickle, slowly, slowly, until I'm panting with the effort it takes. I feel drained and yet, it doesn't feel like there's a lot that I've put in the stone. If any at all because, to be honest, I have no idea if it's worked. Maybe it's just leaked out of me and become part of…well, the air.

I open my eyes again. It looks like Jimmy's gone back to sleep but when I touch his hand, he looks at me.

'What was that about?'

I put the stone against his hand.

'What does it feel like this time?'

'It's warm.'

I sigh. Maybe that means it worked. 'Good.'

'Because you've been holding it. Why is that good?'

Crap, I hadn't thought of that. Fox. I need Fox. Not Gep because I'm not telling him I've got the stone, especially after what he said last night. I'm not letting him know I'm using my power to try and help Jimmy because then he'll want me to do other things – things I don't want to do. I know that without a doubt, because all he thinks about is himself and his power. Not matter what else he says, that's what it always comes back to. His addiction.

'Hang on.'

I go out into the hallway, legs feeling like they're made of frigging jelly, and stick my head into the kitchen. Gep's standing at the back door but Fox is sitting at the table, book in his hand. It must be a pretty crap one because he looks up straight away. I jerk my head and he glances at Gep before getting up and following me back into his and Jimmy's room.

'What?'

I take the rock back off Jimmy and hold it out to Fox. His eyes widen without me needing to say anything.

'What the hell did you do?'

'I don't know. I think I put some of my energy in it?'

'You've put a *lot* of your power in it. I don't know if that's the same thing. Maybe. But you haven't let yourself with much.'

I shrug. It doesn't matter that I feel like I could go back to bed right now. All that matters is that Jimmy can use it.

'Do you think it'll help Jimmy?'

'I don't know. I can only see power. That's it. You probably know more than me.'

I stifle a frustrated grunt. It's not Fox's fault that I know bugger all about this. I press the rock back into Jimmy's hand.

'Here. Hold it. Hopefully it'll help you feel stronger.'

Jimmy pushes it back at me. Well, he tries to anyway. 'No way. Fox said you haven't left yourself with much. I can't take it.'

'Don't be an idiot. I'll be fine. You need it more than me. It's only until we can work out what we need to make you better.'

He must be feeling really bad because he doesn't put up another fight. He just sighs and closes his eyes again. Christ! I can't lose him. I can't. I won't survive that. I won't be able to live without him. And I know I'll do whatever I have to do to make sure he's okay. But there must be another option except for Gep.

Gep and the corruption he has in his power and how he uses it. All I can think about is the spirit saying there are consequences to using the power. Which, if I'm truthful, scares the shit out of me. There must be another way.

I head towards the door, determined, in my mind at least. My body feels like it's being dragged along for the ride.

'Where are you going?' Fox is still standing near Jimmy, protecting him. It makes me feel better.

'To see Selti. To see if I can get her help.'

CHAPTER 28

I call her on the way over to her house. She answers in only two rings.

'Hey you.'

'Hey.' Even the sound of her voice brings a smile to my face. 'What are you up to today?'

'I was planning to do my English assignment actually, considering I haven't even looked at it yet. I've been distracted.'

The smile on my face gets bigger. 'Well, I hope whatever's been distracting you has been worth it.'

She laughs and my guts clenches, as if the sound is a string wrapped around my stomach, pulling it tighter and tighter. 'Yeah, it's been worth it.'

'Do you want a hand with studying? I did the assignment at my last school already. Even got a B for it. And then you can give me a hand with something else.'

'That sounds intriguing. I've got Emily coming over as well, though. Is that okay?'

'Sure,' I say even though it's not. But I'm not that selfish. I can be patient. For a few hours anyway. Jimmy has the stone and Fox is watching him. He'll be fine. Fine...

When I get to her house, Emily isn't there yet. Neither are her parents. Perfect. I can feel the book, still in the bookcase, crackling, humming…calling to me, and wonder if I'll have a chance to get it today. Probably not. It's too obvious and there's still a small part a small, stupid part – that wonders if I'll be able to take it and still be able to be with Selti. It's the same small, stupid part that thinks maybe I should just ask her for it. Tell her everything. Trust her. And I do, but I have to protect her too. I can't drag her into all the shit that is my life. I can't expose her to Gep and his pyscho-ness. It's bad enough that I'm in her life, bringing her closer to it. But hopefully I can get her to help me with understanding my powers.

She kisses me at the front door. A short one that transforms into a longer one which leaves us both breathless. Which isn't great when I'm already struggling with keeping upright. The further the morning goes on the weaker I'm feeling. Maybe she can help me with that as well.

We're standing there, smiling at each other, when Emily walks up the stairs behind me.

'Oh, hi.' She doesn't look entirely pleased to see me.

'Penn's going to help us. He's already done the assignment,' Selti rushes the words out and I feel sort of bad for crashing their party. Not bad enough to leave but guilty just the same.

'Hope that's okay.' I try and give her the nicest smile I can and she blinks for a moment, looking a bit stunned that I've actually spoken to her, before her eyes flick away again.

'Yes. I mean, sure. That's fine.'

Selti takes my hand and leads me through to the lounge room, where she has her books spread over the coffee table. I sit down beside her on the couch and Emily sits across from us and starts to pull her books out too. I, of course, have none. Stupid. But when I pick up Selti's assessment sheet I remember most of it anyway and start to talk about what I did in my assignment. They disagree with me over some things and it's cool. Probably the first study group I'd ever been a part of. It's kind of fun which is not something I ever thought I'd say but there you go. This town is bringing a lot of firsts into my life.

I don't know when it is that I start to nod off but the next thing I know, Selti is running the side of her hand down my face and I'm blinking my eyes open.

'What time is it?'

'A bit after two. You've been asleep for about four hours.'

'Shit. Sorry.'

'It's okay. You must have needed it.'

'Has Emily gone?'

Selti nods. 'She just left. She said to say goodbye.' She grins at me. 'It's a wonder she could make herself heard over the snoring.'

I can feel my face get hot. 'Christ. Really?'

She laughs then and shakes her head. 'No, not really but you should have seen your face.'

I grab her and tip her back onto the cushions of the couch, tickling her until she calls for mercy and then, my lips are on hers and my tongue is flicking at her lips, tasting her, teasing her until my heart feels like it's pulling all my other organs to it – each beat pulling them closer and closer. My lips go down, tracing along the side of her jaw and down her neck to the ridges of her collarbone. Her breath is fast in my ear and I can feel her fingers tracing the bottom of my spine, pulling my shirt up slightly. Christ! I come up for air, forcing myself to stop. Her eyes are dilated and her cheeks have a pink tinge to them. The sight of her almost undoes me. Almost. But I can't do this. As much as I want to. Just in case…just in case something happens, and I need the book after all, and then we have to leave. I don't want to take this too far and leave without her understanding why. I might be a thief but I'm not a bastard.

'We should stop,' I say and she nods at me but neither of us move.

She licks her lips – I don't think she does it consciously – but that simple movement has everything clenching again. Jesus. I feel like a walking hormone. I sit up before my resolve disintegrates into ashes under this damn heat she creates in me. She sits up to, straightening her shirt and her hair, which makes me want to dishevel her all over again. I grit my teeth. It shouldn't be this frigging hard!

'Um, so, what can I help you with?'

I'm so distracted with trying to keep my hands to myself that, for a moment, I have absolutely zero idea what she's talking about.

'What?'

'You know, you said there was something I might be able to help you with.'

'Oh, yeah.' I look down at my hands, unsure how to bring this up without sounding totally lame. 'You know, last night, when you said maybe I was blue because of...power. Because of a shift in energy.'

She nods but she's really still, like she's afraid of scaring me off.

'Well, if that's true; if I do...have power...do you think you could teach me some stuff.'

'What sort of stuff?'

I can't make out her tone of voice. It's almost neutral. And I have no idea what that means. I wonder if this is too weird for her. Maybe she doesn't want to do this. I mean, it's not really a boyfriend/girlfriend thing. If that's what we are...

'You don't have to help me if you don't want to. I mean, if it's too weird. You know...'

But I don't know. Not really. Because there's this soppy part of me that really wants her to say yes – that wants her to *want* to help me with this thing that's apparently part of who I am now. Not only because it means I might be able to use them to help Jimmy – to save Jimmy – but because it'd be nice if she was the one to teach me. Rather than Gep.

'No, it's good. I'm happy to.'

But that's not what her voice is saying. Her voice is saying it's the last thing she wants to do. And I feel…stupid. Stupid and weird and not anywhere near good enough for her. I try not to let it show on my face but she's better at picking up these things than I am at hiding them from her.

'Do you want me to help you?'

'Not if you don't want to. It's good. I'll work it out.'

She sighs and slides closer, putting her hand on my chest, flat, silent for the moment like she's trying to work it all out in her head.

'It's not that I don't want to. It's …'

'What?'

She looks down at her hand so I can't see her face.

'I don't want you to think I'm strange. That's what everyone's thought about me my whole life.'

I put my fingers under her jaw and gently bring her face up to look at me.

'Me, think you're strange? Jesus! You are so normal in comparison to me. I'm the one who was a frigging glow stick, I'm the one with a psycho step-father…it's a wonder you still want me around!'

'I do,' she says quietly.

'You do what?'

'Want you around.'

And my heart feels like it balloons at her words. Like it's literally filling up my whole chest. Because she wants me. I try to ignore the crappy side of my brain that's telling me she probably wouldn't if she knew everything. If she knew about Gep and the spirits and Jimmy fading and what I've done for Gep, year after year. If she knew the evil that's surrounded me for as long as I can remember.

'Okay. That's good then.'

God, talk about smooth. She smiles at me though and it doesn't matter if I know the right things to say or not.

'Well then, powers. What do know so far?'

I don't want to tell her anything I've got from Gep – the rituals he does, or the words he uses or the burn. All of it's evil shit. So I shrug.

'Nothing really.'

'Okay. Well then, probably the first thing to know is that every living thing in the world has energy and it's that energy you use in magic – whether it's your own or something else's.'

Which would probably explain why I was so frigging tired this morning. Why Fox freaked out a bit when he said I'd used a lot of my power.

'Energy. Gottcha.'

'The next really important one is that any spell or magic you create will come back to you threefold. So, it's important not to harm anyone or anything in what you do.'

All I can think about is all the shit Gep's done over the years – all the harm he's done to all of us. And how he never seems to pay for it. Although maybe my mum paid the price for him, if it's true when he says he loved her as much as he did. Which only makes me hate him even more.

'Are you okay?' Selti is looking at me with concern on her face and I realise the hatred must have shown on my face for a moment. It's getting harder and harder to keep things from her.

'Yeah, sorry. So, don't harm anyone.'

She nods. 'There's a lot more. Things about the moon and protecting yourself and herbs and...well I could go on for ages. Was there something you really wanted to know?'

I lean back, trying to act cool, trying not to let her see how that one word makes me feel like getting up and pacing. 'Protection? What did you mean by that?'

'Spells have the capacity to be both negative and positive. And spells from other people can impact you, as well as other things… spirits, like you said your stepdad called sometimes?'

Her voice is tentative, like she's afraid of upsetting me and my jaw clenches for a moment. Me and my frigging big mouth – and the fact she remembered it – when I'm trying so hard to keep her away from it.

'Right. What can you do then?'

Not that I'm thinking about it for me – whatever – but if I can use something for Jimmy…

'Well, you can cast a circle around you. That provides you with protection in that spot. And there are certain herbs you can use to provide protection too.'

'What sort of herbs?'

She chews on her bottom lip, thinking for a moment. 'Rosemary, acacia, larkspur, sage. Wolfsbane as well, except it's poisonous. Mum knows more than me though. If you want to know more, we could ask her.'

'No!' The word shoots out of my mouth. It feels like it ricochets around the room. But Jesus, if her mum knew, then she'd probably ask questions and there's no way I'm going there. 'I mean, it's not something I feel comfortable with sharing yet. Except with you.'

'Okay. Just us then. Do you want me to get you some of the herbs?'

'Do you have them? Here?'

She smiles. 'Of course. Mum has a special affinity with herbs. Come on.'

She grabs something out of a drawer of the coffee table and I follow her out the back to a garden filled with plants. I have no idea what any of them are – herbs haven't featured big in the chuck-something-in-the-microwave cooking that's been my go-to – but Selti knows. She bends down and cuts them with the knife she must have grabbed.

'Here. Sage, rosemary and I've added some thyme and mint as well.'

I take them in my hand. They smell amazing.

'And what do I need to do with them?'

'Well, you can burn the sage and most of the others you dry out. But even putting them all in a small bag and keeping them on you should provide some protection.'

'A small plastic bag?'

'A fabric one would be better. I've got one if you want to us it.'

I smile at her. 'That'd be great.'

She smiles back at me and it feels awesome. Like she's happy to help me. Like we have this secret that belongs only to us. She puts them in a small leather bag for me.

'It's important you believe in it though. It has more power if you do.'

'I believe,' I say. For Jimmy, I'd believe anything.

CHAPTER 29

 'm still tired when I wake the next morning. Not as tired as I was yesterday but putting the energy into the stone isn't something I'm going to be able to do every day. Not if this is how it leaves me feeling. Even though it worked. A bit. Fox said Jimmy was sitting up and had lunch yesterday but he was still tired last night. Tired enough that he was back in bed and asleep by six o'clock. I gave him the bag of herbs in his room, so Gep didn't see. Jimmy laughed and asked how a salad was going to protect him but maybe if I believe, that's all he'll need.

And maybe that'll help him be okay this morning.

Maybe his energy will improve as well.

Maybe.

The kitchen's empty when I walk through. I grab an apple and bite into it, the juice running down my throat, making me feel half way human. Fox is lying on his bed, dressed for school, when I stick my head in. He looks over at Jimmy and then back at me, shaking his head. And like that, I feel shit again, although it has nothing to do with energy. Or it has nothing to do with *my* energy.

Jimmy's face is not as grey as it was yesterday but he still doesn't look well. The herbs are sticking out from under his pillow and the stone is beside his hand on the bed and I pick it up, rolling it in my palm.

'All your energy's gone from it.' Fox sits up on the edge of his bed, forearms on his knees as he leans forward. 'Gep was in here last night. I think he knows about the stone. He came in here for a while and then left. I heard the front door.'

'Shit.' Definitely not something I can keep doing then. Not if it only lasts Jimmy one day. And now Gep knows…I'm amazed he didn't come and whack me over the head with it last night if he saw it. I shake Jimmy. He comes awake easier than he did the morning before. Something at least.

He opens his eyes for a moment to look at me and then closes then again.

'God. Is it morning already?'

'Yep,' I say, trying and probably failing at keeping my voice upbeat. 'Monday too. Time for school.'

He groans as I help him sit up. His left arm is shaking, spasming, and I massage it for him until the spasms stop. Fox has already got his clothes out for him and I pull his pyjama top off and help him with his school shirt. By the time we finish, he's sweating like he's been for a hard sprint and his jaw is shaking with the effort he's had to exert. I stop and sit down on the bed beside him.

'I can't do it. Not today. Maybe tomorrow. I feel a bit better today. Thanks to you. And my salad.'

I can only nod, my throat too thick with emotion to laugh at his lame attempt at humour.

'It'll be alright,' he says, like he's not the one in pain. Like he's the one who should be doing something to protect me.

'Sure,' I manage to get out. 'Sure.'

But I feel like a real shit. There should be more I can do for him. What's the use in having all this frigging power if I can't actually help him. It's fucked.

Together, Fox and I help him back out of his school shirt and get him comfortable.

'Do you want breakfast?'

He hesitates for a moment and then shakes his head.

'I don't think I could manage it. Sorry.'

And I'm angry that he feels like he needs to apologise to me. Like this is all his fault or something just as stupid.

'Don't apologise. Ever. Just don't do it.'

'Okay.'

'We'll see you later then.'

He nods but he's already closing his eyes and I feel so useless I want to punch something. Anything. Preferably Gep's face. These things Selti's teaching me aren't strong enough for this. Or aren't working quick enough. And I'm not asking her to help anymore. I'm not bringing her into all of this – I've done that enough already.

The book then. That's my only choice now. I have to trust that the very person I don't trust at all is telling us the truth. For once.

'Just rest. I'll be back this arv. With the book Gep needs. Okay?'

He doesn't answer me and for that split second, I think I've lost him. That's he gone already, even though that's stupid. But the panic has me rushing out of the room, even though I try and look calm. Trying to keep the panic to myself. I hurry to the drawer where I know Gep put the photo album. Reefing it open so hard it almost comes right out except that it sticks a bit at the end. I grab the album, not even bothering to close the drawer again, and flip over to the front photo. The one that had the four of us. Except there really only looks like two of us now.

Because Jimmy has become even fainter.

CHAPTER 30

Kat keeps on trying to get me to talk on the way to school, chattering away, asking questions, trying to make everything normal. It's only when Fox punches him that he shuts up but he looks like a dejected puppy and for a second, I feel bad. Only for a second though. I've got more important things to occupy my mind and I need the silence to sort them out.

The book. That's what it comes down to. Well, if I'm going to believe Gep anyway. And, at the moment, it's the only glimmer of hope I have.

So, the book. Even if it means I lose Selti.

Shit.

We're almost at school when I see her. Selti. Getting out of the car. My chest squeezes, tightening to the point of actual physical pain. I don't want to give her up.

Fox steps into me, knocking me slightly, and I turn to glare at him. He glares back at me.

'What are you doing?'

I frown at the question. 'Nothing.'

'Your power was spiking. It felt like you were only just keeping a hold of it.'

I turn to him fully.

'What are you talking about? I wasn't doing anything. I didn't even feel anything.' Except sad. But that doesn't have anything to do with my power.

'Yeah, well, whatever. I can only tell you what I felt. Maybe you need to talk to Gep, even if you hate him. At least he understands all this crap.'

I don't answer him. I don't know what to say. When I turn back, Selti's mum has got out of the car too. She leans in to give Selti a hug. She's dressed differently to how I've normally seen her. More…formal. Like she's going out.

Like no one will be at home.

I swing back to Fox and Kat.

'If anyone asks, I'm sick. I'll get Gep to ring the school. Tell Selti okay.'

Fox nods – no questions – but Kat can't let it go.

'Why? Are you feeling sick?'

'No, Kat. There's something I need to do. Now. When everyone's at work and school.'

'Oh.' I can see the exact time when it filters through his brain and makes sense. 'Oh! For Jimmy. To help him.'

'Yep. Hopefully.'

He nods. 'Do you need a hand?'

I smile at him this time. 'No, mate. You go to school. I'll see you this arv.'

He nods and starts walking. Fox looks at me.

'Just be careful.'

'Aren't I always?'

He grunts and then starts walking too. I watch them go. And it hits me that I do have a family. Even taking Gep out of the equation, Fox and Kat are my brothers. Not blood like Jimmy.

But my brothers. And I don't know how I ever thought I could leave without them.

I'm half way to Selti's house when I ring Gep's mobile. He answers before it hits the second ring.

'What?'

I resist the urge to ask him where he is.

'I need you to ring the school and tell them I'm sick.'

'Are you going to get it?'

That's one thing about Gep – he's not slow.

'Yes.'

'I'll ring them now.'

'And Jimmy's at home. He didn't have the energy to come.'

He grunts and then hangs up on me. I look at the black screen and put the phone in my pocket. I don't know why I keep expecting something different from him. Stupid, I guess.

I open the gate to their house and slip through. It's nice they've got no close neighbours and no dog. Makes it a lot easier. But I still need to be careful. No point in tempting fate. I walk through the bush beside the driveway, just in case Selti's mum comes back, or her dad's still at home, and stand there for a while when the house comes into sight, hidden by the bushes at the edge of their garden. I stand there for long enough, watching for any movement, that the insects forget about me and start to call out again.

I'm pretty sure it's safe but I scoot around the back of the house just to be sure. I move cautiously to the back stairs, staying close to the wall and under the windows. The French doors that run along the back of the house don't offer me any protection if someone happens to be inside. And I've got no idea what excuse I can use if someone does catch me.

I try the handle. It moves easily under my hand. That's the thing about small towns and people who live on acreages. They think they'll never be broken into. And I'm spoiling that for them.

Spoiling it for someone I care for. A lot. Love maybe. That thought stops me for a moment, frozen with the door half open.

Love.

Christ!

But I can't think about it now. Maybe not ever if this all goes wrong.

The book feels like it's shouting at me from the bookcase. My power calling to it. Not that I really understand what's going on. How can I have this thing happening in me and not know what it is or how it works?

It's still quiet when I move across the floor but I go over to the entry to the kitchen anyway and stick my head out, looking both ways down the hallway. Holding my breath. Waiting. Still nothing. And I start to relax a bit. Enough that my heart slows to an even beat anyway.

It's only when I grab the book from the bookcase, my arm tingling, like bubbles under my skin, that I realise I have another option. An option that might let me help Jimmy as well as keep Selti.

I put it down on the table and grab my phone out of my pocket, bringing the camera up. Flicking open the front page of the book, I line it up, taking the photo before turning to the next page. It's not that big. Probably take me an hour at the most but it means I can leave it here. And Selti and her family will never know what sort of person I really am.

But I can't help but read it as I go through. A sentence here, a paragraph there. More than the first couple of chapters I read the other night. I'm caught up in the science of it, even though it was obviously written a long time ago. The way they write and the words they use make it pretty obvious, even if it didn't already look like an old book that's going to fall apart at any moment.

But the way they describe the power – the energy – that every living thing supposedly has, like Selti was talking about...it's amazing. There're even diagrams, for God sake, showing the internal organs of animals and humans and where the energy is made in the body and where it leaves. And then it moves on to spirits and the paranormal plane and how energy is used to and from there. Talking about things like temperature changes and 'soul' energy, whatever that means.

I can't help myself – I know the time between each photo is getting longer and longer and I'm leaving myself open to being discovered but it's like I can't tear myself away. Especially when I get to the chapter entitled 'Creating a constant energy loop'. It has some messed up stuff. But messed up stuff that sounds terrifyingly familiar. Because it sounds like Gep.

It's only when I glance at my watch that I realise I've been here for three and a half hours. Three and a half frigging hours! I flick through the pages like a maniac, clicking photos of the last two chapters I'm not even sure are going to be really clear. But I need to get out of here.

There are still three pages to go when I hear the sound of the front door. And voices. One of them Selti's, even though school's not supposed to be finished yet.

Crap. Crap. Crap.

I try to shut the book while cramming my phone in my pocket and don't succeed at doing either. The book flops open again and my phone falls on the floor, making a loud clunking sound on the wood.

Shit!

I scoop it up, starting to run out the door at the same time, and then I remember the book, still sitting on the table. They'll know, they'll know! That's all I can think.

Before my brain even has a chance to ask 'What the hell are you doing', I'm back at the table, grabbing the book.

And that's when they walk into the room.

Selti and her mum.

CHAPTER 31

I freeze. Caught mid stride, book in hand, eyes so wide they feel like they're popping out of my head. I look guilty, no doubt about it. I *am* guilty.

The silence feels like it goes on forever. Even my heart feels like it's stopped beating, like it's keeping really still so it won't be noticed. Waiting to see what their reactions are. The reaction to me being in their house. Breaking and entering. Well, not breaking but I feel like that's clutching at straws. I'm not sure Ellen, Selti's mum, will see the variation.

She steps slightly in front of Selti, like she's protecting her.

From me.

'What are you doing here, Penn? Why are you in our house?'

I'm tempted to say I was waiting for Selti but that's the feeblest excuse on the face of the planet and my brain doesn't seem to want to work fast enough to come up with a lie that's even close to believable. Once again, my skill at getting myself out of shit situations has deserted me.

'Penn?' Selti's voice holds the hurt I can clearly see on her face. And I can't believe I'm the one who's caused that.

My body sags, the tension falling away with the knowledge

that I can't lie to her. Not now. I put the book back on the table and rest against the edge – feeling like I need it to hold my body up – looking at her.

'I had to read the book, the one I started the other night when I was here, with your dad. I needed to see what it said.'

Ellen is frowning at me.

'So you thought it was perfectly appropriate to come into our home, when no one was here – trespassing into a place we'd previously welcomed you to – and read it. And where you planning to take it too? Even when my husband specifically told you that you couldn't?'

'No, I –'

But she doesn't wait for me to finish.

'I can't believe we welcomed you into our home and this is what you chose to do. I think you should leave. Now.'

'Stop, Mum.' Selti moves forward and touches her mother's shoulder and even though her mum frowns, she stops talking. 'I think we need to let Penn tell us why he needed to read the book.'

'I hardly think…'

'Mum, please.'

Her mum's lips go tight but after a moment, she nods. I hear the air sigh out of Selti's mouth, like she's been holding her breath. And then she looks at me. Expecting the truth.

And I know I have to give it to her, even if it makes her want to run away from me – leave me and all my screwed-up-ness in the dust. Protect herself.

'Jimmy's really sick. I think he might be dying. That's why I asked you about the protection stuff yesterday.'

I can see the shock on Selti's face

'Why would you think that?'

I shrug, trying to find something in the silence that makes sense. I don't want to tell her about the photo.

'He's…fading. Can't get out of bed. Doesn't want to eat. Doesn't want to even go to school. Doesn't have the energy to.'

My voice breaks at the last bit – a crack in the ice, making me feel off balance, like the ground is moving under me. Selti goes to move towards me but Ellen holds her hand out.

'Who's Jimmy?'

'My brother. My twin.'

'And why would you think reading this book would save him?'

I drag out the chair at the table and sit down, my energy seeping from me, like I'm the one who's fading. I run my hands over my face, through my hair. Buying time. Anything that means I don't have to tell them. But my brain is empty. A cavernous void, filled only with air and silence. It's no good.

'Gep, my step-father, he is…well, he calls himself a sorcerer.'

The words sit there, swelling, taking up room, like me saying them has given them substance. As soon as they're out, I want to pull them back in, swallow them whole again, hide them away from sight. If only. Selti and her mum are both staring at me, mouths slightly open. You can tell they're mother and daughter. Which is such an inane, stupid thing to be thinking at this point, but there you go. My brain is an idiot.

'A sorcerer?' It's Ellen. Selti's still just looking at me and I can't work out what her expression means. But she's not trying to move towards me anymore.

'Yes.'

'And that's the word he used. Not shaman or something else.'

I shake my head and I can see the doubt on her face. It's stupid, but now that it's out, I want them to believe me. I want them to understand. I lean forward, elbows on my knees, hands pressed together.

'All my life, all I can remember is him doing stuff. Stuff with spirits, stuff with powers and energy.'

Ellen takes a breath in. Short and sharp and not very loud, but loud enough that I can hear it. Probably because I'm watching for their reactions.

'What sort of things?'

I take a deep breath. This is it. No going back now.

'He calls spirits, asks them questions. Does these…rituals to get them there. And he makes us do them, most of the time. Be the ones to do the ritual. He calls us the conduits. The spirits come into us.'

The shock on both of their faces is clear, which actually makes me feel a bit better. If they're into all this sort of stuff and even they're shocked by what I'm telling them, then it must be as bad as I've always thought. Like I said, my brain's a moron.

'Are you telling me you've been possessed by spirits? That your step-father calls to them and makes them enter your body?'

I grimace.

'I don't know if it's a possession. They sort of…use my voice. But yeah, I guess they're in me. I can feel them.'

Ellen is shaking her head. She comes over to sit at the table, on the opposite side to me, leaning her forearms on the top. Selti comes over too. She sits next to me but doesn't touch me. And even though I want to reach out and take her hand, I don't. Mainly because I don't want to take the chance that she'll pull away. So, I'm a coward as well as a moron.

'What else does…Gep?' She pauses and I nod at her. 'What else does he do?'

'He does this…energy type of thing. We call it the burn. He puts his hand on you and it sort of sends this power through you. Like electricity, I guess. It's sort of hard to explain. Hurts like hell though.'

'And he does this to you?'

I take a deep breath.

'He does it to all of us. He's a fucking psycho. Sorry for swearing.'

And I am. But it feels so good to get it out. To let go of the secret. To not be the only one responsible for making sure the boys are okay. Not that Ellen will probably do anything. Or even *should* do anything. I mean, I still don't know that I want to bring them into Gep's world. But at least there's someone else who knows. Just in case.

'Did he give you that black eye?'

Her eyes are narrowed, looking at me. It feels like a test. Like she's waiting to see how truthful I'm going to be. I glance at Selti and she nods at me.

'Yes.'

Ellen leans back in the chair, the air sighing out of her in a long, narrow stream. I wait. I'm good at that – plenty of practice with Gep. She's looking at the table, a small frown marring the space between her eyes. Finally, she looks up at me.

'I'm sorry you've had to live with all of this.' I nod. I don't know what to say to that. Thanks? But it's nice that she realizes it hasn't been a great childhood. Nice that someone else understands how shit it's been. 'Tell me why you think Jimmy is dying. And why you think this book will help?'

I lean forward, onto the table, and grip my hands in front of me, the bones in my fingers hurting slightly under the pressure. It's a good hurt. Keeps me focused.

'The last time Gep did the ceremony, he made Jimmy the conduit, even though he wasn't strong already. And I could see it, the spirit, taking even more strength out of him. It said Jimmy had clean energy, whatever that means, and that it liked being in him. When I told Jimmy to push it out, it laughed and said he was too weak to do that.'

'What happened?' Her voice is deeper, quieter.

I look down at the table, at my hands.

'I pushed it out of him. It was the only thing I could think to do. I pushed it out of him like I've pushed it out of myself before. It worked but it didn't help. He's been really weak ever since.'

'You pushed it out? You have some powers yourself?' I can hear the surprise in her voice.

'I guess. It's all new though. Like, really new. I don't know anything about using them.' I don't want to tell her that Selti started teaching me some stuff yesterday in case she wasn't supposed to. 'Gep keeps on saying he wants me to use my powers with him but I don't want to. I don't want to do anything the way he does. I just want to save Jimmy. And I'm not doing a great job at that.'

'It's not your fault, Penn.' Selti is looking at me, her eyes wide.

'I know. I know. But I can't lose him. Not like we lost Mum. Not the same way. I need to save him.'

'What happened to your mother?'

I look back at Ellen.

'She died, when we were three, in a car accident. That's when Jimmy got his brain damage. But Gep told me the other day that a spirit wanted her, whatever that means. I don't really know how it all happened but he showed me a photo.' I shake my head and stare up at the ceiling for a moment, trying to stop the damn water that seems to want to leak out of them. 'It sounds totally weird…it is weird… but there's this one photo, with Mum and Gep and Jimmy and me. And my mum's image has faded so much it's almost like she was never there, even though the rest of the photo is okay. And now Jimmy's image is fading too.'

This time a tear does leak out. Just one. Down my cheek like an explorer on a solo expedition. Selti goes to touch me but I pull away. Because if I let her, I don't know if I'll be able to hold myself together. I do a half grimace, half smile as way of apology and she gives me a small nod, like she understands.

Ellen is shaking her head. 'It sounds like your step-father is mixed up in some quite dark magic.'

I nod and then shrug, like I can't make up my mind. I mean, I always thought he was doing some crappy things but I'd never really thought about it being dark magic. I've never really thought about it *being* magic until last week.

'Can you help, Mum? Do you understand any of this?' Selti's voice is soft but I hold my breath at her question, waiting for her mum's answer.

She frowns. 'Perhaps. You said your step-father thought the book might be a help?' I nod. 'Well, that might be a place to start. I'll have a look through it, see if I can find anything out.'

The pressure around my rib cage loosens off slightly. To have someone else offer to help – someone else who probably has a better understanding of all this crap; someone who I can probably trust – is amazing.

I nod, a small one, trying not to overplay how great it is. Just in case she can't help…

She picks up the book from the table and starts to flick through the pages, like she knows what she's looking for. Selti and I sit there, watching her, not saying anything, until finally Ellen looks back at us, a frown on her face.

'Why don't you two leave me to this? Go outside. Perhaps Selti can help you with the use of your powers, since you've only newly come into them.'

Selti nods at me and doesn't say anything about yesterday so maybe it's good I didn't mention it earlier. Her hand is warm in mine when she leads me outside, to the table I sat at with her dad.

'Did the herbs do anything?'

I shrug. 'I don't know really. He said he felt a bit better but I don't know that he believes in them. I think the stone had an effect but maybe it was both.'

She frowns. 'What stone?'

I forgot I hadn't told her all of that. 'Gep had this stone. It felt different. Warm without being warm. And yesterday, before I came to see you, I put…I don't know, energy, I guess… into it for Jimmy, hoping it might help him.'

She nods. 'Okay. How did you put your energy into it?'

I shrug. 'I don't know. I sort of pushed it in until I couldn't push anymore. It sort of felt like it was just trickling in but Fox said I'd put a lot in it.'

The shock on her face is easy to see and she takes my hand, gripping it.

'Don't do that anymore. You can't. Promise me!'

'Sure. Okay. Okay. I won't. I promise.'

Her grip loosens a bit and she nods. 'Sorry. But it's dangerous. Really dangerous. If you don't have safeguards in place you could drain all your energy. You could die. That's why you must have been so tired yesterday.'

I swallow hard, feeling my pulse jump into my throat. Shit. That's what I get for mucking around with things I know crap all about.

'Okay. It didn't work so well anyway. Jimmy wasn't great this morning so it didn't even last one day.'

She frowns at me. 'That can't be right. If you put that much energy into the stone, it should've lasted him for ages.'

My heart rate jumps up another notch. 'Do you think Gep was telling the truth then? Do you think a spirit's draining Jimmy?'

'I didn't see a spirit on him last week at school.' She bites her lower lip as she thinks. 'And if you say you pushed it out of him… maybe Mum will find something.'

I nod. But I can't say anything for the moment because if I open my mouth, it's going to rush out of me – all this emotion I'm trying to hold in. Rage towards Gep who's the reason we're all in this fucking mess to start with; worry and frustration for Jimmy and probably guilt as well. Guilt that I have this power and still can't keep him safe.

'Tell me about your power. How does it feel?'

I go to shrug and stop myself. That's not going to help and I need to understand my power if I'm going to help Jimmy. I close my eyes, trying to focus on it.

'It's… warm, I guess. Like I've been in the sun except it's inside me. And it moves. Sometimes it's slow, sometimes it's faster.'

She nods, like that makes sense.

'Can you make it move?'

'I don't know. I guess I did when I put the energy into the stone for Jimmy. But it was hard.'

'When you pushed the spirit out, how did you do it?'

'I ...pulled my power to me, like tensing a muscle, and then pushed it. Pushed it out.'

'Good. And how were you after you did it? Pushed it out?'

'Tired. Really tired.'

Selti nods. 'That's what happens. Whatever you do, there'll be an equal reaction. Using heaps of energy will make you tired. The more you use, the tireder you'll be.'

'And how do I get it back? The energy?'

She laughs. 'Sleep helps. Eating. Being out in nature – standing barefoot in the grass, swimming in a natural water flow. It helps to restore you.'

'So how come Gep never seems to be tired when he does something?'

'I don't know. If he uses dark magic then perhaps he gets it from there. Negative spells create negative reactions for the person casting them though.'

'That probably explains how he gets off on the power from the ritual. It's like he needs it. Like a drug.'

She touches my face. 'It must suck to live with that.'

I lean into her hand, the feel of her skin on mine reminding me that not all my life is totally crap.

'I don't want to be like him.' My voice is so quiet it's a wonder she can actually hear the words. But I want her to know. I want her to understand that just because I've been around Gep for most of my life, I'm not like him.

'I know.'

She's looking at me – her brown eyes wide open, serious, trusting. And I see her. I see the freckles on her nose, the different colours of brown in her eyes, the different shades of pink on her lips. And then she's kissing me. Wanting to, even though she knows everything about me and this pathetic life that's somehow been mine. It makes me feel stronger, better, to know she still wants to be here, with me. She leans into me, letting me take her weight, holding her…

That's probably why her mum's shout, telling us to stop, striding out onto the veranda, crushes me like a coke can being stomped on. Making me remember I'm not good enough, even if Selti thinks I am. She stands beside Selti, the book clutched to her chest like a shield, eyes narrowed.

'What did you do? Just then?' Her voice is higher now. Worried. Panicked almost. My heart races in sympathy. Or maybe with its own fear. Christ, what's her problem?

'Nothing. I didn't do anything!'

'Mum, what's going on?' Selti doesn't seem anymore clued in than I am.

'What did you do to her?'

She's looking at me like I'm a psycho killer or something. I look at Selti and then back to Ellen. I don't know what the hell she's talking about. Absolutely. No. Freaking. Idea.

'Nothing. I swear!'

I go to take Selti's hand again, not even thinking about it, only wanting her touch but Ellen holds up her hand up.

'Don't touch her!'

CHAPTER 32

Selti takes a step back from me. Slowly. Like she doesn't want her mum to freak out again. It makes my heart clench but I don't say anything. I'm watching Ellen, whose eyes are flicking between the two of us.

'What's wrong?' Selti's voice is constrained, like she can't take any more surprises. Like I've thrown her enough already.

But Ellen doesn't answer her. She's still looking at me.

'You told me you hadn't developed your powers. That they were new!'

The accusation is back in her voice.

'What? I haven't developed anything. Truly, I haven't! I've only realised I've got my own bloody powers in the last week. I told you, I used them to push the spirit out of Jimmy. But that's it. And then my brother, who can see powers or something, he said he could see mine. That's all.'

'So, before you came here, to our town, you didn't have any access to your powers?'

I feel like this is a trick question except I don't know what to say to make sure I'm safe. Or to make sure Selti's safe. I look at her, hoping she'll help in working out what her mum's looking for, but she's frowning, looking at the ground. I look back at Ellen. Her eyes are tight around the corners.

'No. I don't think so. I mean, not that I can think of.'

And yet, as I say it, I think of Jimmy. And about what he said I did after the car accident. But that can't be true. Not if I haven't done anything since then. Can it?

She looks at her daughter.

'Selti?'

She shakes her head, understanding the unspoken question even if I don't get it.

'I hadn't seen anything that made me think he had powers. Not till probably a week ago. We were in the park and Penn glowed. I think that's when his powers came in.'

'You glowed?' It feels like her mum is only just keeping it together. Like she's trying really hard not to lose her shit. My internal radar, the one that's kept me safe all my life, is telling me to get the hell out of here. But I stay where I am for probably the first time ever. I can't run away from this. I need to stay. For Jimmy. And for Selti. And probably for me too. I nod.

'What happened when the glow began? What were you doing?'

I see the redness of Selti's cheeks and know mine aren't any better. But there's no way I'm saying anything. This is up to Selti.

'We kissed. For the first time.' Her voice is louder, like she's trying to pretend she isn't embarrassed to say it.

Ellen's mouth tightens this time, as if it's trying to be the perfect match for her eyes.

'That's what I was afraid of.'

Well, shit. I know I'm probably not who they were dreaming for as the perfect match for their daughter but she doesn't need to be so blunt about it! I have a bad enough time wondering why the hell Selti's interested in someone like me most of the time already without a comment like that! I struggle not to tell her to get stuffed.

'Mum!' Selti's voice holds the same level of outrage. It makes me feel a bit better.

'I don't mean it like that.' She looks at me with what I think is an apology in her eyes. I decide to give her the benefit of the doubt. 'I don't know how much Selti's told you of what we do but we're Wiccan. Earth witches. And energy is important. Energy and it's balance.'

I nod. That sort of sounds like what Selti was telling me. But hell, I'd probably nod anyway.

She takes a deep breath. 'And one of the powers I have is to be able to…see people's energy aura, and particularly the transfer of energy between people. That's why the book was so important to us – why we bought it even though it cost a small fortune. When you two kissed there was a transfer of energy – you muddied Selti's aura. Started to drain her.'

Selti's frowning at her. 'What do you mean?'

'I mean, when you touch each other, Penn seems to take your energy. I suspect it happens when he's feeling emotional, so it mustn't happen all the time. I didn't see it the other day when he was here. He probably uses it to stabilise himself when he's feeling strong emotions.'

I step back, moving away from her. Jesus!

'What are you talking about? I don't do that!'

Because I can't be. That's so frigging wrong. Evil, almost. Like Gep. And I love Selti. But then my traitorous mind flicks to the times when being with her, close to her, touching her, has made me feel better. Has made me feel…stable. Just like Ellen said.

I shake my head.

'That can't be right. I wouldn't do that.'

Ellen takes a deep breath. 'The fact that you're saying that makes me feel slightly better. It *is* happening but I'm guessing you're not doing it on purpose.'

'I wouldn't do that.' I'm repeating myself, I know, but I can't wrap my head around the fact that she thinks I'd do this. To Selti.

'Why is it happening? Why with me?'

I'm glad Selti has it together enough to ask logical questions. Ones I probably need the answers to.

'I don't know,' she says. 'But I'm hoping the book will tell me.'

CHAPTER 33

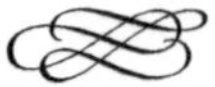

Gep's waiting for me when I get home. It seems like a lifetime ago that I rang him – not just this morning – and my head is teeming so much with everything that's happened today I'd almost forgotten I told him I'd go.

'Did you get it?'

For a second, I don't know what to tell him. Do I tell him yes and hope that if I give it to him, I can trust him, or do I rely on Ellen and Selti now…and hope they can help? His eyes narrow as he watches me and I know I have no choice. If he figures out I'm lying, he might still take it out on Jimmy, no matter how weak he is.

'No, I didn't get it but I was able to photograph all the pages.'

He stands up and stalks around the table towards me. I don't step back from him.

'What do you mean you didn't get it?'

There's no way I'm telling him about Selti and her mum. No freaking way. Because I don't know what he'll do if he knows about them. And that scares me more than anything.

'I'm not stealing anymore. I'm sick of it. This stuff belongs to people.'

He leans in closer, his breath in my face.

'And yet, you thought it was okay to steal from me.'

My heart thuds deep in my chest, like it knows we're in trouble.

'What?'

'I saw the stone. The one you took from me.'

I shrug, trying to not show him how scared I am.

'So what? I stole it in the first place. I figured it was part mine as well.'

He puts his hand against my arm and I wait for the burn but it doesn't come. I don't know if that means his power still isn't back or if he's making the choice not to use it on me. His fingers dig into my skin instead.

'None of it's yours. None of it. Remember that, you little shit.'

I shrug his grip off. 'Do you want the photos or not?'

'I want the book.' It's as if his growl makes my blood vibrate and for the first time I can feel my power rearing up, wanting to match him. I hold on to it, pulling it back. I won't be like him. I refuse to be like the man I despise with every fibre of my being.

'Well go and steal it yourself.'

I push past him, walking towards Jimmy's room.

'Penn!'

I stop and turn, staring at him.

'Give me the fucking photos.'

'I'll transfer the photos to your phone.'

'Just give me your phone.'

'No.' I stand tall, waiting for him to retaliate but he only sneers at me.

'What are you hiding? I don't want to read any idiotic love texts between you and some slut. I just want the book.'

I struggle not to respond. I know he's just throwing words around, hoping something will stick and make me explode. I know he doesn't know about Selti. I know it…

'I'm not hiding anything. But you're not getting my phone.'

He grunts at me before rolling his eyes and heading for his room. I try not to let my mouth hang open. Are you kidding me? That's it? My head can't quite believe it – or trust it.

Jimmy's still lying on his bed when I go in but at least he's awake this time.

'Hey,' he says, 'what was that about?'

'I got the book. From Selti. Or I got photos of it anyway.'

The relief on his face is easy to see.

'Do you think it'll help?'

'Yeah, course it will.' I hope. Not that I say that. 'Selti and her mum came home when I was there.'

'Shit. What happened?'

'I told them. Told them about everything. Selti's mum, Ellen… well, she thinks she can help. She's going to get some info for us. She says Gep's type of magic is dark magic. That it's evil.'

His eyes go wide as he listens to me.

'Did you think she will? Be able to help, I mean?'

'I think so. Did you hear what I said about Gep?'

He nods. 'That can't be right though. Gep's not evil. There's some good in him.'

'Jesus, I can't believe after all he's done to us that you're still defending him.'

'I'm not. I'm only saying he's not totally bad. There's still some good in him.'

I roll my eyes. 'Whatever.'

'When does Selti's mum think she'll have the information?'

'Tomorrow afternoon. I'm going back after school. So, you have to hang on, okay?'

He nods but I can see the fear in his eyes anyway.

CHAPTER 34

I walk home with Selti the next afternoon. It actually feels weird to go back after breaking in yesterday. There's a big part of me that can't believe I got away with this – with getting the contents of the book and still being able to be with Selti. And now I've got extra allies too.

And I don't have to pretend anymore. They know it all.

Ellen is waiting for us in the kitchen when we go in, glasses of iced tea on the bench for us, like a real Mum. She has the book in her hands.

'What did you find out?' Selti sits down on the stool but I can't sit. I try not to pace but it's hard.

'Well.' She draws out the word as she puts the book carefully on the bench. 'I believe I've found the reason Penn can affect your aura and therefore use your energy.'

I hold my breath, hoping the reason's not too crap. Hoping it doesn't make me a bad person that means I'll have to stay away, for her own good.

'You two obviously have...a connection. Sometimes it can happen, especially when one of the two has empathic abilities, which we know you do Selti. And when there is that connection, it can be very strong. So strong that one can take energy from the other to help do things like centre themselves.'

'And can we stop it?'

'Absolutely.' She holds out a bag like the one Selti gave me yesterday. 'I've made you a bag, Selti, based on your own strengths. This should help you to be able to withstand any change from Penn. And Penn, you need to be aware of it. You can stop it if you are aware and make the choice not to.'

'As easy as that?'

She frowns at me. 'Magic is a reflection of the purpose you put into doing it. You've told me you don't want to do it to Selti…' She waits for my response and I nod. 'Therefore, take action not to. But I can also teach you a blocking technique, Selti, just in case Penn isn't aware he's doing it.'

I smile at Selti and she grins back at me. 'Told you she was good.'

'And what about Jimmy?'

'Your brother and what's happening to him is more compli-cated. Largely because I'm not sure what's acting on him – what's causing him to fade. A spell will keep on having an impact unless there's a spell to counteract it. You said there was a spirit who took possession of him?'

I nod. 'But I pushed it out. I'm pretty sure it's not there anymore.'

Selti sits forward. 'I could go see him. See if I can see a spirit around him. Maybe it's not in him but it's still having an effect.' Ellen is nodding at her words but I'm shaking my head like I'm trying hard to shake it off my neck.

'No way. You're not coming to the house. I'm not letting Gep anywhere near you.'

Her mum purses her lips. 'You do have a point. It's not some-thing I'd like either. Is there a way to bring your brother here?'

I shake my head again. 'He's in a wheelchair and I don't think he'd have the energy to make it this far and back again.'

'I can understand that.' Ellen tucks the hair behind her ears, staring at the book for a moment. 'Is there a place outside of your house where we can come and see him? Somewhere where you step-father won't see us or know what we're doing?'

I frown, trying to get my mind to work. 'We're on Tumbler Street and there's a creek down the back of our place. I could probably get him down there.'

'Perfect. I know exactly where you mean. I used to swim in that creek as a girl. The sun and the water will no doubt do him the world of good as well.' She claps her hand together. 'How soon would you like us there?'

'Give me half an hour.'

CHAPTER 35

$\mathcal{I}$ try and sneak in but there's not much chance of that
with the uneven floor boards all over the house. Kat
and Fox are in the lounge room watching TV and look up as I
come in.

'Where's Gep?' I mouth the words, and while Kat squints like
he can't work out what I'm doing, Fox sits forward.

'He's in his room.' His voice is quiet. 'He took the stone off
Jimmy.'

'Christ! So much for caring for him.' I want to punch something although that's not going to help. But the decision not to
give Gep the book feels more and more like a better idea because
I don't trust that he'll do anything to help. I don't trust him at all.
'I have to take Jimmy down the back yard. I'll tell you later. Keep
a watch out for me.'

Fox nods and so does Kat, eyes wide. I can see his need to ask
questions all over his face so I head off before he gets the chance
to start. Jimmy's still in bed. Four days running. Adrenalin,
fuelled by fear, hits my body like a flash flood. At least he's awake.

'Hey. How was school?'

I put my finger in front of my lips.

'I need to take you down the back, to the creek. Selti and her mum are there. Trust me?'

He nods but when I go to pick him up out of bed, he can't help the groan that escapes. His body is so stiff it takes a few minutes for him to be able to relax in my arms so that's he's not like carrying a board and he's panting by the time his spasming stops.

'You okay to go?'

He nods but he doesn't open his eyes again and I move as quick as I can, not worrying about the wheelchair. It'll only slow us down and maybe clue Gep into what we're doing. I forgot to factor in the back door though and struggle for a second, trying to open it with two full hands before Kat comes and opens it for me. He doesn't ask any questions, just nods and I smile at him. Seems like everyone can change.

Gep's room is over the other side of the house so I stick close to the hedge, trying to keep as far away as I can. By the time we make it to the creek, Jimmy still hasn't opened his eyes and my arms are shaking so much I'm worried I'm going to drop him. Selti and Ellen aren't there yet so I put him down as softly as I can and lean his back against a tree. We sit there for another couple of minutes in silence before he opens his eyes again.

'That was tough.'

'I know. I'm sorry. But I needed to bring you here so Selti and her mum, Ellen, can see you without Gep knowing.'

'Why?'

'Ellen thinks she can help make you feel better. She does magic but not Gep's type of magic. I trust her. And Selti can see spirits.'

'Spirits? What does spirits have to do with how I'm feeling? I thought you pushed it out of me. I can't feel it.' I can hear the nervousness in his voice and reach over to touch his arm.

'I did. It's not in you.' I think, but I don't say that. 'Selti can see them, even if they're not in you though, and Ellen can see auras so it might give us some answers.'

'What about the book? What about Gep?'

'I gave Gep the photos of the book and if he can help, well, I guess he will.'

'You don't trust him?'

'No. But you know that.'

He nods. 'I just want to feel better.'

And he's willing to do anything. Even trust Gep. Again. Can't say I blame him. I hear a noise behind us and turn to see Selti and Ellen. I stand and wait for them to come over.

'Ellen, this is my brother, Jimmy.'

'Please to meet you Jimmy.'

'Hi,' he says and there's no mistaking the tiredness in his voice. He looks up at Selti. 'Can you see any spirits?'

She shakes her head and sits down next him. 'No, I can't see any.'

It's a relief and a disappointment all at the same time. Because, shit, at least I got the spirit out of him but if it's not a spirit affecting him, what the hell is it...?

I look over at Ellen. She has her lips pursed, looking at Jimmy like he's a piece of art or something. She kneels next to him.

'Jimmy, I know you're feeling tired but can you tell me how else you're feeling?

He sighs. 'Tired is mainly it. But I'm not hungry either. I can't eat. I feel...like I'm not really here.'

Shit! I want to pick him up and run, run, run. Get him away. Although that might not fix it anyway. So, we're stuck. I push my knuckles against the rough bark of the tree, letting it make dints in my skin, letting the pain ground me, keep me here.

Ellen nods. 'I don't know if Penn told you but I see auras. Yours has white and yellow, which I think are primarily your colours – your healthy colours. But they're very hazy at the moment. And there's a lot of grey and brown in there, blocking out the healthy colours.'

'What does that mean?'

'It means that something is blocking your aura. Something is affecting you.'

I suck in a breath. 'Do you know what it is?'

She shakes her head, frowning. 'No, I don't. But there are some things I can do, some things that might help, until we can work it out. Would you be okay with that, Jimmy?'

He nods and for the next half an hour, she does lots of different things. Things with herbs and stones and cleansing, whatever that means. I don't know if it makes any difference, I can't really see a change, but Ellen nods when she's done, obviously happy with what she can see.

'Okay, I've managed to clear some for you. You should start to feel better within the next couple of hours. But I think we might need to do this again.'

'Is there anything I can do?' Anything. Jesus, at this stage I'd be happy to cut myself open and give him my blood if that'd make him better.

Ellen frowns for a moment, thinking. 'There may be, but I'd like to research this a bit more before we start. We don't want any negative consequences for either of you.'

'What are you going to research?'

'It's about the energy transfer,' she said. 'I'm wondering if you can give your brother some of your energy without it having a negative effect on either of you. Something that will give him the energy to be able to get through this and adjust his aura himself.'

'I've already done that.'

'What? How?'

'Through a stone,' said Jimmy. 'He put it in a stone and gave it to me. I told him not to but it did help. A bit.'

Ellen looks at me and shakes her head. 'That's pretty advanced magic. And dangerous. Especially when you don't know what you're doing.'

I look at Selti. 'Yeah, Selti already made me promise I wouldn't do that again. Not until I know what I'm doing.'

'Idiot,' Jimmy mutters and I can only grin at him. He smiles back but it doesn't quite reach his eyes.

'Yes, please, wait until I've done my research, okay? I'm thinking it will need to be done in a certain way so there aren't negative reactions for either of you.'

I frown. 'Was it dangerous for Jimmy too?'

She tilts her head a little, side to side, like she can't make up her mind. 'It might be. It would affect both of your auras – your energy – perhaps not in a positive way. Please, be patient. I think we've given Jimmy a boost for the moment. We can do the same thing tomorrow if we need to.'

The thought of trying to get Jimmy out of the house again under Gep's nose fills me with dread but if it needs to be done, I'll find a way.

'We'd better get back,' I say. 'Before we're missed.'

Ellen nods. 'Yes, go. We'll see you tomorrow. Jimmy, it was lovely to meet you.'

He smiles at her. The one he has that makes anyone feel on top of the world, even if he feels like shit. 'Thank you. I do feel a bit better.'

Selti comes over and rubs my arm. 'Try not to worry. It'll be okay. See you tomorrow?'

I nod, even if I don't really believe what she's telling me. She's not the one who's had to live with Gep for sixteen years. They watch me pick Jimmy up and carry him back to the house. I'm pretty sure they're still standing there when we're finally out of sight, which is sort of nice. Like they've got our back.

The door's still open when we walk in. I come up short though, stopping even though Jimmy is heavy in my arms. Because Gep's sitting at the table, and he doesn't look happy.

'Where the fuck do you think you've been?'

CHAPTER 36

'None of your business.'

I keep on walking, expecting him to stop us, stand in front of us, do the burn – assert his dominance – but he doesn't. He sits there, watching us as I walk past. I take Jimmy into his room and put him back on his bed. He's looking a bit better, although I don't know if that's true or if that's what I want to believe so bad I'm making things up in my head.

He sighs when I put the pillows under his head a bit more.

'Do you think I'll be able to go to school tomorrow?'

'Jeez, man, you must be the only kid who actually misses being at school.' It's a standard joke between us but he doesn't laugh this time. He just looks at me and it's my turn to sigh. 'I don't know. Maybe. Or maybe you should take it easy again and we'll see what Ellen can do tomorrow.'

He nods but I can see his eyes getting glassy and it feels like my ribs are breaking, one by one, making my chest ache, as I watch him fight the tears. It's not fair. Why do all the shitty things happen to him?

'Hey, don't worry. It'll be okay.' An echo of Selti's words. I'm guessing he doesn't believe them any more than I did but he nods at me.

'Sure. It'll be okay. I'm going to sleep for a while.'

'Yep. Sleep. I'll see you in the morning.'

I stop at his door and shut my eyes for a moment, wondering if I'm better off going to my room and avoiding Gep. But I can't take the chance that he'll go in to Jimmy and...do something just to put me in my place. I mean, I don't think he would – how sadistic could he be? – but history has shown me that what I think is ethical doesn't really apply to Gep a lot of the time. And the longer we've been with him, the less and less of those good moments we're getting. So, I head back to the kitchen. Ready for battle.

He's still sitting there and turns his head to look at me as I walk in the room. The stone I took from the box is on the table in front of him. I don't say anything, waiting for him to talk first.

'What did you do to it?'

Christ, he knows. Of course he does. But there was this little stupid part of me that thought maybe I could get away with it. It's that little, stupid part that answers.

'Nothing. I thought maybe it would help. Since it was one of the things you made us take.'

'Bullshit. I can feel it. I can smell it. What. Did. You. Do?'

'Jesus, what's your problem? You can smell it? That's fucking weird.'

Stalling. Hoping he'll just leave it. My mouth is suddenly dry and I lick my lips, trying to get some moisture happening.

He stands up, coming around the table to me, standing so far into my personal space I can see the individual hairs in his five o'clock shadow.

'Don't fuck with me, boy. I know you've been using your powers. I can *feel* it. You've been using them, trying to save him, but it hasn't worked, has it? Has it!'

His spit is on my face from his scream but I refuse to wipe it away. I refuse to give him that. I stare at him, expression neutral. Well, as neutral as I can make it.

He watches me for a second, breathing heavy, and then takes a step back and another. And another. And then he thumps down in the chair, elbows on the table, his palms pressing into his eyes. He groans and it sounds like he's in pain. Good, I hope he is. Still I say nothing. Finally, he looks up at me.

'I need you to help me save him. I need your power.'

'No.'

'What do you mean no? Don't you want to save him? Your own brother. Don't you love him?'

It's my turn to walk over to him and I lean on the table, getting down into his face.

'Don't you dare ask me about love. You don't love anybody. You never did. Even my mum. It's all about power for you. It always has been. And I won't let you use me or Jimmy just to get your frigging fix. No more.'

And then I turn and walk away. Before I do something I might regret; something that will make me like him. I'm only surprised he doesn't follow me.

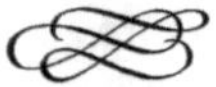

It feels a bit like ground hog day when I go to check on Jimmy the next morning. He still doesn't want to go to school. But at least he doesn't seem as tired. And he's happy to have some breakfast, even if it's not enough to keep a sparrow alive. It's a start. I wish I could see the auras like Ellen. Then I'd know for certain that he was doing okay and it wasn't just a false hope.

I stand at the drawer where the photo album is, scared to open it and see. Scared this might all be wishful thinking and that Jimmy's image might be even more faded. But I can't move away either. So, I stand there, hands by my side, looking at the drawer like it's my mortal enemy.

Eventually, Fox comes over and looks at me for a second before opening the drawer and getting the book out. I take it from him but my hands are shaking and I feel like I'm going to throw up. Kat comes over to join us. I don't know where Gep is. Usually that'd make me worried but I can't concentrate on him at the moment. One shitty thing at a time.

'Let me do it.' Kat takes the album from me after it becomes clear I'm too much of a coward. He opens the book so frigging slowly I almost rip it from him. But then, the page is open and we can all see it.

'It hasn't changed.' I can't stop the disappointment in my voice. I was certain he was getting better. Certain!

'But that means he's not getting worse,' says Kat. 'He hasn't faded more.'

I nod. Yes, at least it means that. That's what I need to hold on to. And hopefully, if Ellen can help him more this afternoon, then maybe… maybe I can save him and we won't need to place our trust in Gep.

'We better get moving,' Fox says and I nod. I want to go to school. I want to see Selti and talk to her about the picture, and about Jimmy eating, and work out how I'm going to get Jimmy to them this afternoon. And, to be honest, I just want to see her.

She's waiting for us at the front gate and Fox nods at her before heading into school.

'Hey Selti,' Kat says.

'Hey Kat. How are you?'

I almost groan – asking a question like that of Kat could mean we'd be stuck here for hours – but, in a way, I don't mind either. I love that Kat is so…optimistic. I don't know I would have done without him over the last couple of days.

'I'm really good. I'm going motorbike riding with Jay this afternoon. I can't wait for that. It should be excellent. He's got a Yamaha TT-R125 and he's going to let me have a go. I've never been on one as big as that before.'

Selti laughs. 'Well, you'd better be careful then.'

He laughs with her. 'Yeah, I will be. See you Selti.'

'See you Kat.' She turns to me then and smiles a smile that feels like it's just for me.

'Hey.'

'Hey back at you.' I tuck a strand of the blue hair that I now love behind her ear.

'How's Jimmy?'

'He ate this morning but he still wasn't strong enough to come today. The photo hasn't faded anymore though, so that's something.'

When I say it out loud, it does give me a bit of hope. It's a start.

'That's great.'

'Can your mum come back this afternoon?'

She nods. 'Of course. She was up all night, reading everything, trying to work out what's interfering with Jimmy's aura in the first place.'

'Did she find anything?'

'No not yet.' Selti must see my face because she takes me hand. 'She will though. Don't worry.'

I nod. It's easy to say that. Harder to follow through.

The morning seems to fly by and it's lunch before I know it. I sit with Selti, of course, and it surprises me a bit when Rory and Alex come over and sit with us too. Selti raises her eyebrows but doesn't say anything.

Alex nods at me. 'Training this afternoon?'

Shit. I forgot it was Wednesday. 'Crap. I won't be able to make it. Jimmy has an appointment this afternoon and I need to go with him.'

'It's the finals next week. If you don't come, you might not get to play.'

'Yeah. Whatever happens. It'd be good to play but...' I shrug. 'You know, my brother needs me.'

Alex nods. 'Sure. I can respect that.'

Rory leans in. 'Can't your dad take him?'

I shake my head but don't say anything else. I learnt a long time ago that the more you say, the more you can get caught out on. Seems like Selti's the only one I can be honest with.

'So, Selti, how are you?'

Selti gives Alex a cool look. 'I'm good Alex. How about you?'

'Ah, you know. Basketball, working at the shop. How's your mum?'

It seems like an innocent question but there's an underlying current there, chucking out sparks, like it's trying to start a fire.

'Yeah,' Rory says with a grin. 'How's your mum?'

And he actually sniggers. Sniggers! Like a frigging eight-year-old. I can feel Selti's hand get tense in mine, even though you'd never know it by looking at her face.

'She's awesome, guys. Hasn't asked the Goddess for any favours lately but you know…there's always that possibility if she needs it.'

I can see Rory physically swallow. As if he's scared. What an idiot! I can't believe they've known Selti their whole lives and yet know so little about her or her family. The fact that they don't know how awesome she is and what a great person her mum is. Their loss, my gain, I guess. But it sucks that she has to put up with them being morons.

'Yeah,' I say, 'when she did that spell over the weekend; man, that was something to see.'

Rory looks at me like his eyes are about to pop out of their sockets but Alex is keeping it cool.

'You've met her, then? You know she's a witch?'

'Wiccan. But, yep. So?'

There's silence for a moment…the silence you see in the western movies, crickets in the background, before Alex nods.

'Okay then.' And that seems to be it. I wonder what reaction they'd expected. Whether they thought Selti had kept it secret from me and that, once I found out, I'd be out of there. Shows they don't know either of us – not that I've really given them a chance.

Selti squeezes my hand and I know I've done the right thing. For once. Sort of makes me want to puff my chest out. Not that I would. Well, only in my head. We walk together to biology and everyone's doing a double take. For once, I have no desire to hide anything. I'm with Selti and I'm happy for everyone to know it. Everyone but Gep.

We sit at the front. Biology's never been one of my favourite subjects but I can tell Selti enjoys it. She leans forward, taking lots of notes…and I can't help but tune out. It's nice to watch her though, even if she turns to me half way through, laughing and tells me to stop it and pay attention.

Maybe it's because I'm actually listening at that moment that it happens. The teacher's going on and on about parasites and parasitoids – a parasite that ends up killing its host, using it all up, when it hits me like a lump of wood to the head. A thought that storms my brain, making it hard for me to breathe, to see, to function.

Gep. It's Gep! Gep who says he loved my mum so much but that she faded; started using drugs. It wasn't a spirit that wanted her. It was Gep, taking from her, influencing her aura, taking her energy like Selti's mum said I was taking her daughter's. Jesus! Being a fucking parasitoid to my mum, no matter that it was killing her. Knowing it's all about the power for him.

My chest is aching, so tight it feels like my lungs can't expand, and I put my fist against it, pushing, pushing, trying to breath. Because that's what he's doing to Jimmy. Maybe even now. Right now. Taking Jimmy's energy like a frigging tick sucking blood. And feeding off the energy I've been giving Jimmy to keep him going. That's why the stone didn't last! He took it; used it.

I stand up so fast the chair falls backward and the whole class turns to look at me. I don't care. I don't care! I need to get out of here. I need to go to Jimmy and stop Gep. Stop him before he kills the one person I've loved my whole life.

Shit. Oh shit! I'm going to throw up. Right here. All over the class room floor. I swallow hard and turn, ready to run. But not away this time. Back to the house, to where Gep is using Jimmy to feed his own pathetic, moronic, *evil* need for power, slowly but surely, leaching the energy out of him until there'll be nothing more for him. Until he's dead. That's all I can picture: Jimmy in bed, eyes open and staring, skin cold, lost to me forever because I didn't leave now. Leave now and do something. Anything. Kill Gep, take Jimmy. Anything.

'Sorry, feeling sick,' I mumble to the teacher before I rush out of the room, not even looking at Selti, looking at the door instead, the way out...

I stumble out and take a breath, confused for a second over what to do. Get my bag? Just go? Go. Leave. Now. And I don't care what happens. I don't care if I get expelled. None of it matters. And I start to run.

CHAPTER 38

J'm half way home before I have to stop, trying to suck in the air my body is telling me it needs. I lean forward, hands on my knees, blood pounding so loudly in my ears it's all I can hear for a moment.

A car coming up behind me has me spinning. I don't know why – except maybe the thought of Gep and going up against him already has my body feeling like it's running on a higher speed, like it's warming itself up.

I see a flash of blue through the windscreen of the car and I know it's Selti. Of course. Coming to help. And even though there's a part of me – a really selfish part – that wants her here, there's a saner side which still doesn't want her anywhere near Gep. Because if anything happened to her…

She gets out and turns to thank the person in the car – Emma, who gives me a nod before turning around and heading back to school. Leaving Selti here. The expression on her face doesn't leave me with much hope that she's going to go back to safety.

'What's happened?'

'Nothing. It's nothing. Just go back, okay?'

'No, Penn. I'm not going back. Not until you tell me what's going on?'

Christ, I don't have time for this!

But I need to tell her. I owe her.

'Gep. It's Gep. He's taking Jimmy's energy; he took Mum's. I know he did. Like I was able to take yours. Except he doesn't stop. He doesn't care. He's going to kill Jimmy, just like he killed Mum.'

I wait for her to tell me I'm crazy, that it couldn't happen, that Jimmy will be okay, but she doesn't. I can see her brain working, filling in the gaps that I didn't say – believing me – and she nods, like she's come to a decision.

'I'm coming with you.'

'What? No! You can't!'

She folds her arms. 'It doesn't matter what you say. I'm coming. You might need help. Even if it's just to get Jimmy out of there.'

And she's got me. I can feel my resolve shaking, splintering…

'You shouldn't. I mean, I'd love to have you with me but…it's not safe. You should go back.'

She starts walking without saying anything else. Walking away from me. Towards the edge of town. Towards my home. I hurry to catch up. Man, she can walk fast when she's angry!

'Selti, come on.'

When I finally catch up with her, the look on her face makes me wonder if I should have. Maybe it would have been smarter to be a coward and walk three steps behind or something.

'Selti…'

'How old am I?'

I don't know where she's going with this. It sounds like a trick question.

'What?' I'm stalling for time and she knows it.

'How old am I?'

'Um…seventeen?'

'Right. And how old are you?'

'Seventeen.'

I think I know where this is going now. But I'm not going to make it easy for her.

'And do you think I'm smart?'

'Yes.' I can answer that one easily. Smarter than me, at any rate.

'And do you think I'm capable.'

I sigh. 'Yes, but – '

'There aren't any buts. People,' she pushes her finger into my chest when she says this, 'should stop trying to tell me what to do. I'm not a little girl and I'm not easily scared.'

'You should be. Gep is psycho.'

She doesn't even bother turning to look at me this time.

'I'm coming, Penn. Get over it.'

There's this part of me that's jumping up and down with joy at the thought of her being there. I wonder if I'm selfish enough to let it win. One last try…

'But what if you get hurt?'

'What if *you* get hurt?'

Fair point. 'Yeah, but this is my family. Not yours.'

She stops this time. Pulls herself up so quickly it's a wonder she doesn't leave a skid mark on the bitumen. I stop with her, hands shoved into my pockets, waiting to see what she's going to do. Unsure, like I always seem to be with her, the manipulation skills I've built totally useless.

She takes a step forward, close enough to reach up and put her hands around my neck. And then she's on her toes, her lips coming to mine and I dip my head, meeting her half way. My stomach clenches with how she makes me feel – that I'm not alone in this; that she knows everything about my life and still wants to be with me – and my hands go to her waist, lifting her, holding her against me, her arms wrapping tighter around my neck.

It takes a car coming along the road to draw me back and when I put her down, we're both breathless. She touches my face, her thumb tracing the outline of my eyebrow, her hand trailing down my cheek until it cups my face and I lean into it slightly.

Her eyes are serious as she looks at me. 'I love you.'

'You love me?'

She smiles. A shy one, but I can't believe how brave she is. Braver than me to put herself out there like that...to be the first one to say it...risking rejection.

'Yes.'

I take her hand, looking at her fingers rather than at her. And take a deep breath.

'I love you too.'

It's only now that the words are out there that I look up at her. Her eyes are serious again.

'You're important to me. I would hate for you to get hurt. And,' she hesitates, dropping her head and looking down at the stray stones littering the side of the bitumen, before meeting my eyes again. 'And...I sort of feel like that makes me part of your family.'

That sounds so good, so insanely awesome, that it scares me. Stupid. But this is what I've wanted for what feels like my whole life. And all I can think now is what if it goes, what if something happens and I lose it? Lose her? I need to send her home. I need to make sure she's protected.

I go to open my mouth but she beats me to it. 'And don't tell me to go home again. I'm not doing it.'

Damn! How can she know me so well when I'm still clueless with her? But I know when I'm beaten.

So I do the only thing I can. I take her hand.

'Come on then. Let's go get Jimmy.'

CHAPTER 39

We stop at the front door and Selti squeezes my hand. I give her a tight smile.

'Are you okay?' she asks.

I nod. 'Let's do it.'

The floor squeaks at our entrance, like it's telling him we're there. Paranoid much! Jesus.

I circle around through the lounge room and look in Jimmy and Fox's room before making my way to the back of the house. Jimmy's still in his bed, curled up, a grimace on his face, like his muscles are already causing him pain, even before he wakes up. But he looks okay – his skin a better colour. I'm hoping I'm right.

I don't disturb him. I don't want him to hear this. And I don't want him feeling bad if something goes wrong. The last thing he needs is to blame himself and I know he would. Damn conscience always gets him doing things he shouldn't or feeling guilty about things that aren't his to own.

I lead Selti round to the back of the house. Gep is sitting at the kitchen table, all of the artefacts we've stolen in front of him, spread out like a study of all things magic. I glance at my watch, realising that Fox and Kat will be home from school at any moment. Probably a good thing they're not here yet. Maybe I can have it out with Gep without them having to witness it all. They've seen enough already.

He looks up as we stand in the doorway. His glance flicks from mine to Selti's and I can see the slight widening of his eyes, even though he tries to hide it.

'Penn.'

He doesn't say anything about what's on the table but then, I wouldn't expect him to. Not in front of a stranger. I take a deep breath, letting it fill my lungs like I'm trying to build armour over my chest from the inside out. And then I talk, letting the words rush out of me while I still feel like I can say them.

'I know what you did to Mum. And what you're doing to Jimmy. I know you're the one killing him.'

I want it all out – no more secrets, no more bullshitting.

He stays absolutely still. Doesn't even blink. It's unnatural. I'm almost at breaking point when he looks down at the blue stone, holding it in his hand, examining it, like he's thought about what I've said and hasn't deemed it worthy to reply.

'Aren't you going to introduce me to your friend?'

I go to tell him no but Selti beats me to it.

'I'm Selti. And I'm not just his friend, I'm his girlfriend.'

I don't know whether to grin or be shit scared of what he might do with that information. My grimace is probably a bit of both.

He watches her for a few seconds, eyes narrowed, and I want to pull her behind me – block her from his view; protect her. I pull on her hand slightly, trying to get her to move, but it's like she doesn't even notice. She's focused on Gep as much as he's focused on her.

'You're a…witch.'

She nods at him and I wonder how the hell he knows that after meeting her for five seconds, when I had no idea until she told me.

'And what stupidity have you been filling his head with that he comes in here and accuses me of trying to kill one of my sons?'

Even though the question is directed at Selti, I get in first this time.

'She hasn't been filling my head with anything. I know what you're doing. I figured it out myself. And he's not your son. Neither of us are.'

I know I probably shouldn't have added that last bit but I can't help it – he doesn't get to lay claim to us anymore – not when he's doing what he's doing. It's stupid though, like poking a bear with a stick. A really short one. The stick, not the bear.

His eyes latch onto mine, blazing like the burn is happening to him internally. I swallow hard, determined not to step back. Not this time. Not ever again. Even when he stands up and I can feel his power, pushing into me, trying to force me back... or force me to fight. Somehow, he's got it back. And that means he must be using Jimmy again. Sucking him dry...shit, shit, shit!

'I'm going to try and forget you said that.'

I don't know who he thinks he's trying to fool. Selti maybe? He never forgets anything.

'How come you've got your power back? I thought you'd lost it.'

It's not a question. It's a challenge. And he knows it. He pushes his chin up.

'It was obviously a short term thing. Perhaps a repercussion of you using your power the other day when I wasn't prepared for it. But I know now.'

And he's prepared. That's what he leaves unsaid.

And then it clicks into place in my head, like a puzzle finally fitting together. Maybe he's got it wrong. Maybe it wasn't just when I used my power that made him lose his. What if he lost his power when I protected Jimmy from the spirit? What if I didn't only push the spirit out but I pushed Gep's power away from

Jimmy too? Blocked him from taking Jimmy's energy, even if I didn't know what I was doing? Only for a little while. And that's why Jimmy looks a bit better the last couple of days. Not only because Selti and Ellen have been helping but because Gep has only just been able to access it again and Jimmy's been able to…recharge.

And the more I think about it, the more I know I'm right. Gep killed my mum. And he's killing Jimmy.

'I know you're taking Jimmy's energy – using it to make yourself stronger. That's why he's fading. Not for any other reason – not because of the spirit or a curse or anything else. It's because of you. And I'm guessing that's what you did to Mum too. That's what killed her.' I look at him, really look at him, watching for his reaction. Watching for his guilt. 'You killed her. It doesn't matter how much you say you love her. You took all of her energy for yourself until she was dead.'

He bends over the table, his forearms cords of muscle as his whole body becomes tense.

'I would be very careful what you accuse me of.'

His voice is low, controlled, but I know he is anything but. I can see it in his face. I'm done with being careful though. Done with doing what he wants me to do to keep Jimmy safe. It's not working anyway because I've been looking in the wrong area. It turns out that I just need to stop him.

I take a step forward, closer to the table, determined to do whatever I have to do to make him understand that I know what he's doing. And that I'm not scared of him anymore. Well, I am. But I'm trying to bluff. Because I don't *want* to be scared of him. I can't afford to be scared of him. Jimmy's life is on the line.

The sound of the front door opening and of Fox and Kat's voices make me pause. I turn slightly when I hear them stop at the kitchen door. I'm guessing they can feel the tension – it'd be a bit hard to miss and neither of them are stupid.

Kat is the first to talk – trying to smooth things over like he always does – a tentative smile on his face when he looks at Selti.

'Hi Selti.'

'Hi Kat.' Her voice is soft, like she doesn't want anyone to really notice she's here. I don't know if that means she's starting to wonder whether she was having a crazy moment when she said she wanted to come – when she said that she wanted to be part of our family – or if she's just letting me do what I need to do.

'I didn't know you were going to be here this afternoon. I was going to go bike riding but it got cancelled. So it's nice you're here.'

I want to tell him to shut up but Gep has started to move around the table, closer to Selti, and adrenalin is spiking through my system, infecting every organ. I move closer to her too.

'What's going on?' I can hear the tremor in Fox's voice and I feel bad. Bad that they're going to be involved in this, no matter how much I wish they weren't. But that's not going to stop Gep. It never has in the past.

'Gep's killing Jimmy,' I say. 'He's taking his energy and using it to feed his own power. That's why Jimmy's fading. And I think he did the same to my mum.'

There's silence from behind me and I don't need to turn to know they've probably both got their mouths hanging open. Not that I'm going to turn around to check. I'm not game to take my eyes of Gep.

'You don't know what the hell you're talking about,' he says, sneering at me. 'You come into a miniscule amount of power and you think you know everything. I would never hurt her. Never. I loved her!'

I wonder, for a second, whether that might be true. Whether he wasn't really aware of what he did to Mum; what he's doing to Jimmy – after all, I didn't know what I was doing until Selti's mum saw it.

But I've had too many years of his lies to trust in anything he says. Maybe he did love Mum, in some warped way, but power has always been more important to Gep than anything else. Always.

'You might have. Maybe. But you still killed her – stripped her of all her energy until she was so weak she had to use drugs to feel better. Stripped her of all of it until she faded away. And that's what you're doing to Jimmy.'

I can see the anger in his face. It transforms it, turning it into something ugly. Demonic almost.

'I did not kill her!'

I notice he doesn't even mention Jimmy. Bastard. He takes another step towards me, Selti beside him now. I want to tell her to move – to get away from him – but I don't want to draw attention to her either. Shit. I don't know why I bought her...I knew I shouldn't have...or I should have warned her more. Told her everything about him, so she'd know to keep herself away from him – so she'd be more prepared.

Shit, shit, shit. My heart's in my throat. I never knew what that saying meant until now. But it feels like everything's there – heart, stomach, spleen – all of it, crowding in, making it nearly impossible for me to breath. He is so close and my eyes flick to her. It's like I can't help it, even though I know I shouldn't. And he notices. Like he notices everything. His mouth shapes into a smile, warped by the anger still in him.

And he grabs her arm.

I don't hesitate. Don't give him a chance to hurt her. I can't. If something – anything happened to her...

I step forward, my hand on his chest, like I'm about to push him away. And even though my brain doesn't seem to have a clue what it's doing, my body does. I feel my energy – just mine – push into him, burning him like he's burnt all of us in the past, scorching his insides like he's scorched mine hundreds of times.

The shock on his face would be almost comical if it wasn't for the fact that he still has Selti's arm in his hand.

I keep going, keep burning, keep hurting – needing him to let go. When he starts to sink to the floor, his hand falling away from her, and it registers that she's safe… she's okay…she's safe… I jerk back my hand.

That's when I realise what I've done. That's when I realise I'm as bad as this sadist that's pretended to be my dad for the last sixteen years.

And that's when I turn and run.

I run like I'm being chased except I don't know what I'm running from. From myself probably.

My whole body feels like it's on fire by the time I stop. I have no idea where I am. On the edge of the town somewhere. The houses around me are spaced further apart, not as hemmed in as the houses around us, like opening the buttons on your pants after a Christmas day lunch.

I lean over, hands on my knees, trying not to vomit. All I can think is that I'm evil. As evil as Gep.

As corrupted.

I used my power to hurt someone else, even if I didn't know how I was doing it. All that matters is that I didn't stop until he collapsed. Shit. He could even be dead. Not that that would be a bad thing for Jimmy, Fox and Kat. Even for Selti. But it would be bad for me. Big bad. Enormous bad. Going to jail and never seeing my family again bad. Never seeing Selti. Alone. Never mind trying to explain how I killed him.

Shit. Shit!

This can't be happening.

My thoughts are going so fast I can hardly keep up, hardly make sense of them. What have I done?

And how can I be around anyone now. Jimmy. The boys. Selti. My chest aches with the thought of having to stay away but I can't chance it. What happens next time I get angry – will I do the burn on one of them? Will the power make me do it – control me – like the more it happens, the harder it is to control? Like I've let loose a monster that's been living in me but isn't really part of who I am. Of who I want to be. Maybe that's what happened to Gep. Maybe that's how he started. And now I'm on the same path. Except I know…know with every part of me…that it's not a road trip I want to take.

The words the spirit said ricochet in my head – that you can't use the power without consequences. And that's what I've done. Used the power, called it to me, even if I didn't know how. And now I have to face the consequences.

I need to go. Disappear. Get away from them so I can't hurt them like Gep's hurt us over the years. Suddenly, I feel like I understand those moments when he seemed a bit more like a normal human being. And I don't want to understand that. I don't want to imagine that I'm going to end up like him – only partially Penn while the rest of me wants the power and will doing anything to get it. Even taking it from people I love.

Staying here isn't an option. Not now. I need to prove I love my brother as much as I say I do.

I can feel a sob forming in my throat and swallow it back down. If I give in to it, I'll be lost and I'll go back because that's what I really want. I want to be back there…with my family. Keeping them safe.

It's that thought that has my legs buckling, sending me to my knees, the rocks on the road digging into my skin, not that I really notice them. Holy shit, what if they're not safe? What if Gep's woken up, if they haven't got away, if he's hurting them now, taking it out on them!

What if I've left Jimmy vulnerable to him? Who's going to keep him safe? Selti? Her mum?

I stand again, trying to stop the panic that's bubbling inside me, trying to think logically…trying to make the right decisions. Because if I go back, I'm not going to be able to leave. I know it. I won't be strong enough to do this again.

My hands are shaking and I lace them together on top of my head. God, if anyone is watching me now they're going to wonder what the hell I'm doing.

I can still feel the remains of the power I used on Gep coursing through me. It makes me feel strong inside, like there's something warming my blood; fire inside my soul.

I hate it.

I don't want it.

And yet, my body seems to like it.

Shit!

I'll go back then. Just to check on them. Just to see if they're safe. But I won't let them see me…not unless I need to get them away from Gep. I'll sneak back – one thing I've had a lot of practice at – and check they're okay and then go. I can make that sacrifice.

I can!

I shut my eyes, trying to shut out the fact that my heart doesn't want to agree with me, and then whirl around when I hear my name called. Whirl around and take a step back from Kat and Selti.

They're safe, at least. And if they are, then Jimmy probably is too. And now they all know what Gep's doing, they can keep him that way. I feel my body sag a bit, relief and regret all parcelled up together. Because that means I can't go back now. There's no need.

Kat's got his hands out like he's trying to show me he won't hurt me. If only that's what I was actually worried about. My eyes flick to Selti – she's watching me, eyes narrowed, hair moving gently in the soft breeze. Looking at her makes me want her so badly I take another step back. Because the power's responding to her too. Flaring up like it can sense she's near. Like it wants her. Kat's hands fall to his side as I do.

'What are you doing here?'

It comes out harsh – angry. Not that I am. I'm scared but it's probably better they don't know that. Better if they think I'm a bastard they shouldn't be around.

They look at each other, like they have a secret message passing between them, which just serves to piss me off. I don't want to see them being friends – having secrets. Not now.

'Just go!' The words are rough in my mouth, like my tongue's coated with sandpaper.

Kat takes a deep breath. 'We want you to come back. Come home.'

I'm shaking my head before he's even finished talking.

'No. I can't. You saw what I did. You have to go.'

'You aren't Gep, Penn.'

Selti's voice is firm, like she has all the facts behind her. But she doesn't. She can't begin to understand what our life's been like, waiting for Gep to snap and hurt us again and again and again. And she doesn't know how tempting that feeling of power is. How much I want to use it again, now I've felt what it's like. How much I want to hurt him for what he'd done to Mum. For what he's doing to Jimmy.

'You don't know…' My words falter and I try again. 'I did that back there. Me. No one forced me to. I was angry – I thought he was going to hurt you. So I hurt him first. I did it. I used my power to hurt someone else. Just like he does.'

'You saved me.'

I stare at her for a second, wanting to believe her, wanting to think I did it for all the right reasons. But I can still feel the power in me, struggling to get free – to claim me.

'I need to go. Before I hurt somebody else. One of you. Or Jimmy.'

Because that can never happen. Never. I'm not willing to take that chance.

'You're not going to hurt anyone else.'

'You don't know that.'

Kat takes a step towards me.

'But *I* do. You've been there my whole life, sharing a room with me most of the time. I know you'd never hurt us – all you do is protect us over and over, even when you don't really want to. What happened back there with Gep…that was different. He doesn't think twice about hurting one of us. And I was afraid he was going to hurt Selti too. He had that look on his face. There wasn't anything I could do though. But you could. You protected her.'

I take a trembling breath in. This is so unlike Kat. The Kat I've known the whole of his life doesn't like to believe there's bad in anyone. Gep especially. He's always got his rose coloured glasses on, believing the best, even when it's so painfully obvious that that's not true. It's something I've never been able to understand.

I look at Selti and she's nodding.

'It's true. I haven't known you for as long as Kat has but I do know you're not a bad person. You're good – one of the most protective people I know. And I'm not afraid of you, Penn.'

'You should be. I'm not who you think I am. It's all an act.' I need to make her leave. Protect herself from me, rather than moving closer like she is. 'I don't even love you.'

That makes her stop and I almost take the words back. But I don't. I can't. I need to convince her they're true.

'I don't believe you.'

'That just shows what a good liar I am.'

'Stop it. You're not going to convince me. I know you're scared of hurting someone. But you won't. You won't!'

It sounds like she's trying to convince herself. I don't say anything and I can see the frustration flit across her face, like she wants to hit me. She should. Hit me and hate me.

And leave.

I ignore the need to take in a shuddering breath. This blank face – this nothing boy – this is who I know how to be. This is what I've done my whole life. And I can lie again.

'I know you're not a bad person, no matter what you say. If you were, you'd be trying to use my energy anyway, even though Mum showed us how to stop it happening. Or use Kat or Fox's energy. Or Jimmy's.'

'I would never do that!' The words spill out of my mouth before I can stop them.

Selti moves forward, standing right in front of me, and puts her hand on my chest. I can feel the warmth of her through my shirt. Feel her melting me, even though I shouldn't let her. But I can't step back. My legs aren't listening to me.

'I know you wouldn't. That's how I know I'm right.'

She reaches her other hand up, wrapping it around the back of my neck, pulling me forward. I don't resist, even though my brain is screaming at me to just turn. Turn and run.

And then her lips are on mine. At least I have enough wits about me not to kiss her back. At least I can do that for her.

'I love you,' she says and leaves another kiss on my lips.

'I love you.' And I can hear the tears in her voice before I see them in her eyes.

'I love you, Penn.'

And I don't care then. I am a totally selfish being, it seems. Because I'm kissing her back. Kissing her like I love her, even though I told her I didn't. Kissing her like she is the only thing that's going to keep me safe, even though I know that's not true.

'Come back with us,' she whispers as she pulls back slightly from me. 'Don't leave.'

Those words bring the fear back full tilt. She grabs my arm, like she knows what I'm thinking.

'Please.'

'I don't know that I can. I don't know that I can trust myself.'

It's not Selti's voice I hear then. It's Kat's.

'You can't leave Jimmy alone with Gep. If you do, he'll make Jimmy pay for what you did to him. And Jimmy's really weak, Penn. He won't survive it.'

'Gep's still alive?' There's that mixture of relief and regret again. God, I don't even know what I'm feeling!

Kat nods. 'He's still out of it though. We left him on the kitchen floor. Fox is looking after Jimmy but what happens when he wakes up? Who's going to keep us safe from him?'

Kat knows me. He knows what to say to make me give in before anything else would. How could I even think about leaving Jimmy when he's so weak – thinking he could stand up for himself and not get hurt by Gep? Or that it should be up to Ellen and Selti, when they're not responsible for my family? When they could get hurt by Gep just as much? Stupid. Stupid and selfish. I need to make sure he's safe before anything else. Because that's what I've always done. He needs me. I need to get them all away – make them safe – and then I'll leave. But not yet.

'I'll come back. But we need to get out of there. All of us. You, me, Jimmy, Fox. I don't know where we're going to go but we can't stay there anymore. He's going to kill Jimmy if we don't.'

'Mum and Dad will let you stay. For a while anyway, until you can sort something out.' I can see in Selti's face she honestly believes that and maybe she's right. But I can't see them being very impressed with four teenage boys turning up on their doorstep, even though they know what's been happening for us.

We can think about that when we're out of there though. Because I don't think Gep's going to let us go. Not now. Not when everything's changing. I get the feeling that, even though I've hurt him, he's going to want to use my powers. And that scares me more than anything else except maybe losing Jimmy. Or Selti.

I hold up my hand to Kat and Selti.

'I'm not using my powers. At all. I don't care what Gep does. We'll find some way to get out of there. But I'm not going to become like him.'

Selti steps forward and takes my hand. I wrap my fingers around hers, drawing on her strength.

'You'll never be like him.'

And I want to trust in her words and in the promise they hold so badly my head hurts with it. I want to grip them to me and hold them like a talisman. But I don't know that I can.

CHAPTER 41

I can hear someone in the kitchen when we get back and the panic spikes in my chest, like a defibrillator to a fading heart. Gep's awake. He's awake and he's hurting Jimmy and I'm too late. Except if he was hurting Jimmy, I'd know. I'd feel it.

I turn to Selti. She has an eyebrow raised at me.

'Don't even think about telling me to go home.'

I don't argue this time, knowing there's no point. I just nod.

Kat's still standing back by the door, like he doesn't really want to come much further. He looks really young. I forget sometimes, that he's only twelve.

'Do you want to stay here?'

For a second, he looks like he's going to say yes, but then he shakes his head.

'Nah. You might need help.'

I nod once and take a deep breath. Our steps echo on the floor – he'll know we're coming. If he's still here.

I stand at the doorway to the kitchen, trying to take in what I'm seeing. Fox is sitting at the table, facing me. He looks up and there's a dark red mark on his cheek, like he's been punched or slapped. The anger simmers in my guts, tempting me to use my power so Gep doesn't get the chance to hurt anyone else. I push it back down, deep.

At the end of the table, Jimmy's in his wheelchair. He's white – ghost white like there's nothing much left of him – no substance. His eyes are shut but he opens them as I look at him, and they're still bright green. They widen slightly and he jerks his head towards the kitchen bench. Towards Gep. Who is standing there making a sacrifice, like that's the thing you'd do at this time. Yeah, really worried about Jimmy and making sure he's safe!

And the anger roars back up in me, like a dam wall being opened, driving the blood through my body like it's trying to blast the walls of my veins clean.

'What are you doing?' It sounds more like an accusation than a question.

He doesn't answer me. And he doesn't stop what he's doing. His hands continue to coat the chicken entrails, practiced and sure – and it hits me with a sense of sick realisation that this is a normal part of our childhood – all of ours. And I know there's no choice left anymore – we're getting out of here tonight.

One way or another.

'I asked what you think you're doing.'

Finally, he turns to me. His eyes are dark.

'Don't think your little display of power has given you any authority here. You caught me by surprise before but let me assure you, it won't happen again. You know what I'm doing. And you can't do anything to stop me.'

It's a challenge – loud and clear. Either I step up now or none of us will ever be safe.

'We're leaving. All of us. Me, Jimmy, Fox, Kat. Tonight.'

A snort of laughter is the only response I get.

'We are.' I know I shouldn't repeat it. It makes me look weak – feel weak – but I want him to be…afraid. Afraid of losing us. Afraid enough maybe, to want to change. Not that we'd stay. But still… At least then, I'd know he feels something for us. Something beyond the power stuff. I don't know why I still need that – I should be way past it – and yet, there's a part of me that still craves his approval. Love? Not that he's ever given that. And I have Jimmy, Fox, Kat. Selti. He'll have no one.

He turns around, the chicken in his hands, the honey dripping from it onto the floor in golden drops. It feels like a warning, a foreboding of death, somehow. A shiver quakes over my body, making my hair stand on end. Drip, drip, drip. Die, die, die.

I give myself a mental shake. Jesus, talk about melodramatic. No one is going to die. No one. We're leaving. That's all.

'Don't be stupid. None of you are going anywhere. You think it would be easy to go and live your own life? Well, let me tell you something. It won't be fucking easy. I've fed you, housed you, got you to school. You think you're going to be able to do that. Look after Jimmy, work, provide for you all. That's why I laughed. Because you are fucking delusional.'

'I don't care. It's better than staying here, letting you drain Jimmy. Letting you kill him like you killed Mum.'

'Stop saying that! I did not kill her! And I'm not killing Jimmy.'

He moves the chicken to one hand and it squelches in his fingers. With the free hand, he grabs one of the handles of Jimmy's wheelchair, and swings him out from the table.

'I'll fucking prove it to you.'

'Penn!' Jimmy's voice is soft, broken, but I can still hear the panic in him. It infects me, like a fast-moving virus, pushing its way to every corner of my body.

Stop him, stop him, stop him!

My power reaches up in me, pushing forward, begging me to use it.

'Gep, stop! You're not making him be the conduit. I won't let you. I won't let you do it to any of us anymore.'

I grab the other handle, not letting him move. Anger flashes across his face but there's more than that. There's fear as well.

And in that moment, I realise that he'll never be scared of losing us – there's only ever fear for himself. Fear of losing the power he's gained at the expense of everyone around him. Everyone that he might have loved – everyone that might have loved him. Fear of letting it go and being weak in a way that would never be acceptable to him.

And yet, that's all I want.

He takes his hand off the handle and rips a piece of chicken off, bringing it around to Jimmy's face, trying to stuff it in his mouth. Jimmy turns his face and tries to push Gep's hand away but there's no strength in him. I reach out to help him, pushing against his arm, but the desperation is making Gep stronger than he already was and before I can even react, I can feel his power pushing into me, burning me.

I can't stop the grimace coming to my face and I can hear Selti yelling my name through the haze of the pain. It's different this time though. Different to his past attacks. Because this time, I have my own power to protect me. And even though I swore I wouldn't use it, I know there's no choice. Not if I want to save Jimmy. Save my family.

Save myself…

I push my own power to meet his, pushing against it, forcing its retreat. His eyes are wide and I can see the disbelief on his face. Because I am stronger than him. Stronger than he thought I could be. And as I feel my power force its way in to him, he raises his hand and pushes me away. The unexpectedness of the physical attack knocks me off balance and I stagger backwards, losing my grip on the chair.

It's enough to give him the space to try and force the chicken in Jimmy's mouth again and I know for certain that if that happens, I'm going to lose my brother. Even if the sacrifice isn't done properly, it will be enough to kill him. And that can't happen. It can't. Not Jimmy! The best of me. Not him!

But Fox is there before I can even get up, pushing himself in between Gep and Jimmy.

'No, you bastard. Not Jimmy.'

I get up to help him, scrambling on the honey mix that's splattered all over the floor, trying to get traction. Before I even get close, Gep is flinging him aside, like he's just a minor disturbance, nothing worth much attention, and I hear the crack of Fox's skull hitting the table, watch as his head bounces on the stained lino on the floor, feel my heart stutter as I watch the blood pool under his red hair, hear myself begging, begging, begging for him to open his eyes.

He doesn't.

No, no, no! I promised him!

Promised to keep him and Kat safe. I should have let him leave when he wanted to that day at school. Should have let him get away from here when he had the chance.

I rush at Gep, throwing my body into his, launching him into the air, hitting the floor together and skidding with him until we reach the far wall, Gep's head crunching against it. And then I am up, crawling my way towards Fox, touching his head, his face, my hands turning red with his blood.

My fault. It's my fault.

And then Kat is beside him, tears soaking the skin of his cheeks, his hand shaking as they hover over Fox, like he's too scared to touch him. I want to say something to him, comfort him, but I don't know the words that would do that. What words would make this better? I'm lost in a vortex of guilt that's not letting me breath.

That's why I don't hear Gep when he gets up. Don't hear him make his way over. All I hear is Jimmy's voice, warning me. And I feel Selti at my back, throwing herself on me, protecting me. There's a roar from Gep and I feel Selti go stiff against me before I hear her grunt. I can't move with her against me and it's not until her weight has slid from me to the floor that I can spin around.

She's on the ground, white and motionless, but breathing. Still breathing. I want to touch her, reassure myself that's she warm but my hands are covered in Fox's blood and I'm paralysed by the shock of all that's happened – unable to move. I have no idea what I need to do next.

'Penn.' I look up at my brother, still in his chair. He's shaking, arms and legs stiff in front of him, the adrenaline in his system making it hard to control his body. But he's not looking at me. His eyes, wide with shock, are looking beyond me.

I turn to look and that's when I see him.

Gep.

Lying on the floor, eyes open, staring at nothing.

Dead.

I don't know how long we sit there, surrounded by death and blood. Seconds, maybe. Minutes. Hours. I can't make my brain work, even to get up to wash my hands.

It's only when Kat moves to the phone and is talking to someone on the other end, asking for the police, that my body seems to kick into action. Even then, I can't think. It's all I can do to move. To just barely function.

I check on Fox. He's breathing. Alive. Although there's lots of blood. And suddenly all I want is for everyone to get here and hurry up before we lose him – to do something, to fix it, because I don't know how to anymore. I grab a towel, putting it under his head, trying not to hurt him but thinking it might stop the blood. Somehow.

I wash my hands then, scrubbing them in the sink, over and over and over until there is not the slightest stain of pink.

I touch Jimmy's arm and I can see the tears in his eyes – I'm not sure if it's shock or pain. Probably both. But he is alive. And he will get stronger. Now at least, he has that chance. I keep my eyes diverted from Gep. I can't look at him. Because if I do, then I have to wonder what happened to him.

And I can't get the answers for that without Selti awake.

I go to her, sitting on the floor beside her and sliding her head onto my lap, stroking her beautiful blue hair back from her face, whispering to her that she should wake up, that's it okay. That she's safe.

But her eyes stay closed.

Kat lets them in. Police, only two, which I guess makes sense for a town this small. They take one look at the bodies littering the floor of our kitchen and then they're calling for the ambulance as well.

They try and make me move from Selti's side to question me. I shake my head, unable to talk, until the ambulance arrives and they put her on a stretcher, taking her away from me. It feels like it's a permanent thing and for a moment, I'm tempted to fight my way to the ambulance, pull her free and take her away. But that's stupid. It's not about me. It's about her. About making sure she's okay. She only got hurt because she was with me. And maybe it's better that she goes. Even if I feel like it's breaking my soul into pieces, cracking like dirt in a drought.

They take Fox too, wrapping a bandage around his head before they do. I don't even ask them any questions. I watch them take him. Numb. Stupid. Wasted. That's all I feel.

It's not until they put Gep in a stretcher, pulling the blanket up over his face, that my words return.

'Wait.'

They pause, watching me as I stumble over to them. I pull the blanket back, looking at his face. At his eyes. At the blankness in them. I put my hand against his face. Even now, his skin is cool. Clammy almost. And while I know I should feel some sadness that the only person I really knew as a parent is dead, all I can feel is relief. A body sagging, weight lifting relief.

Because we're free.

They want to take Jimmy to hospital too but he is protesting so much that when I say I can take care of him, they're happy to leave him with me.

The police question us and I tell them all I can. About Gep attacking Jimmy and me and Fox helping and Fox getting pushed. And I tell them that he attacked Selti too. Because what else could it be. I don't mention magic or powers though. As if they'd believe me anyway. And if they notice the chicken on the floor and on the bench, they don't ask me about it. Which is good. Because I don't know that I have it in me to find a lie to cover that.

The house is quiet when they leave but we still don't say anything to each other. I get the mop and clean the floor, washing it four times before I feel like there's none of Fox's blood left. And Kat massages Jimmy's arms and legs for him, stroking, stroking, stroking until they start to relax and the intense pain is gone from him.

'I'll carry him to bed,' I say to Kat, my voice tired. 'Do you want to go and have a shower or something?'

It feels like I should say more. Comfort him in some way. My twelve year old brother, even if it's not by blood, but I can't think of anything to say. I can't say I'm sorry about Gep, because I'm not. And there doesn't seem to be anything else.

He nods, hesitant.

And then he comes over to me, wrapping his arms around my waist. Hugging me. I hug him back, pulling him tight against my body, trying to hold in the emotion that is suddenly pushing its way up in me like my power had, pushing against my skin, trying to break free. But there's only one sob that manages to break free before I hold it in.

'I love you, Penn. I'm glad you're my big brother.'

'I love you too, Kat.'

They're words I should've said in the past. Words I should've told him. He pulls away from me, giving me a weak smile, before heading towards the bathroom. I go over to Jimmy. The other half of me. The good half. Although maybe…just maybe…I might have a bit of that in me too.

I lift him out of the chair and carry him to his room, lying him in the bed.

'Jesus, this room is so freaking bubble-gum purple it makes me feel sick.'

He chuckles. It's good to hear. It feels like it's been way too long since I've made him laugh.

I sit there on the side of his bed, looking at my hands, silent for a second.

'I can't believe he's gone.'

Jimmy is watching me, like he's knows there's more to come.

'I'm not sorry he is.' The words rush out of my mouth, like saying them quickly won't make me as bad a person as I know I am for thinking that.

'I'm not sorry either.'

My head jerks up at his words.

'He wasn't a dad to us.' Jimmy's voice is strong, despite the tiredness I know he feels. 'He wasn't anything to us in the end, except bad. You saved me, Penn. Again. There's nothing to feel guilty about.'

It's amazing that he knows I do, without me having to say it.

'But Selti…' I swallow hard.

Unable to say it. Unable to say that she got hurt because of me.

'She was protecting you because she wanted to. Because she loves you.'

'Did you see what happened?'

He frowns, thinking for a moment. It feels like forever before he answers.

'It looked like Gep went to use his powers on you. But he got Selti instead, when she threw herself on you. I could see him, doing the burn, the pain on her face.' He shoots a look my way at that, guilty, trying not to make me feel worse. It doesn't work.

'And then she…I don't know… it looked like she threw it back at him. He went all stiff and then collapsed.'

The blocking technique she learnt from her mum. That's what it must have been. Enough to save her but not before it affected her. And it's my fault. If I hadn't met her, made her be my friend, confided in her, loved her…

'Stop it.'

I look at Jimmy and he's frowning at me.

'You're not the reason she's in hospital. That's Gep's fault. Not yours.'

'Yeah but – '

'No! Stop it. She loves you. And like all of us do for each other, she protected you. Like you would have done for her. Don't let Gep get in the way of that. You've been happier than I've ever seen you before.'

'Yeah so happy that I left you here, getting drained by Gep!'

'Enough. No more guilt.' He's tired. It's plain to see on his face. 'We did what we could. And now it's over. Now we get to have the real life you always said you wanted. Don't spoil that with guilt that isn't yours to own.'

I nod. It makes sense. Even though I can still feel the guilt gnawing at me. But I can try. For Jimmy and Fox and Kat. And me. I can try.

I GO UP to the hospital after school. Go up and sit with Selti, just as I have for the past one month, one week and five days. Sit with her and hold her hand and tell her about what's been happening. I don't know if her mum and dad are happy that I'm doing it or not but they don't stop me, so that's something at least.

Fox was released two days after everything happened. He's been quiet for a long time but he's slowly starting to come back to being the Fox we know and love. Kat fills the silences like he always has. And Jimmy is stronger. Stronger and going to school with us.

The whole town has been amazing, rallying around us like we're part of the community rather than just some blow-ins that have only been here for three seconds. We're getting the house rent free for the next year and they raised enough money that we can look after ourselves. Nothing flash but enough. And they're still bringing us dinners every now and then…the four orphan boys who lost their father due to a heart attack – that's what the death certificate says anyway – and for the moment, we're happy. Happier than we've ever been before. And that's a start.

I brush Selti's hair back from her face and perch on the side of her bed.

'Hey there, you. How are you feeling today?'

Nothing. Like usual. I promise Jimmy every day that I'm letting the guilt go and I'm trying really hard. But I need her to wake up. That will make it easier. I stroke her hair back again.

'Selti, I need you to wake up okay. Wake up and be with me. I miss you.'

Nothing.

'Selti.'

And like a freaking miracle – like something you see in the movies – she blinks. Once, twice. Really slowly. And then her eyes are open, looking at me.

'Penn?'

'Welcome back.' I can't keep the smile of my face and I lean down, kissing her forehead before sitting back up. 'Jesus, you had us so worried.'

She glances around, taking in the hospital room.

'How long have I been here?' Her voice is croaky – unused. I don't care as long as I get to hear it.

'Almost six weeks.'

She raises her eyebrows. 'Wow.'

And then I can see her thinking about it. Thinking about that day. She frowns at me.

'Gep?'

I take a deep breath.

'He's dead.'

Her hand goes to her mouth.

'Was it me? Did I do it?'

I shake my head. Firm. Understanding suddenly, what Jimmy's been trying to tell me.

'No. It was Gep. It was his choice to do what he did. All you did was protect me. You have nothing to feel guilty about.'

Her eyes scan my face for a moment, like she's trying to find the lie there somewhere. Finally, she nods.

'Are you okay? You and Jimmy and Fox and Kat?'

'Yep. We're all okay. Just waiting for you to wake up, Sleeping Beauty.'

She smiles at my lame joke and I feel the rush of emotion I always do when I'm around her.

'I love you,' I say.

She takes my hand, kissing each knuckle in turn until everything in me is clenching with longing for her.

'I love you too.'

And I know my real life has begun.

ACKNOWLEDGMENTS

Being an author means you're often stuck in your own fantasy world with characters only you can hear (until they're on the page and then you get to share the voices in your head!). So this page is about saying 'thank you, thank you, thank you!' to all the fabulous people who've encouraged me to keep going back to this world.

My husband, Adrian, and my gorgeous children, Jack, Gabrielle and Lawson – for the joy, laughter and love you bring to my life and your patience with sharing me with the characters.

Mum and Dad, who've always been encouraging and loving and who made me believe I was capable of anything I put my mind to.

Every woman needs a great group of goddess girlfriends and I'm lucky enough to have more than my fair share:

Net, Col and Cass – my cheerleaders since the start of this journey and who have helped me celebrate each win with a good glass of wine and a mean game of Blitz. Honestly don't know what I'd do without you.

Bec, Bernie, Arlene, Leanne, Sue, Lisa and Shaunagh – for all your fabulous love, support and great story ideas (looking at you especially, Arlene!) and for making a line at the book signings. You guys are awesome!

Toni – sister-in-law/manager extraordinaire! I'm unbelievably grateful for all the support, reading and championing you've given me. You rock!

Shelley, Sandy, Kris, Cher, Ally, Linda, Cass, Dana – my author tribe; my writer family – for your unwavering support, your feedback and for all the laughs along the way!

And finally, for all of you – the readers, without whom we'd just be people who hear voices! I hope you had as much fun reading as I did writing. Big (massive, huge!) love to you all!

ABOUT THE AUTHOR

A writer of copious amounts of words – just because if they didn't come out, she's sure they'd make her head explode – Sue-Ellen is an international author with seven published YA and adult stories: *Aquila, When Henry Met Gina, The Jade Goddess, Streamer, The Flight, Talon Marked* and *The Rise*, with her children's picture book, *The Jacket*, released in Australia, UK and the US.

In her 'other' life, Sue-Ellen is a social worker living in Central Queensland with her family, two dogs, a bird and a snake. A lover of tea, wine, chocolate and slightly weird shoes, she's an eternal optimist who enjoys making things difficult for her protagonists but loves a satisfying ending.

She loves to connect with readers and you can find her on facebook, goodreads or at www.sueellenpashley.com.

www.ingramcontent.com/pod-product-compliance
Lightning Source LLC
Chambersburg PA
CBHW072351110726
47909CB00003B/667